CHASING
AFTER
MORE

THE ABERDEEN RANCH DUET
BOOK ONE

ELLE F.SUN

Editing by Ellie Rich, @byelliesedits

Cover Design & Interior Formatting: Elle F. Sun

Paperback ISBN: 979-8-9936774-0-8

(This book is intended for audiences 18+)

chapters

Content Warnings

- Adult/explicit language
- Suggestive sexual themes and remarks
- Loss of a parent from cancer (off page)
- Loss of parents from a car accident (off page)
- Grief (as a parent, spouse, child, and friend)
- Panic attack (on page)
- Alcohol (consumption, abuse, and mention)
- Self-harm (off page)
- Mental health topics (therapy)
- Divorce (off page)

This book is intended for an 18+ audience.

***

If you or someone you know is struggling with any of the topics above and would like to talk to someone, you can text HOME or HOLA to 741741 to reach a live volunteer Crisis Counselor. Free, 24/7, confidential.

PLAYLIST

The Archer by Taylor Swift
Bindi in the Dirt by Mikayla Pasterfield
Blindsided by Bon Iver
The Bolter by Taylor Swift
East Chicago, IN by Michigander
EMPATH by Lea G
Fade Into You by Mazzy Star *
The Fall by Gregory Alan Isakov
Fool by Djo *
Hot Blooded by New Constellations
Keep The Rain by Searows *
Little Current by Bay Ledges
Lump Sum by Bon Iver
Marble Arch by Erin LeCount *
Neon Moon by Cigarettes After Sex
Pool by Samia
Rein Me In (with Olivia Dean) by Sam Fender, Olivia Dean
Sidelines by Phoebe Bridgers
Subliming by Richy Mitch & The Coal Miners
Summer Begs by Sarah Jaffe
Take Me Home by The Paper Kites, Nadia Reid
twenty four by Nick Kent
Vienna (In Memoriam) by The Army, The Navy
Wash. by Bon Iver

* mentioned in the book

For the empath who can't help but feel everything and anyone whose grief made them want to feel nothing.

one

ENGAGEMENTS, WEDDINGS, AND BABIES

DELIA

I have never felt so stuck in my life.

It's like there's this invisible force keeping me from moving forward, but at the same time, I can't figure out what to do to break the spell.

"What if you did a semester abroad?" My best friend's cheerful voice breaks through my momentary pity party.

"I'm not in school, Clara." I laugh, knowing she's trying to give me a reprieve from the emotional turmoil I'm experiencing. I take a sip of my hazelnut iced latte and let my eyes roam around the coffee shop, the faint sound of rain tapping against the window. April has been so dreary and is not helping this feeling of just *bleh*!

I need inspiration to strike. A sign. Someone to run up to me and shout, "Do this!"

Clara waves her hand as if shooing my response away like a bothersome fly. "People move out of the country to work all the time! You know, get a change of scenery, and come back!"

My lips twitch in amusement. She makes it sound so simple.

"I *do* know, but that's not what I feel like I'm supposed to do." I close my laptop, taking a much needed break from my fruitless search. Steepling my hands under my chin, I close my eyes, letting out another dramatic sigh.

"Okay then," Clara starts, "you take a moment and do…whatever it is you're doing, and I'm going to get a refill of my tea." She scooches back in her chair and it isn't until I know she's out of earshot that I let out a small whimper. I hate this. This nagging feeling that I'm out of place in my own life.

And I know…*I know* that I'm not supposed to have everything figured out right now–not that I ever have. But I thought I'd feel more established in my life at this point, like I was living out my purpose or something. Instead, I've been living in a sort of limbo since I graduated high school and realized college wasn't for me.

I don't know if it's the approach of my 25th birthday or the latest smattering of posts on social media of engagements, weddings, and babies, but something isn't quite right inside me. Like my soul is searching for more.

My phone buzzes causing me to peel my eyes back open and return to reality. When I see it's a notification that the store had a sale, another ache pangs in me.

I used to love my job. I loved showing up and working with people, making them happy. I was basically the living, breathing model of "if you love what you do, you'll never work a day in your life."

I've been with the same boutique since I walked away from college. I started as a sales associate and worked my way up the ladder, becoming a manager almost two years ago. And it really sucks because there's no logical reason for leaving my job. It's all based on a feeling. Which isn't something I'm unfamiliar with because I'm often driven by my emotions and feelings, but usually in a way that leads to fun and enjoying life. It also has its downsides, but I don't focus on that–at least I try not to. Instead, I focus on being in the moment and making the best of things. There's so much heaviness in the world, why not leave a little sparkle everywhere you go?

"Does anyone know you're thinking about leaving?" Clara asks as she sits back down with her topped off mug of earl grey tea.

I arch an eyebrow as my best friend reads my mind, per usual.

"What?" She holds her hands up as if to show she means no harm.

"Get out of my head," I jest while swatting her hands down with my own. "But no, I haven't told anyone."

"Ugh," she groans. "I don't like being the only one who knows. It's making work awkward!"

Oh, yeah. Clara is also my co-worker. She's the visual merchandiser and keeps our store organized and pretty. So while I run the ship, she makes sure it always looks like something you'd see in a magazine. We make a really good team, and she's part of the reason I've hung on these last few months.

"Well, no one at the store knows," I start, "but a few weeks ago during one of the management meetings, I did mention to Diane that I was considering taking some time off during the summer– so it was on her radar."

"How did she take that?" Clara's eyebrows raise.

"Surprisingly well. She said that she'd feel comfortable with you and Lola taking over while I'm gone, which is what I'd thought too. She posed an interesting question though," I say.

"Hm?" Clara tilts her head.

"She asked me, if I didn't take this time away, would I be more likely to quit? And I thought about it and my answer was yes, because I feel like I'll eventually become so unhappy that I'll want to walk away. So, she said she was in favor of me going for it, if that meant she'd be able to keep me at her company for longer."

"I mean, yeah. I can definitely see that side of it. We're lucky we work for someone who's so understanding," Clara offers. "Probably why people work there for so long. But still, I don't like having to keep a secret like this."

"I know, I know. I need to make a choice before the end of the month so I can give at least two weeks' notice." I open my laptop back up, going to the spreadsheet I made of potential jobs. I skim over the top three I've narrowed it down to and clear my throat like I'm about to give a speech when Clara interrupts me.

"Do your parents at least know?"

I shrug. "When I was at my dad's last weekend, I mentioned I was looking for a change."

More like I cried on his couch and told him I felt like I've been running in circles lately.

"And what about Val pal?"

I huff out a small laugh. My mom's name is Valerie, but a few years ago I started calling her by the nickname, remarking instead of my gal pal, she was my Val pal, and it stuck, even with my friends who know her.

"She thinks that if I can sort it all out financially, I should do it. Take the chance. While I don't have any true commitments, all that stuff."

I love how my mom always manages to keep me grounded with practicality, while also being a shoulder for me to cry on. She's definitely the logical one out of my parents, whereas my dad offers more emotional support.

My heart squeezes just thinking about them *and* the possibility of us being more than an hour away from each other. It's funny, in the past I would've never batted an eye about not having them nearby. But something shifted the last few years, and it's made me realize more and more that they're in my corner. And I'm so grateful for that, lucky even.

When they got divorced, I thought I'd never recover. I was so angry. All. The. Time.

But our family therapist helped me realize something, among many things. While I'd been so hung up on wanting them to stay together, I'd neglected the reality that even if they separated, I would still have a mom and dad who love me. Fiercely. And at the end of the day, that was more than a lot of people could say. Talk about perspective…

"Do you really have to move away?" Clara breaks me out of my thoughts, giving me a pouty face before chuckling. I roll my eyes, then focus my attention back on my laptop, and start my debrief of the best options I have.

"Okay, first up is Key West, Florida."

Clara raises her eyebrows enthusiastically.

"I would take a bit of a pay cut, and I'm not entirely sure if I'd be a good waitress…but living near the beach would be nice. There are long term condo rentals that aren't too expensive and I'd probably get free food during shifts."

Clara butts in, "That one gets my vote 'cause I would have a place to vacation. Atlanta is feeling a little crowded lately."

I shake my head. "Right, yes, of course. Let me add that to the pros. But wait, if you take a vacation, there really will be nobody to run the store," I say, quirking up an eyebrow.

"Pshh, Lola could run that store with her eyes closed. Honestly, I'm surprised Diane hasn't promoted her from assistant manager and moved her to another location," Clara says.

"That might be because I'm not ready to let her go, but anyway, moving on," I quip. "We have Nashville, Tennessee.

Bartending sounds like it could be fun, the money would be great, and I found someone who's subleasing their place for the summer and it's actually a few hundred dollars cheaper than my rent here."

"And! And!" She waggles her finger in the air. "Aren't there cowboys there?!"

A mixture of a snort and laugh escapes me. "I mean, not really. Maybe country singers?" And then I sigh because *cowboys*. That word triggers the dream of what I really want–to move out west.

While I've spent time narrowing down my search to a few options, the truth is, I'm not completely sold on any of them. All I want is to find a ranch to live and work on, ideally in Montana.

Why? Other than it feels like something is tugging on me to go there, I couldn't really tell you.

But I can see myself riding horses in my spare time, rocking a pair of cowgirl boots, and chasing that sense of belonging that's been evading me. I feel like if I could ride a horse through a field with my hair blowing behind me in the wind, I would be healed.

Now, what I would do on said ranch? Unsure. But I'm a fast learner, *and* I'm also willing to do whatever is needed, even if that means cleaning up poop all summer. I'm that desperate. The only thing I really have to offer is that I took equestrian lessons in middle and some of high school.

The daydreaming vanishes almost as quickly as it began, though, because the reality is, I haven't had any luck whenever I search.

But it's been awhile and I'm feeling a little hopeful, or maybe it's the jolt of caffeine from my latte kicking in. Regardless, it can't hurt to look again. I abandon my presentation and switch back to the job site I've been hunting on.

"I'm going to see if there are any new listings in Montana," I blurt out.

A grin breaks out across Clara's face, knowing how badly I want to go there. Crossing her fingers while I start my search, she looks up to the ceiling and whispers, "Universe, if you're listening, send our girl out west."

The universe must be wearing noise canceling headphones.

Five minutes later, I'm discouraged and frustrated. Maybe Key West, Nashville, or my third choice, Boston, will be enough of a getaway that I'll forget the pull out west.

Except, I know it won't. Because I've been fighting this feeling for a lot longer than I've let on.

"What about Wyoming?" Clara points to a patron who's just walked into the shop wearing a sweatshirt with the state on it.

Okay, coffee shop! I'll take the sign.

"I didn't even think about that. You're right. I've been so stuck on Montana, that I didn't even consider that there are plenty of other states to explore." I huff out a breath to move a piece of hair that's fallen in front of my face as I change the job search location to Wyoming. I click my fields of experience: retail and management, child-care, customer service, and press search.

The screen refreshes, a few posts popping up and immediately catching my eye, but there are things about them that don't give me a good feeling. I know, again with the feelings. I scroll a little more and all of a sudden, it's like the heavens part and a ray of light shines down on my laptop screen.

There, staring back at me, is perhaps the answer to every cry, wish, and dream…and I'm not sure it's real so I spin the laptop to face Clara, needing a second pair of eyes.

Her eyebrows fly up to her hairline as she starts to read the listing out loud.

"Jackson Hole, Wyoming. Single mom looking for a jack of all trades. I have a 5-year-old daughter and my grandma lives with us, as well, on a small ranch. We do have a few animals, if you're afraid or allergic. I also own a small boutique on Main Street. I'm looking for someone who would move in for the summer and basically become part of our family. You'd help with my daughter and grandma, but this is where the tricky part comes in—I need someone who could help run my store. The start date is tentative, but ideally, I'd love for it to be as soon as possible. If you're still reading, interested, and qualified, please call for more details. "

My mouth hangs in suspension, my best friend meeting my eyes again and grabbing my phone to type the number in and pressing call before I can even argue.

Maybe the universe is listening after all.

two

UNCLE OF THE YEAR

GRIFFIN

"Nineteen. Twenty. Alright, time's up!"

A giggle rings out on the main floor of the house and I make my steps louder than usual to add to the dramatics of the game. I glance over at my grandma, who's sitting on the couch with a book, and she snickers.

I raise my voice before asking, "Grams, you haven't seen a little girl anywhere, have you?"

More giggles.

"Never in my life," she responds, before pointing in the direction of the hall. I laugh, not actually needing her help, and continuing with my pretend search.

I slowly make my way through the kitchen, opening and closing cabinets while calling out, "Where's Libby?" I take a few more steps. "Is she under the kitchen table?" I look even though I know she's not there. *I can't believe this is my life lately,* I think to myself.

Even more giggles bounce off the walls.

"I think I lost her, Grams!"

I turn back toward the living room when my niece calls out, "Griffy, I'm in here!"

The worry in her tone has me shaking my head and laughing. Sometimes, she takes things so literally for a five-year-old, and other times, she takes nothing seriously. I guess that's the good thing about kids. They're usually not thinking about anything past what's in front of them, so if they are upset, they're easily redirected.

I stomp down the hall, making each step louder than the last to build the anticipation of finding Libby. I push open the door to my sister's office and spot two little feet poking out from under the curtains. Before I can even pull the fabric back, Libby pops out and darts past me, squealing as she makes her way through the door.

"Hey, that's cheating!" I shout after her and wait a few seconds before trailing behind. But the glint of a gold picture frame has me stopping at the edge of my sister's desk. I pick up the framed photo of our parents with us at my Cathy's high school graduation. I was thirteen at the time, and if I only knew what the next couple of years held, I would have done so much differently.

Now I'm thirty-one, the same age that my sister was when she had Libby, and nothing could have prepared me for the position I'm in.

I don't mind helping her out right now. I know it's temporary. Plus, I would do anything for her, Libby, and Grams. But there's still a part of me that feels like when I'm not working and supporting our family name, I'm letting someone down. It's an unspoken pressure that's weighed on me for a long time and I don't see it easing up anytime soon.

"She's with me!" I hear Grams call, and it brings me out of

my thoughts, reminding me I was supposed to be chasing after the little blonde bundle of joy.

"Oh, good, you caught her!" My voice echoes out into the hall.

I set the photo down and head back into the living room, where Libby has now tucked herself into Grams' side and is pretending to read her book.

My phone buzzes in my pocket, and I take it out to see a few texts from Cathy, letting me know she will be finishing her day soon, and also has exciting news. I'm hoping the news is she found someone to help her out and I can resume my life as usual.

"Do you mind if I step out for a second?" I motion to the front door and Grams chuckles.

"Griffin, you don't need my permission." She shoos me away with one hand, holding her book for Libby with the other.

Nodding in response, I duck out through the front door and sit in my grandfather's rocking chair on the screened-in porch. Pop always liked to come out here and watch the horses when he'd had a long day. He would eventually get my dad to come over, who'd bring me with him. I spent countless nights out here listening to them talk about the ranch, the shit they were dealing with in their businesses—anything and everything, really. Their voices mixed with the sounds of different bugs and critters, as well as the wind-chime my mom made, became one of the most familiar backtracks to my life.

I run a hand through my hair, pulling down on the ends where it's longer. An ache I've worked hard to get rid of threatens to stir in my chest. It doesn't help that I can't shake the heaviness from the moment in the office, and I'll be damned if I have to carry this with me for the rest of the day.

Not wasting another second, I take my phone back out and

call the number I know will go to voicemail. When the familiar beep sounds, I lower my voice and start speaking.

"Hey, Dad. Just sitting on the porch and thinking about you. I've been helping Cathy out the last few weeks since her manager up and quit with no notice. People these days. I swear having a good work ethic is becoming more and more rare. But I'm not complaining that it's given me time with Libby and Grams lately. I know I see them almost every day, but it's been different having to help get them both up and moving in the morning. They're very similar even at such different stages of life. You'd laugh, but I also think you'd be proud. At least that's what I tell myself. I miss you and Mom—oh, Cathy's calling. I'll talk to you later. Love you."

I end the call and quickly pick up my sister's.

"Hey, Cath. What's going on?"

"I think I found someone!" She screeches so loudly into the phone, I pull it away from my ear on instinct.

"That's great! For everything you're needing?" I know what she's looking for is somewhat a shot in the dark, but not impossible to find.

"I think so! I briefly spoke with her on the phone and, gosh, I really hope this works. How's the day been?" I don't miss the lightness in her voice, and it eases the ache from earlier knowing that her burdens hopefully won't be as heavy here soon.

"Great, Lib is inside with Grams and I came out to the porch for a few minutes to catch a breath. We were playing a pretty intense game of hide-and-seek." I laugh but it catches in my throat when I see the empty hook where Mom's wind-chime used to be before a storm blew through a few months ago and broke it. "It's so quiet out here now."

Cathy hums in response, not needing me to elaborate because she's shared the same sentiment.

"Well, I'll be home in a few hours. I was thinking we could do home-made pizza? Libby has been asking to make her own since she saw that Curious George episode and he was throwing the damn dough in the air."

I snort in response. "Yeah, that sounds fine. We'll be here."

"Okay! Love you, baby bro."

"Yeah, you too, sis."

I hang up and take one more deep breath before getting up and walking back into the living room. Libby's head perks up and she gives me a sleepy grin, one that Grams is also wearing.

"Is it nap time?" I plop down into one of the recliners and kick it back.

"No!" Libby whines and Grams shakes her head.

"Rookie mistake, my boy."

Little does she know, I've got the upper hand.

"Well, here's the thing, Libs. The sooner you take a nap, the faster your mom will be home, and she said we're making…pizza for dinner!" I raise my eyebrows at Libby whose entire face lights up. She scrambles off the couch and makes a beeline down the hall for her room.

"Wake me up when Mama's here!" The faint sound of her jumping into her bed makes me laugh. I give my grandma a look of victory and she closes her eyes, resting her head on the back of the couch.

"Well played," she murmurs.

"Uncle of the year," I muse before closing my eyes as well.

three

"MOTHER'S INTUITION"

DELIA

"We're going to miss you so much!" Janie, one of my sales leads, says while cutting another slice of cake and sitting down next to Clara who's trying not to cry for probably the tenth time today.

"Yeah, what are we supposed to do without you?" Lola chimes in.

I can't believe how quickly the last five weeks at the boutique have flown by.

When I–or should I say, Clara–called Catherine, the mom who posted the listing, it only took a few phone calls back and forth before I secured the job. I explained to her my current situation and we settled on my start date being the Saturday before Memorial Day weekend. I sent Diane an email as soon as I found out letting her know that I would be taking that leave of absence after all. Just like she'd said during our meeting, she supported the decision and told me she would be eager to hear all about it when I returned.

"You'll all be fine, I promise. Besides, it's only a few months and I should be back." I move to hug one more girl before sitting back down.

"Key word being *should*," Clara shouts and I glare at her.

"The position is only through the summer while her daughter is out of school. So come the second week of August, they won't need me anymore, and I'll be back!"

At least, I *think* that's the plan.

"Are you nervous?" one of the girls asks, and my stomach dips.

"I'd love to say I'm not, but of course I am."

Everyone nods in understanding, but only Clara has been along for the ride from the beginning and truly knows the whirlwind of emotions I've been experiencing.

She's witnessed it all. That initial nervous excitement at the coffee shop, the butterflies I felt when I sent my resume, and finally the hope that turned into certainty when Catherine offered me the position and said that finding me was like her own "heavens parting" moment.

There was a small part of me that felt like maybe I was hurting Clara's feelings in the process by making it seem like I couldn't wait to get away from here, but I know that's not how she thinks. I find my best friend's sapphire eyes framed by her strawberry blonde curtain bangs and smile. When she returns it with one full of sentiment, sadness nips at me, but I continue on with my optimism and put on a cheery face. It's what I do best, after all.

"But I'm also excited. I really think it's like fate or something." I beam at the girls and they make similar expressions, putting their hands over their hearts and sighing.

"Are the clothes cuter than ours?" Janie asks and I shake my head, laughing.

"I haven't really looked, but I'm hoping I get a decent

discount so I can build my western wardrobe up. When I video called with Catherine, she was wearing a floral print dress I'd kill for, so I'm hopeful."

They all *ooh* and *ahh* before Clara interjects. "Speaking of…"

Lola suddenly produces a very large box, shoving it toward my lap. My faithful assistant manager gives me a watery-eyed grin. "We all thought these would be a great going away present."

My own eyes water with the tears I hoped were not going to come as I open the gift and see a beautiful pair of crimson cowgirl boots. I can't help but laugh at the color–they know me so well. I love bright tones and often use my clothes to help express my personality.

"They're perfect, I love them. I love y'all. Thank you so much. Seriously, this means the world to me because you're all supporting not just my trip, but me."

We all hug again before I try on the boots, earning me whoops and hollers while I strut in them, pretending I'm on the runway. But there's a moment of silence when everyone has turned away to gather their stuff and clean up before we leave, and I stop in front of the mirror and look myself over.

The crimson boots don't necessarily go with the yellow sundress I have on, but I don't care. I smile at my reflection and imagine a cowgirl hat nestled on top of my wavy blonde hair. Once again, a strange feeling washes over me. Like I'm connecting with a version of myself that already exists, but I haven't met yet.

"You ready to lock up?" Lola's voice breaks through my thoughts and I turn, giving her a soft smile.

"Cuh-losing time," I sing the lyrics of the Semisonic song dramatically, like I do every shift when I'm here until close.

Clara snorts and we all file out to the parking deck before parting ways.

"See you in a few months!" I call out one more time as I watch their cars drive away and a few honks ring off in the distance.

"I'll follow you?" Clara helps me put my bags in the back seat of her car, since I'm planning to leave mine at my mom's house while I'm away.

I nod and get into my front seat, starting the drive to the suburbs. My parents still live in my hometown only an hour away from the city, which makes for easy visits whenever I want to see them. But unlike most of my drives there—usually spent listening and singing to my favorite songs—I spend this one in silence as I chase after the various thoughts spinning and whirling around in my head.

The fear that slowly trickled in a couple days ago of being away from family and friends in a new place, where I don't know anyone, starts to creep back up.

What if I get to Catherine's and realize I've made a mistake? What if her daughter doesn't like me? What if I don't like them?

I shake my head to rid myself of these thoughts and instead focus on my sense of courage I've been holding onto since the coffee shop.

Turning into the driveway, I hop out and wait by the hood of my car for Clara to pull up. The front door swings open, Mom flurrying out, and I notice her red, puffy eyes. My heart twists into a knot because I *really* did not want tonight to go like this. Mom notices the unease now written on my face, throwing her arms around my shoulders when she makes it to me. She squeezes tight before pulling back and smiling at me.

"I know, I know. I'm not supposed to cry, but I'm so proud of you." She reaches out with both hands, tucking my dirty blonde hair behind each ear then cradles my face in her palms. "Delia, my dreamer."

Tears rush to the edge of my eyes and I blink them out of vision.

If I start crying now, I don't know if I'll be able to stop. *And* I'm worried I might psych myself out of going. I need to get through this night and on the plane tomorrow, and then I can have a breakdown later on. *Problems for future Delia.*

Clara arriving gives me the interruption I need and I quickly pull away from my mom before saying, "Gotta pee after that drive!" and escaping into the house.

Once I'm in the bathroom, I stare down my bleary eyed reflection and speak to myself.

"You will not fall apart tonight, Delia Rose Fairchild."

After glaring at myself and rambling off a few more pep talk phrases, I walk out of the bathroom and join Clara in the kitchen with my mom.

"How're you feeling, honey? You all packed and ready to go?" my mom asks while loading the dishwasher.

"Mhm, absolutely," I murmur, but the waver in my voice has Clara glaring at me.

"You're not packed at all are you?" she accuses, and I hate how well she knows me.

"I have my things…together," I argue back, turning to face Mom again. "I have to tell you something, though, both of you."

My mom shuts the dishwasher and gives me her attention as Clara also turns to face me completely.

Well, shoot. Now that I have the floor, I'm finding it hard to deliver the news.

"Go on," my best friend urges.

With a sigh, I drop the bomb. "I won't have the best cell service while I'm on the ranch. Maybe when I go into town and am at the boutique 'cause there's better Wi-Fi, but outside of that, I won't have a great connection."

My mom squeals at the same time Clara groans.

"You should write letters!" Mom continues, clapping delightedly and darting over to one of the drawers.

"There's no Wi-Fi at the house? Only at the store?" Clara whines. "That's crazy! It's literally 2025."

I roll my eyes. "There is Wi-Fi at the house but it's not the most reliable, hit or miss. Maybe it'll be good for me, ya know? I can really focus on being present and disconnecting for a little while I do my soul searching."

"Yes, yes, yes!" my mom agrees enthusiastically, joining us back at the counter with a pile of paper–*stationary*–in her hand. "Here! Take these." She slides what I now see are multiple sheets of stamps in my direction. "This is exciting, Delia! Writing letters is a dying art, you know. There's something so beautiful about waiting to hear from the ones you love."

Swiping up the stamps, I chance a look at Clara who still has her eyes narrowed.

"Thanks, Mom. This is super helpful because I didn't really have any sort of back up plan."

"Ha," Clara scoffs. "No back up plan, so you were going to go off the grid and not tell me?"

"No, I was going to tell you tonight. And I just did." I look back at my mom who's trying to stifle a laugh.

"Clara, sweetie, you're going to be fine. If you really miss her, come over and we'll have dinner." She pats her hand before leaving the kitchen and heading to her room.

"Are you actually upset?" I turn back to my best friend, trying to get a read on her expression.

"I mean, a little, but not at you. You can't help the service will be spotty, but I don't know why you waited to tell me. Doesn't that freak you out a little though? Going somewhere new and you won't really be able to contact anyone?" She quirks up an eyebrow.

"I would say yes, but after I had a video call with Catherine, and she also spoke to both my parents and gave them all her information, I don't think there's much to worry about." Except there's a lot to worry about, but I refuse to show anyone that I'm having doubts. I've made these plans, I've committed to them, and I'm going to see it through.

"Catherine is so lovely, too," Mom chimes in, joining us back in the kitchen, this time with a bag stuffed full of tissue paper. She sets it on the counter and continues on, "Awful though, about her ex-husband. I mean, really, so sad. I bet her daughter is an absolute delight and it's a shame he's missing out on that."

"What happened?" Clara's eyes widen and she gives me a look of concern.

"Oh, it's nothing bad. I'm sorry, I don't know if I should have said that," my mom speaks up before I answer Clara's question.

"Catherine's pregnancy was unplanned and her ex was comfortable with them being child-free at that point in their marriage and didn't want to change his life. So, she cut him loose and was going to raise the baby on her own. But then her grandfather passed away, so she moved onto their ranch to be there for her grandmother. I guess it worked out in a way because she didn't have to technically go through everything on her own." I wince at sharing such personal details of someone else's life, but I'm sure Clara would have heard this story sooner or later.

"But I'm sure it's been such a treat—the three of them in the house navigating life together. It really does take a village." Mom smiles and continues, "Now time for your parting gift."

I pull out the tissue, reaching inside the bag and gasping when I take out a Polaroid camera. I've been wanting one forever since

I started journaling but haven't got around to buying one yet. It's the perfect gift for the summer.

"How did you know?" I ask with almost a wistfulness to my voice, beaming at my mom.

"Mother's intuition," she answers. "Now, I think you two should probably get a move on since you haven't packed." She cuts me a playful glare before rounding the counter.

"I'll go wait in the car so you can have a moment," Clara hugs my mom then sneaks out through the front.

"Delia, baby, listen to me, okay?" Mom comes closer and places her hands on the sides of my face like earlier. "I know that things haven't always been easy for you since your father and I split."

I feel my bottom lip starting to tremble, so I sink my teeth into it and focus on keeping myself together.

"I know you feel things so deeply, and in turn, that has left you with this longing for more—and I hope you find what it is you're chasing after. But hear me when I say this, life will still be *just life* no matter where you go. It's in here," she moves one hand to place it over my heart, "you have to make peace."

I nod, knowing the weight of her words and the truth behind them. Maybe there is a part of me that's running from pieces of my past that still linger within me. Maybe leaving will finally help me let go. Maybe it won't actually matter where I go and all I really need to do is make peace with things like Mom said. But despite all of that, there's still a tug on my soul drawing me away from where I am and I won't deny it any longer.

"Mom, do you think they…" I start, but think better of it. I can't have this conversation now, not when I'm so close to leaving things on a positive and endearing note. I step away from her touch and reach for the camera.

"No," she answers confidently, somehow knowing my

thoughts. "I don't think they were right, and you know that, Delia."

I offer her a smile while pushing away the lies that have begun to tiptoe back into my mind. The same phrase that not one, not two, but multiple ex-boyfriends used when calling things off with me and leaving me to question myself.

I reach out to pull her into one more hug. "I love you, Mom."

She squeezes me tighter. "I love you, most. My dreamer girl."

* * *

"And you leave tomorrow?" Clara says, motioning to the chaos in front and around us.

We both stare at my three open suitcases and the copious amounts of clothes strewn across my apartment.

"Like I said, I have things together." I point at the piles and push past her to start filling my luggage.

"Ugh, I still can't believe you're leaving me." She follows behind me and flops down on my bed. I stop my packing and move to sit next to her.

"You're acting as if you don't get to come visit me." I nudge her with my elbow.

That is by far the best perk Catherine mentioned. I'll have a few weekends to myself and as long as we plan in advance, any friends who want to visit are welcome to come stay at the house. Though, they will also have to go through a background check like I did, but hey, that's small potatoes compared to the pay off.

"I know," she groans, sitting up. "But I'm going to be lonely before and after."

Shrugging my shoulders, I get back up and continue packing. I'm basically taking everything I own minus my winter pieces. It should be fairly warm and Catherine told me to make sure I had things for horseback riding, ranch chores, swimming, working, and going out if I wanted to. So simple, right?

I take a slow and deliberate deep breath, shaking out my hands. It's in these moments when I start to list off all the things I'll be doing that I get a little anxious, like maybe I've bit off more than I can chew. But I know I'm capable and this is what I want.

"Should I bring a few formal dresses, you think?" I look over at Clara who's holding up one of my bikinis.

"I don't know, but do you have a one-piece? This feels a little risqué for a nanny." She dangles the fabric held together by thin strings in my face before I snatch it from her and throw it into the suitcase.

"I bought three, and they're already packed. But I'm still bringing a few bikinis for when I've got alone time." Except I'm not entirely sure when that will be, but I don't care. I'm just eager to see where I'll be living for the summer.

The "small ranch", as Catherine put it, has a house with six rooms and sits on a lake. They have horses and chickens, all of which I'll have to also help with in various ways. Her grandma lives in a separate wing of the house. Yeah, she said wing. So, clearly, "small ranch" is an understatement. My excitement starts bubbling back up to the surface and I let out a small squeal.

Clara ambles onto the floor, helping me pack the rest of my things, and we move my suitcases by the front door.

"Thank you again for subleasing my studio while I'm away," I call over my shoulder while walking back into my kitchen, pulling open a drawer and grabbing what I need.

"I'll admit, I'm excited to live in the city for a few months," she says, and softly laughs. "My mom is also very excited to have me out of the house for a little. She said maybe I'll realize that I miss having my own place and leave her alone." She rolls her eyes as I turn around, and joins me next to the counter.

"Ooh, maybe! Or we could find a place together when I get back since my lease will be ending." I playfully pinch her arm and smile, knowing that her staying at my studio while I'm gone is a bigger deal than we're making it out to be.

Clara's dad passed away last year after a long battle with cancer, so she moved back in with her mom. And while it was good for Clara and her mom to be there for each other while they grieved, I also think her mom wants Clara to go back to having her own life and stop worrying so much. Being a caregiver for your own family member is sometimes one of the most over-looked sacrifices one can make. It's why I have so much respect for Catherine's decision to move in with her grandma.

"It helps that you offered to still pay for half the rent while you're gone." She winks at me.

"Yeah, well, I knew there had to be some sort of incentive, since technically there's no reason for you to move here. It's only two months after all. Anyways, welcome home!" I deposit my spare key in her hand, and pull her into a tight hug. "It's going to be great, for both of us. I just know it."

"WHO'S OLD?"

GRIFFIN

I shut the fridge door and look at the calendar with the date circled and Cathy's handwriting scribbled in the square.

Cordelia arrives.

A mixture of relief and annoyance courses through me.

On one hand, I'm relieved I finally get to go back to work—a little frustrated it's the weekend, but I'm too behind schedule to really complain. The last few weeks spent helping my niece and Grams were special, and I'd do it again, but damn. The projects I need to get done are looming over me. And while I'm fortunate to be my own boss, I don't like playing catch up or seeming unreliable.

On the other hand, I'm annoyed that there's going to be someone unfamiliar in my space. Not directly, but present enough that I'll have to dust off my people skills. There are few things that I dislike more than small talk and meeting someone new. It's always awkward, especially with the older generation because they've lost their filter and think it's okay to say or ask whatever they want.

Grams is the exception to that, she can say whatever she wants. And I guess my clients too, because they pay me well.

I move to the kitchen table, sitting down with my bowl of frosted wheat cereal. I don't care what anyone says, this cereal is the best and I'll take that to my grave with me. I shovel a spoonful into my mouth when my niece rushes around the corner and collides into my side before rearing back and thrusting a very colorful piece of paper in my face.

"Do you think my new friend will like my drawing?" I pluck it from her hand and hoist her up into my lap.

"Well, hey to you too, Libby-Loo." She giggles at the nickname I've been calling her since she was about three as I hold out the artwork and examine it like it's a rare piece of undiscovered treasure. In reality, it looks like she took a bunch of markers and drew her version of a flower over and over again. "Wow. I think she'll love it. Older people always enjoy this type of stuff anyways." I press a soft kiss onto the top of her head before she wiggles out of my lap and gives me a funny look.

"Who's old?" she asks, raising her eyebrows to the best of her ability. She recently learned the motion from me after spending so much time together. Now she does it anytime she can. Except it looks more like her eyes are about to pop out of her head, making me laugh.

Grams chuckles from across the kitchen while pouring water from her kettle into a mug, looking at Libby before speaking.

"No one's old, sweetheart. Don't fuss with your uncle." She smirks while dropping the tea bag in, making her way over to join me at the table. "We'll be fine waiting for our new friend." She raises her drink in Libby's direction who grins like a fool. I shake my head and sigh. I don't have enough time to figure out what those two are up to today. They're thick as thieves anyways and I doubt they'd fill me in on whatever secret it is they're sharing.

I walk over to the sink as I finish my cereal, rinsing out the bowl and putting it in the dishwasher. When I turn around, I hear the sound of a car arriving. I should probably be a gentleman and help this lady with her bags but I'm sure she can handle it. She's probably done this a million times in her life, and I'm already running behind schedule.

"Love you both," I call over my shoulder, grabbing my cowboy hat off the counter with my keys, and booking it out the back door toward my truck. As I'm starting it, my phone lights up. I answer, switching it to speaker while shifting into gear, and head down the gravel path on the backside of the house.

"What's going on, sis?"

I hear shuffling and a squeaking letting me know she's in the middle of moving things around her store, before her bright voice breaks through the phone.

"Did Cordelia make it there? I feel so bad I wasn't able to get her from the airport. The store was so crazy and that lady from last week, you know the one, she spent nearly three thousand dollars? Anyways, she came back and so I had to help her again. But I feel awful, I really wanted to be there to welcome her and make sure she felt comfortable."

By the time she's done with her long winded spiel, I've made it off the gravel path and onto the main road.

"Yeah, Cath. She was getting in as I was taking off. I couldn't wait around much longer, but I think she'll be fine with Grams and Libby. I'm sure she has loads of experience from her own kids and this is nothing new for her. Good idea on your part finding someone closer to Grams' age. That'll give her a friend, too."

There's a long pause on the phone and it gives me the same feeling I had moments before in the kitchen. Like there's something I'm missing—but I'm sure it's nothing.

"Wait, what?" Cathy finally speaks up.

"Cordelia? The woman you hired?"

There's another long pause and I glance at my phone not sure if I've already lost her with the service here, but she cuts back in.

"Right…Well, you ready to get back to work? I know Mack's been on you about finishing up that new fence for his property."

That would be an understatement.

"On me? He's basically been hounding me day in and day out about getting it done. I offered to have Callum go over there to keep things moving, but he doesn't want anyone else helping. You know, so he can attach Aberdeen Crook to the project." I clench my hands tighter around the steering wheel and bite back a handful of other things I'd like to say.

"He values your work," she's quick to dispute, and I admire my sister's 'see the best in people' outlook, but that's just not true at all.

"And you know that's a load of bullshit."

"Whatever the case is, we help our community. That's what we've always done."

"Right. Like they helped us?" I can't stop myself.

"I'm going back to work. I don't like talking to you when you're worked up about this stuff. Are you planning to stop by the house or go straight to your place? I was hoping you could at least meet Cordelia."

My lip involuntarily turns up in disgust. I have absolutely no interest in that, so I give it to her straight.

"I think the lady will be fine. I'm sure I'll run into her at some point. But, yeah, I'm gonna head back to my place since you're not alone anymore. Listen, Cath, I'm probably about to lose service."

"Sure you are. I'll let you know later if we're doing anything you might be interested in."

I give her my agreement before hanging up. Seriously, I don't know why the hell she thinks I'd want to hang out with some woman named Cordelia who's probably in her sixties.

The rest of my drive I spend in silence knowing that when I pull up to Mack's, I'll get an earful. Maybe he won't be around today while I'm working and I'll get some peace for once.

When I pull up to the Kofford Ranch, Mack is waiting for me with a large styrofoam cup in his hand that I know is full of spit and sunflower seeds. I shift into park and reach over to grab my tool belt from my front seat. Not even a second after I've opened my door, he hollers at me.

"Boy, you're about two weeks behind schedule. Wouldn't think you'd take your sweet time getting started today." He spits into the cup before laughing so hard, his gut shakes.

I clench my jaw, and the anger simmering just under the surface from my phone call with Cathy threatens to boil over. It's days like these I wonder if following in my father's footsteps will pay off or end up taking years off my life from all the nagging and people pleasing.

"Give it a rest, Dad." The sweet voice jars me and I turn around to find his daughter who I've known since grade school. She stops in front of me and gives a small bow of her head in greeting.

"Hey, Cadence." I nod in response and a shy smile graces her lips. She's a couple years younger than me, but growing up in a small town meant you ran in the same circles as pretty much everyone else.

There was a time when I thought I could be interested in her, but work seems to be the only sensible relationship for me outside of my family. Her father hasn't given up trying to get us together though, which I know is more for his benefit than hers. But I still enjoy her company and we've been friends now for over ten years, getting a little closer over the last two months while I've been working on her family's property.

I clip my tool belt around my waist, the leather contrasting with my faded work jeans, and make my way over to where Mack is resting against his new fence. *Thanks to me.* He narrows his eyes then casts his gaze beyond me to his daughter before speaking under his breath.

"You'd be wise to accept you two are a good match and bring our families together."

There it is.

He pushes off the wood, not giving me a moment's pause, walking back to his house and leaving me alone with Cadence.

She joins me at the fence and shakes her head, the light brown braid over her shoulder moving with her. For the first time in a long time, I take a second to look her over, Mack's words still lingering in the air. It's not like she isn't attractive. She's got a great body from years of working on her family's ranch. A pretty face that I know gets her free drinks when she's at the bar. The fact of the matter is, she's the girl that most guys in town would kill to take out. I should be one of those guys. But my heart is about as calloused as my hands, so what's the point?

"Ignore him," she quips. "I know my window of opportunity with you has long passed."

"You know it's not like that," I start, considering what to say next. "I don't have time for a relationship. I mean, look how much helping Cathy set me back." I turn around and face their house, resting my forearms against the top wooden rail. "Not that I regret that, but you know what I'm saying."

Cadence leans back herself and turns her head to get my attention. "So that's your plan then? Work for the rest of your life? No romance or love?"

"I could say the same thing for you." I turn to meet her stare. "I know there's plenty of guys more than willing to take you out, yet here you are. Still single."

"And I go out with them." A smirk takes over her face before she adds, "Sometimes."

"Well, your father is ready to marry you off." I chuckle.

"No thanks," she responds quickly. "Being single has its perks and I don't want to be tied down." She thinks for a second, and then adds with a wink, "Well that's not *entirely* true."

I go to open my mouth but she cuts me off.

"What I'm saying is, you've been on your own since you were nineteen, Griff. You don't ever get lonely? You don't ever wish you had someone to come home to or spend time with?" She pushes off the fence and starts walking toward the house, clearly done with our conversation.

"I've got three ladies in my life who keep me on my toes enough," I call after her.

"You know what I mean, Griffin! You'll need someone one day!" she yells as she puts more distance between us.

Yeah, I do know what she means, but I'm not interested and I don't see that changing.

"And I tell you that as your *friend*." I don't miss the way she emphasizes the last word.

I wait until she's inside before pushing off and walking the property. Now that I'm alone, I can finally take a breath. I need to clear my head before getting started so I can make sure I get as much done as possible. I've got about thirty more post holes to dig out for the west perimeter of their ranch fence and will need to mark up the south perimeter this afternoon if I want to even try and get back on schedule.

Cadence's words echo in my mind as I head back to my truck to get the rest of my tools and throughout the next hour as I start working.

You'll need someone one day.

Hell will freeze over before I ever *need* anyone.

five

PUFFY RED EYES

DELIA

"Ma'am, do you need some more tissues?"

The flight attendant gives me a sympathetic smile while holding out my second pack of Kleenex over the seats. I haven't stopped crying since the plane took off from Atlanta...and that was two hours ago.

I sniffle and accept the gift, shrinking into my seat and pulling one out to dab at my under eyes. I thought I was well and ready for this adventure. I mean, I've been dying to get away, but then what happens? I get on the plane and suddenly I'm overwhelmed with emotions.

I know I should cut myself some slack, but I'm frustrated that I haven't been able to keep my brave face on.

I swipe up on my phone and send a message to my dad.

Question

Do you think I'll stop crying anytime soon?

At the same time, my mom texts me.

MOMMA

How's the flight? Feeling okay?

This causes my sniffling to turn into crying again, and suddenly I'm thankful the flight wasn't full and the middle seat is open between me and the woman in the aisle seat.

I lean against the window and take a deep breath when I feel a light tap on my arm. I turn to face the lady who's unlucky enough to be my seat mate.

"I don't mean to pry, but I do want to make sure you are okay?" She's a little older, her voice kind, and it makes me miss my mom even more. An awkward sob escapes me.

Delia, get a grip!

"I'm moving to Wyoming for a job over the summer, and leaving my parents and friends is hitting me harder than I thought it would," I manage to say.

She nods in understanding. "What will you be doing?"

I realize she may not actually care—and is only trying to distract me so I'll stop crying and give her a moment's peace— but I tell her anyway. "Nannying and working at a store in Downtown Jackson Hole."

Her eyebrows rise with what looks like interest. "Which one? I shop at those boutiques quite often. Wyoming is home for me."

I'm surprised when a smile takes over my face and some of the heartache subsides. "Lasso the Label, near the ice cream shop, I think?"

Her hands fly up in the air before she gasps. "Oh my goodness! I love that store! I've been shopping there for ages. Their family is so special to that town. I actually saw Catherine last month."

I turn to face her fully, butterflies taking flight in my stomach.

"Really? That's crazy. Even crazier that you know Catherine! She's going to be my boss. I'm excited but don't really know what to expect. I looked online at the store and the style is different from what I wear back in Atlanta–which is home for me–but I love fashion in general. It's such a fun way to express yourself, all the colors and patterns. My friends got me crimson cowgirl boots before I left." I give her a goofy grin before that all too familiar feeling quickly takes over and makes me add, "Sorry. That was a lot."

She clicks her tongue. "Please, don't apologize. I love your enthusiasm. It's refreshing. Are you staying in town?"

I clear my throat, suddenly feeling nervous. "I'm actually staying with the family. Apparently they have a small ranch but have space for me."

The lady snorts. "Is that what she said?"

I tilt my head, unsure how to answer. "Yes?"

She gives me a wide grin. "Well, you're in for a real treat."

I want to ask more questions, but I don't get the chance when she continues to ask me about my life in Georgia. She tells me about her latest travels and life growing up in Wyoming. We talk for what feels like an hour, all while I try to make sure I don't over share. At the end of our conversation, I feel settled and more confident that I'll be okay.

"The last thing I'll say is, instead of focusing on how hard it is to say goodbye, maybe think about how lucky you are to have people that make saying goodbye so hard." She smiles before turning back to her video screen and putting her headphones in.

I've heard that phrase before but I didn't realize how much I needed to hear it now. I pull out my journal and quickly jot it down, tucking in the tissue package and the wrapper from my snacks to tape down later.

I close my eyes and lean against the window again. I think

back to some past therapy sessions from when I had to go after my parents split. At the time I was annoyed, but I quickly realized how helpful they were. I do some of the deep breathing exercises I learned and tell myself over and over that it's going to be okay. It's like I told Clara, I have this feeling it's going to be great.

I try to doze off, but the combination of eagerness and uncertainty has left me with shaky hands and a knee that won't stop bouncing. I sincerely hope I'll be able to find what it is I'm looking for.

I've been thinking back to what my mom said about making peace within myself if I really want to find that sense of purpose and fulfillment. I'm sure there is some truth to that, but why is there a tug on me to move away?

The plane touches down and my seat mate taps my arm before we part ways. "You're going to have the best time. Soak up every moment."

I thank her again and make my way to baggage claim. Checking my messages, I see a slew of texts from my girls at the clothing store wishing me well and sending me pictures of them frowning. I laugh but send a selfie back, doing my best to smile, and hope they don't notice my puffy red eyes.

As it delivers, a picture from Clara comes through, her wearing one of my shirts and expressing her appreciation for my closet. While I'm laughing at her antics, I notice Catherine has texted me quite a few times. I quickly scan them, reading that she's caught up at the store, but to go ahead and get a ride-share to the house where Libby and Marge are expecting me. I freeze.

Okay, I wasn't prepared for this, but it's fine. I take ride-shares all the time in Atlanta. This is just another city, where I don't know anyone. *It's fine!*

I find my luggage and navigate to the outside of the airport, stopping for a second to fish my sweatshirt out of my bag and throw it on over my head. I read online that even in May the weather can still be cool, but I didn't anticipate it actually being this chilly.

Before I open the ride-share app, a video call comes through from my dad. I pick it up and plaster a smile on my face.

"Hey, Dad."

"Oh, sweet pea, you don't have to put that on for me. I know the flight was rough, but I got your text that you landed. Feeling any better now?"

Sighing, I let the smile slip off my face. My dad always seems to see right through me.

"Yeah, I'm here. I have to take a ride-share to Catherine's, though, because she got stuck at the store."

"Well, you made it. Isn't it beautiful? I remember your mother and I flew there years ago and I couldn't get over the view."

It's at that moment, I realize I haven't even stopped to look around. I pick up my gaze from my phone and the sensation that overcomes me is one I've never felt before.

"Oh my gosh," I can't help but say, and my dad chuckles.

Something about the vastness of the mountains and the size of them makes me feel so small, but not in an intimidating way. In a way that floods me with awe and wonder.

"There ya go," my dad cuts back in. "Remember what you've always said."

"Be where your feet are," I recite the little phrase I've been trying to live by for the last few years.

"I'm proud of you, Delia. I know your mother is, too. If you're able to send us your location when you make it to Catherine's, please do. I love you."

"I will. I love you, too. Thanks, Dad."

We hang up and once I have my bearings, I put the address into my phone on the app and it doesn't take long for a car to arrive. The driver graciously hops out and helps me put my bags into the trunk. I climb into the back seat, sending my ride details to my parents and Clara. I take a few more calming breaths, but the serene moment evaporates when the driver speaks.

"Heading to *the* Aberdeen Ranch?"

"Excuse me?" I squeak out.

The driver reads off the address again. "That's where you're going, right?"

"Yes, but I don't know what you mean?"

He meets my eyes in the rearview mirror and smiles. "Well, you're in for a surprise."

My stomach drops, the nerves swelling back up in me. This is the second time someone has made me feel like I don't know what I'm getting myself into. I'm getting the sense I should have done more research on the Aberdeen name itself, but I was more focused on Lasso the Label.

Opening up the browser on my phone, I try to do some last minute research, but my service is already becoming patchy as we drive away from the airport. I set it down in my lap and pull out my junk journal, flipping through a few of the pages, making sure nothing I stowed in there during the flight fell out. Once I know everything is safe, I tuck it away again. I lean my head against the window and watch the mountains pass. When we make a turn down a side road, I pick my head up and look out the front window.

Holy. Shit.

Surprised is a far cry from how I'm feeling right now as we make our way up a gravel driveway. There are mountains in the background, a beautiful lake, a gorgeous stretch of land. My jaw is on the floor from the scenery in general, but now it's unhinged when probably one of the most beautiful homes I've ever seen comes into view.

The car stops in front of the house and I have a brief moment of panic, that I'm out of my depth here, but I look out the window again, where a beautiful horse catches my eye, and my stomach flutters. This was what I wanted, and I found it. I'm here.

I take a deep breath and open the car door, walking to the trunk where the driver meets me and helps me unload my suitcases. Once I have them, I thank the driver who nods before waving in the direction of the house.

"Good to see you, Margaret," he calls out, before getting back into his car and driving away.

I turn around to find an older woman has come out of the house, standing in the frame of the screen door that's been propped open, and waving back. I had a video call with Catherine last week and she introduced me to her daughter and grandmother, who I was told to call Grams. But after seeing my wide eyed expression, the older lady cut in and told me to call her Marge, short for Margaret. She is even more beautiful in person, her silver hair not aging her but only making her look regal.

Making my way up the path that leads to the steps of their porch, I can't help but notice the little girl I know to be Libby hiding behind her great-grandmother. I stop at the bottom with my luggage, not wanting to scare her.

"You must be Marge," I say, tucking strands of hair behind my ears and wondering if I look presentable.

"I am," she responds. "And this is Libby." She gives the little girl a pat on the back and she emerges with a piece of paper clutched in her small hands, a sheepish look on her face.

"Hi, there," I say, a grin splitting across my face as I meet the brown eyes peering at me. "You look like the Libby I met on the phone." I speak with a playfulness and she nods in response. "Can I come in?"

She nods again, spinning around, and darting toward the front

ELLE F. SUN

door of the house. I grab my things, carrying them up the few steps onto the porch. Marge walks ahead of me, holding the door open as I roll my luggage in, and once I have all my bags inside, I stop and take in the house itself. The main floor is wide and expansive, stretching out to show off the living area, kitchen, a more formal dining space, and other rooms that I'm sure are as captivating as the rest of the house. I'm waiting for someone to jump out with a camera and yell "Gotcha!" but before that can happen, Marge clears her throat and garners my attention.

"Welcome, Cordelia. We're so glad you're here." She extends a hand and squeezes my arm.

"I'm so excited to be here! I'm not sure it's real yet," I answer truthfully. Because really, *I'm not.* "Oh, and you can call me Delia, if that's okay."

"Of course," Marge says, looking down at Libby. "Would you like to give Delia her present?"

"A present? For me?" I move to my knees, making myself eye-level with the little girl and hoping it makes me seem less intimidating. I'm not surprised that she seems uncertain of this new person in her home. I don't know many five-year-olds who are receptive to strangers.

She moves toward me, before relinquishing the piece of paper and holding it out in front of me. "I made this for you," she says, her small voice making my heart squeeze.

I take the paper from her and raise my eyebrows. "Wow, Libby! This might be the most beautiful picture I've ever seen. Are you sure *you* made this?"

She gives me a small smile, giggling as she answers, "Yes."

"Then I'm going to keep this forever." I stand back up, tucking another loose strand of hair that's fallen out of my claw clip behind my ear when I notice Libby staring up at me again.

She tilts her head and blurts out, "You're not old."

42

I blink multiple times, caught off guard by the statement, as Marge snorts.

"I'm sorry?" I look between the two of them and Marge speaks up.

"Nothing, you'll have to excuse her. She's only making an observation." She winks at the little girl who tries to do the same back, but ends up just blinking really hard. I stifle a laugh.

"Can I put your drawing in your room?" Libby redirects her attention to me, bouncing a little on the tip of her toes. I nod, handing the paper back, and watch her take off up a set of stairs. Well, she's clearly past the whole stranger thing.

"She's great." Marge chuckles to herself. "A lot of life that one—she gets it from her mother, who got it from her mother, who got it from me." She smiles wistfully before she turns and starts walking toward the middle of the house, stopping to rest against the wall. She gives me a look over and chuckles again. "This is going to be so fun for me."

"What is?" I quickly reply, looking around the house to make sure I didn't miss something.

"Cathy and her ideas. I'm capable of taking care of myself, so you're aware. But I know she worries about me." She waves her hand in the air dismissively.

"Well, we can figure out our own routine, but I was hoping we could all have breakfast together in the morning. I love to cook and breakfast is my favorite meal of the day." I give a shy smile, hoping I'm not coming off too strong right off the bat.

"That actually sounds lovely," she says. "I'm usually up early anyways, but it'll be nice to have a busy kitchen."

The sound of feet coming down the stairs interrupts our conversation, Libby coming up to me, bouncing on her toes again with a grin on her face. "Can you braid hair?"

"I sure can, but let me put my things away first," I answer with a smile.

After taking my suitcases to the guest room, which is a bit of a pain considering the stairs, I change into some sneakers, and come back downstairs to braid Libby's hair.

She has me help her put on her rain boots–sparkly pink ones at that. She then leads me outside to show off the ranch and all her favorite spots.

Marge hangs back on the porch with a cup of tea, clearly content. At first I thought maybe I shouldn't leave her, but after a very polite scolding, I realized that there's not going to be much I can't keep her from doing.

Libby takes me around the property and gives me an incredible tour. She shows me an old rope swing and does a wonderful demonstration of how to use it, nearly falling off in the process. *A little clumsy*, I note in the nanny part of my brain.

Then she shows me an area by the horses that's been fashioned to allow her to climb the fence. She also demonstrates how she scrambles up the wood and again, almost falls. *Very clumsy*, I correct myself.

Next there's a fire pit, and she gives me a raving review of the s'mores her mom makes.

We pass the chickens and she rattles off all the different names she's given them, and while most of them are silly like Clucky or Fluffy, I can't help but laugh when she points at one in particular and says, "That's Pam."

She gives me a confusing look. "We don't mess with her."

"Okay," I adopt a more serious tone. "I'll remember to respect Pam."

Libby nods dutifully and then drags me, literally, over to the edge of the lake where there's a dock and a canoe. She makes a big deal informing me that she isn't allowed near the water if someone isn't with her and she has to be wearing her life jacket. I'm a little taken aback by her independence, but I guess living on land like this and growing up here has probably given her a freedom that turned into confidence.

I notice a house sitting off the edge of the lake, but Libby either doesn't care to point it out, or is too distracted. I'm thinking the latter because a 4Runner comes up the drive and she takes off back toward the house.

The woman I recognize from our video call as Catherine steps out and envelops her daughter in a tight hug. I hang back for a second, admiring her and her style. She's wearing this amazing rust colored sun dress with a jean jacket, tan boots, and a stunning turquoise cowgirl hat. I wonder if those pieces are in her boutique and if so, can I buy them all immediately?

I jog over and try to act like I don't feel seriously underdressed to be meeting her. "Hi, Catherine! It's so nice to finally meet you." Part of me wants to stick out my hand to be polite, but I also know I'm in desperate need of some hand sanitizer.

To my surprise, she reaches out her arms and pulls me into a hug. When she lets go, she beams. "Wow, you're even more beautiful in person! It's so good to have you here, Cordelia."

"Delia," her daughter cuts in. "We had her name wrong, Mommy."

A flush creeps up my neck, an awkward grin following suit.

"What's that?" Catherine says, still smiling.

"You can call me Delia. I don't really ever go by my full name, it's a little too mature for me. I figured I'd share that with you when I arrived." I anxiously tuck some loose strands of hair behind my ears before shaking my hands out as if to rid myself of the nerves tickling me.

"Funny you should mention that," she says while reaching

into her car, pulling out her purse and some fresh flowers, and shuts the door. "It's a lovely name, though. Family?"

I want to ask why it's funny but hesitate. "Mhm, my great grandmother."

"Well, Delia, I'm so excited you're here. I'm sorry again I couldn't get you from the airport, but we had a customer who always prefers my assistance and I didn't want to leave her hanging. You know how it is, I'm sure." She starts toward the house, Libby trailing behind her.

"I do know how that is," I call after her, breaking into a light jog to keep up. "I used to have a few ladies who would come every week at the same time to have me style them."

"Ah, how lovely," she remarks over her shoulder then kisses her grandmother on the head, who is still comfortably sitting in the rocking chair I left her in. I smile at Marge as we pass through the porch and she gives me a quick nod.

Once we're in the house and Catherine has set everything down, she turns toward the kitchen and starts to rattle off the details for the rest of the week while putting the flowers in a vase with some water. She tells me what I should expect and plan for, and we sit down at the table to come up with a schedule to test run and it sounds doable.

Monday through Friday, I'll be with Libby from when she wakes up until mid-afternoon whenCatherine will come home. She'll take over with Libby, and I'll go to the boutique until the store closes at 7 PM. On Saturdays, I''ll spend the majority of the day at the boutique again—minus today since I just got here. Sundays, I'll be off as the store is closed so everyone can have a day to themselves. Which means I'll be able to sleep in tomorrow and take things slow while I get adjusted.

At first, I was a little overwhelmed, adding up into my head how many hours I'd technically be working, reaching somewhere around seventy. But Catherine told me there'd be a lot of down-time and we could always rotate some of the days if needed.

"Oh, there's one other thing," she interjects, slightly smirking. "I know I mentioned on our video call that family lives here."

I nod, unsure of where this is going.

"I didn't feel the need to specify at the time because he usually doesn't like to socialize much. He's also gone a lot because of his work, so I doubt you'll interact with him, but he does live on the property and pops by every so often to check on things."

He?

My brows knit together, but before I can say anything, she continues.

"My brother, he lives on the property. That funny thing I mentioned earlier about your name? It's him. He thinks you're a grandma I've hired. I could have sworn I at least told him you were young, but I guess I really only shared your name and that you were going to be helping out. Then on the phone earlier, he made a remark about you having kids, and I put it together that he thinks you're an older woman. And I've got to be honest...I didn't correct him."

"Wait, what? Why not?" Now I'm really confused, but a little intrigued, and slightly concerned.

"Because, truthfully, things have gotten a little dull around here," Marge chimes in, joining us in the kitchen. Catherine snorts and I look between the two women wondering if I should go along with this?

"He's not going to like...be upset that I'm here or something, is he?" The panic on my face must be clear because Catherine quickly responds.

"Oh, no! Not at all. He–Griffin–is very kind. But lately he's been more grumpy than usual and I have the oddest feeling you'll somehow change that." She glances over at Marge and they both laugh.

"Well, alright, I guess I'll wait to meet him. Is he my age?" I have to at least ask a few questions.

"Thirty-one," Catherine answers.

"Ah, okay. Well, thanks for the heads up."

I leave the two of them to chat at the table, wandering down the hall until I come across Libby's room. I find her sitting at a small table with stuffed animals in the other chairs, engaging in a very serious tea party.

"May I join?"

She points to the chair with a deranged looking stuffed bear. "You can take Kyle's spot. He's had enough."

Kyle? The bear's name is Kyle?

I stifle a laugh similar to earlier when she announced the chicken's name is Pam. I'm not sure where this little girl is getting inspiration for these names, but it's certainly comical.

I move the bear and take the seat before she serves up some special tea that apparently turns my hair purple. I squeal and gasp, rushing to the mirror and examining myself.

"Libby, what will I do? I can't have purple hair!" I cover my face and pretend to cry, peeking through my fingers to make sure she knows I'm playing.

"Quick, drink this one instead!" She runs over with another cup, sans anything. Making exaggerated slurping sounds, I hold the back of my hand up to my forehead.

"Now I feel like I could faint! What's happening?" I slowly crumble to the floor, picking up a rogue coloring book and fanning myself with it.

Libby giggles delightedly before poking me in the cheek with her chubby finger. "You're silly, Delia."

I huff, sitting up. "Silly? I thought I was poisoned."

She shakes her head, giggling again, but then adopts a serious look. "There wasn't anything in the cup. You know it's pretend, right?"

I can't help the snort that escapes me. "Right, yes. Of course."

Catherine pops her head in the door frame and lets me know that she wants to head into town to show me the boutique, and finish the night with a welcome dinner. Libby cheers and shoos me out of her room so she can pick out her outfit and get ready.

"She already has the fashion itch," Catherine comments as I walk past her toward the stairs.

"We're all just girls!" I call back before heading up to my room to get ready for the night.

"Isn't that the truth!" Marge shouts from somewhere in the house.

A smile splits across my face and, even though it's only been a few hours since I got here, I already have this gut feeling that I'm exactly where I'm supposed to be.

BRING IT ON

GRIFFIN

By the time the sun is setting, I'm not nearly as far along as I'd like to be. Probably because Mack wouldn't stop coming outside and harping on me. For someone who wants this project finished as soon as possible, he certainly isn't helping that timeline.

About two hours ago, I finally decided to take his remarks and shove them up his ass, calling my buddy to come out and help me move things along. I know Mack doesn't want anyone working on this except me, but I don't give a damn anymore. I need to wrap this up so I can move onto my other clients.

"You think Cadence will ever stop looking out here like she wants to rip your clothes off?" Callum remarks under his breath as we load our tools back into my truck bed.

"You think you'll ever decide to take up contracting full time instead of as a hobby?" I snap back, not wanting to entertain his comments. Has she wandered outside today more than usual? Yeah. Did I catch her watching us more than once? Also, yeah.

But he, of all people, should know I've got no business involving myself with anyone.

He snorts out a laugh, raising the tailgate and closing up the truck bed before leaning against it. "You want to go out tonight? I was thinking about heading to Tombstones to wind down."

My first reaction is to say no, but this gives me the perfect excuse to turn down Cathy's plans.

"That sounds good. Did you want to head there now, or maybe in an hour or so? I think I should probably shower before." I motion down at my boots and jeans that are covered in dirt. Not to mention, there's been a sheen of sweat coating me for the last six hours. My T-shirt clings to me and the smell of outside is heavy on my skin.

"Probably a good idea. You care if I come back to your place? I've got clothes in my truck." He walks toward his driver's door, pausing to look back at where Mack and Cadence stand on their porch and wave to us. Well, Cadence is waving. Mack looks like he's shooting daggers from his eyes.

"That's fine." I get in my truck, and pull out of the Kofford Ranch, heading to my place.

A few years ago, I built a two bedroom house by the lake on the edge of our property. It's about a two minute drive, or ten minute walk, from the main house. I moved in with Grams and Pop when I was nineteen, but after Pop passed and Cathy came back and had Libby, I felt like I needed my own space. But I didn't want to be far from the girls. And even though they don't let me act like it, I recognize I'm the patriarch of our family and I'd do anything to protect them.

As we pull up to my house, my phone buzzes with a text.

CATHY

We are leaving the boutique soon to get dinner.
You sure you don't want to join?

> I have plans with Callum.

CATHY

Convenient...

Guess I'll see you when I see you

> I'm sure I'll have to get something from the house at some point.

> Don't be so dramatic.

CATHY

Don't be so lame

I roll my eyes and head inside with Callum following behind. We split off into the different bathrooms, ending back in the living room once we're both showered and dressed. I sit down on the couch, putting my watch on and allowing myself a few minutes to take a breath.

"So you're off nanny duty, I'm assuming? Since when?" Callum asks while walking into the kitchen and opening the fridge. He helps himself to a bottle of water and brings one to me before walking back to the counter, leaning against it.

"As of today. The lady flew in this morning and will be here 'til Libs starts school in the fall." I tilt the bottle at my friend to say thanks and he lifts his in response before taking a sip.

Callum and I met about five years ago, after Pop passed. We got put on a house rebuild together, and after the time we spent during the project, I realized he was someone I didn't mind having around–which is saying a lot. I didn't keep a lot of friends after high school and after everything that happened, by my own doing. I liked that Callum didn't know the Griffin from *before*, so I never had to worry about him bringing up shit I didn't want to talk about.

We also worked well together, and I even offered him a job with my family's business. He won't take it though, always going on about how he doesn't want me as a boss, just a friend. But he also really enjoys his main job at Wesland Ridge, one of the bigger resorts outside of Jackson. I'm biding my time until he caves and comes to work for me.

Sixty years ago, Grams and Pop established Aberdeen Crook & Co., an extension of their ranch and our family name. It started with Pop doing construction and helping neighboring ranches get their properties set up. Then Grams wanted to get involved, so she started helping with the business side of things, book-keeping and such. My parents joined in as well, Mom not helping as much after she opened Lasso the Label, but I grew up knowing exactly what I wanted to do with my life. I wanted to be like my dad and grandfather, and I never thought twice about it either.

I started going to job sites with my dad and Pop when I was a junior in high school, ready to take on projects of my own after I graduated. In those couple years, Dad taught me skills that I'll be able to use for the rest of my life and also set me up to take care of myself should something happen. Pop continued working with me and helping me understand the ropes, making sure I knew how to run things on my own. Not a single day has passed where I've regretted my choices.

"Have you met her?" Callum asks, ripping me from my thoughts.

"Nope, and don't really care to. I'm just glad I can get back to working all day and not having to think about much else." I sip my beer and look out the window at the lake.

I'm not a fool. I know that I've hardened myself over the last couple years and it's probably not the healthiest thing. I've heard enough of Cathy's spiels and Grams' comments to understand that all I'm doing is prolonging the day where something snaps and I can't keep it together anymore.

And to that, I say, bring it on.

In the unlikely chance that's what happens, that's what happens. But in the meantime, I'm going to continue drowning myself in work, focusing on staying busy, and avoiding anything and anyone that tries to interfere with that. Push it down and press on. That's what I live by.

"Well, aren't you a friendly little shit." He snickers.

I pick up one of the pillows beside me on the couch and throw it at him. He dodges it, setting his drink on the counter and giving me his middle fingers.

Rolling my eyes, I finish off the rest of my water and stand up, meeting him at the counter. I punch him in the gut before turning to walk out the front door. "Let's go, you're driving."

With a dramatic huff of air, he picks his keys up off the counter, follows me out to his truck, and shouts, "Alright, passenger princess!"

"SHE'S A RIDE"

GRIFFIN

Callum parks in the gravel lot across from the bar, plucking the keys from the ignition. As we climb out of the truck and start walking across the street, I look to my left where Lasso the Label sits around the corner.

A bit of guilt washes over me from blowing off my sister tonight. For a second, I consider calling her to see if she's still downtown, but my actions are halted when I catch a glimpse of a girl wandering around the corner with her phone held up in the air. It looks like she's maybe on a call, showing someone the view. The action alone indicates that she isn't from around here, but the longer I study her, the more out of place she seems.

While most girls wear cowgirl boots and hats, some because they're from here and others because they're tourists who want to try and fit in, she's wearing a blue dress with a pair of pink sneakers and white socks that have little ruffles around the ankle. They honestly remind me of the ones Libby wears.

But it's the light yellow sweater she has wrapped around her that really catches my attention. So much color amidst the darkness of the night.

Cathy would probably appreciate the hell out of the girl's style. I shake my head, realizing at this exact moment how much being around the girls the last few weeks has worn off on me. Except, that's not entirely true.

Mom always wore fun outfits—it's where Cathy gets it from—and would sometimes take me to the boutique with her. So, I grew up surrounded by clothes and women always talking about what they were wearing.

Callum notices my pause and follows my line of sight, remarking, "Well, damn." He moves two fingers into the corners of his mouth and lets out a loud whistle. A few heads turn, including Blue Dress Girl who whirls around, her dirty blonde hair flying while she takes her phone out of the air. I turn to the side, hiding my face as best as I can, observing out of the corner of my eye. Callum tips his head in her direction. Unbelievable.

I open my mouth, beginning to speak to Callum. "You're ridic–"

But a loud whistle interrupts me, my jaw dropping as the girl returns the cat call back to Callum. I look over my shoulder and watch as she gives a little wave with the widest grin on her face, and turns around disappearing behind the corner.

"I think I just found my wife," he mutters, jaw also slack.

I scoff, grabbing him by the collar of his shirt and dragging him out of the street into the place we were supposed to be all along.

Tombstones is fairly crowded, a light fog of cigarette smoke lingering in the air. We start toward the bar and I'm relieved to see our buddy working tonight. When he sees us walking his way, he immediately turns around, and spins to face us with two cold beers in his hand.

"Fisher, my man!" Callum calls out, walking up and hopping onto one of the bar stools. I lean against the bar top on my forearms and do a quick scan around to see if anyone else we know is out tonight.

"Gentlemen." Our friend nods in acknowledgement as we grab the beers and both take a long pull. "Y'all work today?" he asks.

I nod and do another look around the bar, while Callum answers for the both of us. "Yeah, out on the Kofford Ranch. Griff here is putting in their fence and running a little behind 'cause he had to take off a few weeks to help out Cathy."

"How is she?" Fisher speaks to me, but my head is still facing away from him as I mindlessly search the crowd. "You lookin' for someone?"

The accusation has me giving him my full attention.

"Nah, just curious if anyone else was out tonight," I answer quickly–maybe a little too quickly–because Callum snorts into his beer before giving me a look of disbelief.

"Our friend from the street maybe?" he suggests, and I glare at him.

"Who?" Fisher adds in.

"No one," I clip. "He's being a shit stirrer like usual."

Okay, so maybe I *am* looking around to see if the girl from the street made her way to Tombstones, but no way am I admitting that to him. And now that I think about it, why am I looking for her? I don't know what's put my head on a swivel. I don't give most people the time of day, certainly not women. But something about the way she didn't take Callum's shit... And that grin of hers. It was warm and inviting, like the yellow sweater she had on.

What the hell is wrong with me?

Maybe Cadence was right earlier today. Maybe all this time

alone is going to catch up with me. Maybe it happens to be starting right now. I drag a hand down my face as if I can wipe away the thoughts I'm having. I need a distraction. Now.

"Hey, guys," a voice I thought I'd heard the last of today greets us.

"Cady girl," Callum drawls as I turn to face the woman I was thinking about. Well, one of them.

Her soft brown hair is down in waves that fall over her shoulders, bringing attention to the deep-V of the denim dress she's wearing. She's got on black cowgirl boots and I can tell by the look in her golden eyes, she's not here for a drink. She's here to make good on the looks she was giving earlier. Damn Callum and his observations.

"Cally boy," she quips back at my friend who's basically drooling on himself. You know what, maybe it's the little bit of alcohol in my system, but at this moment, I get it. Cadence is hot and she knows it, which somehow adds to it. Probably 'cause it's true when they say confidence makes a girl more attractive.

"What brings you here tonight?" I ask, as Fisher sets a shot of tequila with a lime on the counter for her.

She raises an eyebrow, reaching for the shot and taking it without using the lime. When she sets it back on the counter, she licks her lips and leans toward me. Hovering next to my ear, she whispers, "I feel like misbehaving." When she draws back, she chuckles a little, probably at the redness I feel creeping up the sides of my neck, but I notice her gaze is fixed beyond me.

"Callum, I want to dance." She pushes past me, grabbing my buddy's hand and pulling him out onto the small dance floor.

"Yes, ma'am," he mutters, following after her like a damn puppy dog. Fisher and I both stand there watching, unable to say anything. I don't know why I'm surprised. She basically told me earlier that this is exactly her game. I guess it's been so long since I've gone out, I've yet to witness her in action.

"She's a ride," Fisher mumbles under his breath.

I whip my head around to face him, my eyes widening. "When?" I don't even have to clarify because he knows exactly what I'm asking.

"My dreams the other night and the week before. Oh, and in my thoughts when I was in the shower last night." He picks up her empty shot glass and the unused lime, discarding them behind the counter. "She did actually make a pass at me last year, but I don't know. She seems like the type to sink her claws in you, get you addicted, but not actually want more than one night with you." His eyes gloss over some and I follow his line of sight, watching her dance with Callum.

"I'll tell you what, though," I remark over my shoulder, "she's got the whole 'daddy's little girl' act down good."

"Ain't that the damn truth," Fisher calls back before wandering away to help other patrons wanting to order.

Fisher is a newer friend to me, having met only three years ago through Callum, actually. But Cal's good people, so I trusted that Fisher was too.

I lean my back against the bar, holding my beer in one hand, and using my other to rub up and down the scruff on the sides of my jaw.

I study Cadence and her movements. I watch the way she tosses her head back and laughs at whatever my friend is saying. I observe the sway of her hips, the denim riding up a little and showing off her toned thighs. And I wait. I wait for something to click. Something to stir inside me.

But nothing happens. She's beautiful, sexy even, but not one part of me–not even my dick–deems her a worthy detour from my years-long journey of shutting off the piece of me that would feel something for someone.

Then a flash of blue, yellow, and pink goes off in my mind, jarring me. Like when someone takes a picture of you and you're not ready for the bright light to go off in your face. And almost instantly, a flicker of anger ignites under my skin because I'll be damned if it's a stranger that I'll likely never see again who causes even an ounce of emotion to flare inside me.

I slam my beer bottle on the bar top, marching over to where Callum spins Cadence. When he lets her spin out, I catch her and pull her into my hold. Her palms push against my chest, before settling when she realizes it's me. Her cheeks have a flush to them, a combination of her shock, the dancing, and the tequila. I run my hands down her back and more surprise floods her face.

"What are you doing, Griffin?" There's a hint of challenge in her voice, along with her confusion.

"I don't know," I answer honestly and she relaxes more in my arms. "But I'm trying to figure it out."

She narrows her eyes, snaking her arms up and around my neck, interlocking her fingers there. The song changes to something slower and we sway for a little before she breaks the silence. "I know you don't want me."

My eyes widen and I rush to speak, but she cuts me off.

"I meant what I said earlier. I know the window for us has passed. Yeah, I still think you're ridiculously hot, but I'd be wasting my time trying to get with someone like you." She shakes her head, as if realizing her words, quickly saying, "I didn't mean anything by that."

"It's okay." I give her a soft smile. "I know I'm not Mr. Warm and Fuzzy."

She frowns a little. "Yeah, but Griff, you weren't always like that. I know after…" She lets her words die off as my body stiffens.

"I'm sorry." I step away from her. "I shouldn't have started something I can't finish."

What a dick move, I think to myself as I turn toward the exit.

"Griffin!" I hear her voice call after me, but I ignore it, pushing through the crowd until I make it outside, finding a spot on the wall to lean against.

Closing my eyes, I push the palms of my hands into my eyelids until my vision goes white. What was I thinking? Trying to use Cadence? To what? Prove a point? Prove that I'm not as hardened from all the shit in my life? *God*, I need to apologize to her again. I don't know what got into me.

"Hey, you good?" I hear Callum's voice over the screaming in my head and somehow manage to follow the sound of it over my racing thoughts. When I open my eyes, Cadence is with him, and the look of concern on her face makes me finally feel something. Disgust.

"I fucked up." I ignore Callum and focus on her directly. "I don't know what I was–" She waves a hand in the air dismissing my words and stepping forward to give me a hug.

"Friends?" she asks as she pulls away.

"Yeah," I answer and Callum pulls out his keys and hands them to me.

"If you want to head out, I can find a ride and pick up my truck tomorrow." He glances over at Cadence whose cheeks turn a soft red and it suddenly clicks. It wasn't me she was looking at earlier today. It was Callum, but he's too ignorant to notice. Well, now I don't feel as guilty, considering this new information.

"You two have fun." I smile at her before speaking to Callum. "Tell Fisher I'll give him a call this week."

He nods and turns back to head inside the bar.

By the time I get back to the ranch, it's almost midnight. I take the gravel driveway at the front of the property, driving past the main house and notice the light in the guest room is still on. It's pretty late for that woman to be up, but maybe she's got jet lag. *Whatever.* I don't have enough energy left in me after the events of tonight to care.

But the curtain gapes open for a second and I swear I catch a glimpse of dirty blonde hair like earlier. *Great, now I'm imagining things.* This is why I don't stay out late.

I pull up to my house, wasting no time to get into bed. I rest my hands behind my head and stare at the ceiling. Today was one of those days that leaves me feeling like I'm in my early twenties again–unsure of life and trying to figure it all out. I reach over onto my nightstand and pick up my phone, dialing the familiar number, the beep quickly sounding.

"Hey, Dad. Today was rough..."

clara bug,

I can't believe I'm in wyoming, here, on this freaking
ranch. Oh my gosh. It's literally one of the most beautiful
places I've ever been. I know we got to video call for a
few minutes the night I got in and you saw the downtown
area, but I really need to make a point to take pictures
of the property. It's been weird being offline, but I
actually don't miss it. well, that's not true. I do miss seeing
you and the girls posts, but it's been good for me to
disconnect from life back home. That was the whole reason
I wanted to come here anyways. And so far, it's proving
to be a great decision. If I'd known that a change of
scenery would have helped me not feel so bleh, maybe I
would have taken a vacation a long time ago haha. Except,
I think it's more than just taking a vacation. I think there's
a specific reason the universe brought me out here. I've
already had some really special conversations with Marge
and catherine, and my time with Libby is so sweet. BUT,
oh my gosh. GUESS WHAT? catherine has a younger
brother who also lives on the property and get this, he
thinks I'm like 80 or something because she told him my
name is cordelia. Maybe I should stop using that on my
resume but I feel like it's professional. It's also my legal
name, but that's besides the point. The brother is like illusive,
and I wonder if I'll ever actually meet him. I wonder if
he's nice. Alright well, I need to go to sleep. I'm taking
Marge into town to get her hair done tomorrow morning and
Libby has asked if we can go to some park while we wait
so I'll need all the energy I can get and then some.

miss you, love you
D. pp

eight

TRAUMA MAKES YOU FUNNY

DELIA

"Please, Libby. You have to get up."

I sit on the edge of the little girl's bed, pushing stuffed animals out of the way to lightly rub the top of the comforter that covers her small frame. She whines, rolling over to bury her face in the pillow.

"I don't wanna." Her small voice is even more muffled by the fabric. I wish I could say this was new, but in the past week since I got here, I've realized that Libby is five going on fifteen. She is sassy, quick-witted, and has enough personality for everyone in this house.

"Okay, so, how about this? I'll go make sure Mar–Grams is awake, and when I come back, we'll get up and make waffles for breakfast?"

I don't even know if we have the ingredients for waffles, but I'm sure I can figure something out. I've yet to make a trip to the store for Catherine, which is on the agenda for today.

The first few days, Libby was fixated on showing me around

the ranch, as if worried I might be waking up with amnesia or something, forgetting everything I'd seen the day before. We mixed up the monotony though with different games and crafts, while also taking care of the chores Catherine had left on a sticky note.

On Monday, I cleaned out the horse stalls while Libby watched with Marge. Tuesday, we fed the chickens and I learned why Libby said Pam is not to be messed with. I damn near lost my finger trying to sneak a pet of her plush feathers. Wednesday, we picked wildflowers and I made flower crowns for us. Yesterday, we played countless games of hide-and-seek, which ended with me finding Libby "hiding" in her bed, aka taking a nap. Now it's Friday, and I think it's time we go on our first adventure together.

"What about pancakes?" Libby sits up and rubs her eyes with her little hands.

"I think I can make that work." I smile and get up, heading toward the kitchen finding Marge sitting at the table sipping her tea.

Since she's awake, I figure I have a second to try and call Clara. It's close to nine, which means it's almost eleven back home. She should be heading to the store soon, and I wonder if I can catch her before she makes it in.

The spotty service thing has been no joke. My texts do alright going out, but calls and video calls really have been questionable. The best service I have is when I'm at Lasso the Label, but I've been so busy there that I hardly have time to even be on my phone.

I turn back into the hallway, taking my phone out of my pocket, but before I do anything, I hear Marge's voice.

"Delia? Is that you?"

I pop out of the hallway, walking toward her.

"Good morning, Marge," I say as I round the kitchen island and pick up the coffee pot off the counter. I'm used to my espresso machine back home, but something about traditionally brewed coffee has been doing it for me. I reach for one of the mugs and fill it, leaving a little room for cream. When I turn around, she gives me a wide grin.

"Good morning, Delia. I like your braids," she says. "Reminds me of Catherine's mother–she always wore her hair like that when my son first brought her around." She lifts her mug to her lips but sets it back down, as if distracted. "Has she talked about her parents at all?"

I freeze for a second. Other than a few mentions that her parents aren't around, it hasn't come up. And I haven't wanted to pry because I've only been here for seven days and it didn't really seem like a conversation I should be starting. What would I even say? "Hi, Catherine, I know we just met, but are your parents alive? Or are you estranged from them? I can't really tell." *Yeah, hard pass.*

Funny, though, seeing as that respective boundary for Catherine doesn't seem to apply to myself. I haven't stopped babbling about my own life to either woman. But it doesn't seem to bother them, so I keep doing it.

Catherine usually shares her own relative life experiences, some mirroring my own like how she also didn't finish college. She told me she always felt called to an entrepreneur lifestyle and my heart soared. I felt understood in a way I hadn't before. She seems to have a knack for that, because with every conversation I have with her, I leave feeling a little more sure of myself.

When I talk to Marge, she listens so intently it makes me feel like every word I have to say is the most precious thing she's ever heard. She doesn't offer advice or try to give me suggestions for what I could or should do differently. Instead, she affirms and encourages me, once again giving me a confidence I didn't know I was missing.

"She hasn't," I finally answer, realizing I've been lost in thought and probably staring off into space. "But I think I've pieced some of it together."

I move to the fridge, grabbing the small carton of creamer and adding a splash. After I put it away, I walk over to the table and set my mug down next to Marge's. I know I should go make sure Libby hasn't fallen back asleep, but something is telling me to stay in this moment with Marge.

"Libby's probably asleep," she speaks, somehow reading my mind. When my eyebrows lift, she continues, "I heard you tell her you were going to check on me, and come back to get her."

"Ah," I answer, sitting down in the chair and resting my arms on the table. I wrap my hands around the warm mug and give her my attention again. Deciding to push the envelope a little, I ask, "Were they close? Catherine, her brother, and their parents?"

She nods. "Very much so. I would say that our entire family has always been close. Catherine's mother–my daughter in law– wasn't close to her parents. They didn't make an effort to keep up with her after she left for college, so she was on her own. I could tell it bothered her by the way she took to me and my husband. But I was delighted when she started coming around. We wanted a big family, but after I had my son we didn't have any luck again, so I gladly accepted his wife as the daughter I always wanted."

"I don't want to pry, but…"

I chew on the inside of my cheek, wondering if I should be asking this. If anyone was willing to share, though, I get the feeling it would be Marge. So, against my better judgement, I come out with my question.

"What are their names? Your son and his wife? Catherine's mom?"

"You're not prying at all. I forget that not everyone knows them," she responds, a slight sheen in her eyes. "James and Paige."

The way she says their names, the reverence she carries in her cadence, makes my stomach sink. It reminds me of the way Clara says her father's name whenever talking about him, so I do the only thing I can think of. I do what I did with Clara or her mom any time I visited and they told me stories about him.

I reach across the table placing my hand over Marge's and softly say, "Thank you for sharing them with me."

Her bottom lip quivers as she turns her hand underneath mine, squeezing lightly. It seems words have failed her so I squeeze back, feeling slightly bad for making her emotional. The expression on her face, however, leads me to believe that she's been waiting for someone to let her talk about them.

Clearing her throat, she removes her hand from mine, fishing out a tissue from her pocket and dabbing at her eyes. I take a sip of my coffee to fill the moment and she shifts the conversation to me. "You're an only child?"

"I am, but I have two step-siblings from my dad getting remarried. My parents divorced about ten years ago. Actually, almost *exactly* ten years ago, because it was a few weeks before my fifteenth birthday and I remember being so upset that I wasn't turning sixteen because all I wanted to do was get in the car and drive away. I was a little dramatic back then." I chuckle to myself.

Finding humor in my dark times has always been a coping mechanism of mine. One that I shouldn't really be proud of, but whatever. Trauma makes you funny.

Except when I look at Marge, she isn't laughing or smiling. In fact, her eyes are narrowed and she looks upset again, but for a different reason. So I quickly ramble off the well rehearsed speech I've given so many times, I've lost count.

"It's fine. Really. I'm okay now. I went to therapy and, honestly, I've got a great mom and dad. They both love me so much–I'm really lucky. The timing wasn't awesome when it happened, but it all worked out." I lift my mug and take another sip of my coffee.

"Can I ask *you* something?" She tilts her head to the side as if studying me. Not giving me a chance to answer, she speaks again. "Do you feel like you aren't allowed to admit that was a hard thing for you? Or that you were affected by it?"

My brows furrow together and I consider her words. Once again, she doesn't allow me the opportunity to respond, adding, "Or did someone make you believe that you shouldn't have felt like it was a hard thing? Or at some point, you should have gotten over it?"

My reaction is to blink repeatedly, trying to process her words, and also wonder how she came to that conclusion so quickly.

I want to be honest with her, especially after the moment we just shared. I want to tell her she's spot on with all of her questions, but I hesitate. I seem to be able to ramble on about anything else, but those questions have left me feeling more vulnerable than I'd like. Maybe because it brings up the memories of the people who've made me feel that way.

So instead, I smile–*maybe a little too widely*–and say, "Those are interesting questions, but, like I said, everything is great now." It's painfully obvious that I'm ignoring her completely, but she doesn't push, instead circling back to something I said at the beginning of our conversation.

"So, your birthday is coming up?"

"June 20th," I smile. "The big two-five."

"What are we going to do for it?" She raises her eyebrows.

I'm a little caught off guard, only because I didn't really have any plans to celebrate it since I wouldn't be home. But she asks as if I've spent every birthday here and I'm starting to sense that there will be no period of awkwardness or a 'getting to know' stage with Marge. She's treated me like I belong here since the first day and it leaves me with a prodding feeling in my chest. One that makes me wonder if maybe I do.

"I don't have any plans. Most of my birthdays I spent doing something by myself after the whole divorce. It kinda ruined things. My dad always makes me a Coca-Cola cake though." A smile of nostalgia slips onto my face. "I don't know how that came to be my birthday cake of choice…" I trail off suddenly lost in thought, a wave of sadness hitting me as I realize I won't be getting one this year.

"That's a lovely tradition. We'll have to do something for you here," Marge assures me.

I take a few more sips of my coffee before suddenly remembering that Libby still isn't awake. "I'll be back!" I push away from the table, padding down the hallway, stopping in front of the door frame. Libby is in fact back asleep and I know this won't be easy.

nine

HIS VERY HOT FRIEND

DELIA

Did it take me an hour to get a five-year-old up, fed, and dressed for the day? Yes. Yes, it did. But is that five-year-old now grinning happily in her booster seat, singing along to the music playing in the car while we drive into town? Also, yes. So I will mark this morning as a win in Delia's nanny book.

The plan is to stop by a coffee shop to get something for Catherine, drop that off at the boutique, and then go get groceries for the next week or so.

Marge did not want to come, and swore up and down she was fine being left alone. I didn't tell her that I texted Catherine to confirm this, but I had to be sure. I don't care how comfortable I'm becoming with Marge, I know there are certain things I can't be slack with. It puts me in a bit of an odd position, being that I'm younger than her but also supposed to be "in charge", so I've opted to treat her like my own grandmother and hope that continues to work out like it has been.

As we cruise down the highway, I find myself relaxing into

the seat, enjoying the way this car drives. It's an older 4Runner, likely the previous model of Catherine's current one–not that I'm complaining. When I took the job and she told me a car would be provided, I felt like I'd won the lottery because that's an incredible perk. I also did *not* want to drive across the country–though I would've if I had to–but I can't imagine driving my car in this type of terrain.

The only thing is since it's not a newer car, it doesn't have any sort of phone hook up for music, so I left it on the radio station it was playing when I first drove it to the boutique on Monday. It must be the one Catherine listens to frequently, because Libby sings along to the older country music that plays. It's not my preferred choice, but it's not bad. It reminds me of when I was a kid and my dad would work on the car in the garage. He always played country music, so it holds a certain nostalgia for me.

"Do you like this music?" I glance into the rearview mirror at Libby.

"I like it cause Griffy likes it," she answers, while pulling on the ends of her hair. She asked me to braid it again, probably because I had mine done. It warmed my heart a little because it let me know that I'm being accepted by her–which was one of my biggest fears.

I'm about to ask who that is when I remember Catherine's younger brother is named Griffin, which makes him Libby's uncle. I don't know why that's now connecting in my brain, probably the jet-lag, or the fact that I forgot about him because I'm not entirely convinced he exists.

Since I arrived on Saturday and they told me about him, I've yet to run into him. The few times we've gone out to the lake and Libby finally pointed out his house, no one has been home. When I get back from the boutique around 8 PM, the lights are off. I'm not dying to meet him or anything, but I am a *little* curious. There are a few pictures of him around the house from when he was probably in high school and all I'm saying is, I would have definitely thought he was cute. Yeah, he's like six years older than me, but whatever. Like I said, I'm curious.

When we pull up to the coffee shop, Libby makes quick work of unbuckling herself and scrambling to open the door. Thankfully, she waits until I walk around and doesn't jump out of the car. I help her down and she doesn't let go of my hand as we head into the spot I noticed the other day on my drive in.

The door pushes open and I'm immediately hit with the most delicious smell of coffee, but also cinnamon and maybe even *sugar* cookies? What is this place and where has it been all my life?

"Hi, there! Welcome to Boulder Brewing Co." The barista behind the counter smiles at me as Libby tugs me closer to the pastry display.

"Hi," I respond, and without thinking, lean down, picking Libby up and situating her on my hip. I freeze for a second worrying she might not be okay with me doing that, but my concern is alleviated the second her little voice speaks up.

"Oh, that's better. I couldn't see from down there." She points at what looks to be a blueberry muffin on the top shelf. "I want that, please."

Who am I to say no to such good manners?

"You got it," I say before giving the barista my attention again. "One of those muffins, and can I get an iced vanilla latte and an iced hazelnut one? Regular milk is fine. Please, and thank you."

I pay for everything, and walk over to a small table, setting Libby down in a chair. I give her the muffin while we wait for the drinks, but something about earlier is still bothering me, so I sit in front of her.

"Libby?" I start and she looks at me, muffin in hand. "I'm sorry I picked you up earlier without asking if that was okay."

She wrinkles her little nose and takes a bite of her muffin. "Why?"

I laugh because I realize it probably seems silly to her, but it's important to me she knows this, so I continue on. "Because maybe you weren't okay with that. We just met and you're still getting to know me, which means maybe you don't want me doing things like that yet."

She tilts her head, as if to consider my words. I'm not going to assume because she's five, she doesn't understand what I'm saying. Part of the experience I had to help me land this job was working at an elementary school during my senior year of high school and if I learned anything, it's that kids are a lot more perceptive than we think.

"So if I don't want you to hold me I tell you no thank you?" She takes a bite of her muffin.

"Exactly. But not just me, anyone. If someone you don't know tries to touch you, or even if you do know them and you aren't okay with it, you can tell them no." I give her a warm smile.

"Okay," is all she says, not that I expected much more, and the barista brings over our drinks to us.

"Thank you again," I stand to take the drinks from her and promptly take a sip of mine. "Ohmygosh," I rush out. "This is like the best coffee I've ever had."

The barista laughs. "I'm glad you like it. It's a new bag of beans we got from this shop in Wisconsin called Hey Honey's. We're trying it out this week, so I'll let our owners know it's a win."

"Are you guys local?" I take another sip, Libby now out of her seat and leaning against my leg still holding her muffin.

"We have one other store in North Carolina," she says, "but I think they might open a few more locations in the future."

"Well, thank you again." I move the drinks under my arm to offer Libby my hand. She takes it and we head to the car, getting in and arriving at the boutique five minutes later.

When we walk in, I notice Catherine wrapped up in conversation with someone, but Libby makes a beeline for her anyway. When she sees her daughter, she finds me and smiles. I give her a small wave and set her coffee on the counter that's behind the register.

Saturday night when we came by for the first time, I couldn't stop gushing over how much I love everything. She has a wall of cowgirl hats, shelves of cowgirl boots, racks of dresses with colorful fabrics and playful patterns, and my favorite part, a charm necklace bar.

She added it to the boutique last year after getting tired of not being able to find a necklace she liked and decided to make one herself. After receiving compliment after compliment when she'd worn it, she decided to make it a part of the store. I've already been eyeing the charms and think I know what I'll put on mine.

"Delia!" Catherine walks over and gives me a hug. "Thank you for this." She picks up her coffee and takes a long sip. "Today has been so chaotic and it's not even noon yet."

When she mentions the time, I suddenly realize I never called Clara and mentally slap myself for that.

I tried to video call her last week after dinner to show her where everything was, but the connection was glitchy, and I was cat-called. I gave up and told her I would try again later. And while I was frustrated with the failed phone call, the look on the guy's face when I whistled back at him made up for it. His friend though, his very *hot* friend, might I add, looked like he wanted to evaporate into thin air.

"What's that smile for?" Catherine asks, and I didn't even realize I was grinning.

"Oh, nothing. Sorry. I was thinking about something that happened last week. Anyway, it was no problem. I'll definitely be getting coffee from there more often." I pause, looking at Libby who's wrapped herself around her mom's leg. "I also got Libby a muffin, I hope that was okay."

"Of course! Here," she turns, popping open the cash drawer and handing me a twenty dollar bill.

I hold my hands up, before stammering, "Oh, you don't need to do that."

"I do," she argues, but with a smile still on her face. Catherine might be one of the nicest people I've ever met. I swear, it's like she radiates sunshine and kindness. I'm sure a lot of people take advantage of that, which is why I don't want her paying me back. When I still don't take it, she sighs, rolling her eyes playfully. "Okay, fine. However, I did want to give you money for the grocery store. I know I mentioned in your interview that I'd have a debit card for you to use for groceries and gas, but I haven't been able to get to the bank. Until then, are you okay with me giving you cash for everything? Most places around here prefer cash anyway, a little insider knowledge for you."

"Sure, that's fine!" I take the cash from her, comfortable now that it's for groceries. "Honestly, whatever is easiest for you, works for me."

"I'll write you checks for your weekly stipend though. I'm assuming you know how to deposit them through your phone? Or maybe you'll want to save them until you get back? It's really none of my business what you choose to do with your money," she says with a light laugh. "Sorry, if you couldn't tell, I'm a talker."

I laugh in response, enjoying someone other than me rambling for once. "As a rambler myself, there's no need to apologize. To answer your question, though, I don't know what I'll do with them actually. Although I know I'm going to save them. Maybe I'll fall in love with this town and put it all toward finding a place so I can stay here." My words are meant to be a joke, but Catherine's eyes light up in delight.

Libby also seems to enjoy that idea and blurts out, "You should stay forever!"

Catherine must notice the shift in my expression and quickly speaks up. "She's not staying, sweetheart. She was being playful."

Libby pouts and I feel kind of bad. But, I'm not supposed to stay here. I'm supposed to visit and find myself, do some soul searching. No planting of roots will be occurring.

Not knowing what else to say, I circle back to the original conversation.

"Well, I guess we will head to the grocery store! I think I should be back to the ranch in about two hours and I'll need to change before heading back here to relieve you."

"Oh, about that, there's a bad storm supposed to roll through this afternoon and evening. I was talking to some of the other shops and they're probably going to close early, so I think when I leave, we'll close." She sighs, before continuing, "The weather here is so temperamental. Even when we try to keep up with the radar, it seems we still end up surprised."

"Wait, are you sure? I don't want you to have to close because of me," I rush out. "I've driven in some really poor weather conditions back home."

"I'm not closing for you. I wouldn't want to drive in it either. Especially since we don't have an exact time of when it will start. It's really not a big deal and I'll take over with this one when I get home." She reaches down and tickles her daughter's sides who squeals and giggles. When she stands back up, she reaches for a slip of paper and hands it to me. "I wrote out mostly everything that we need. Feel free to add the things you'd like for yourself or that you think would be good to have. I trust your judgement."

I take the list and we talk for a few more minutes before Libby and I leave the store and head to our third and final stop. On the car ride there, Libby is more chatty than she was earlier and I'm sure it has nothing to do with getting to know me and everything to do with the sugar in the blueberry muffin that was almost as big as her face.

Thankfully, her energy doesn't falter while we grocery shop. In fact, it works in my favor because she's helping me find things in record time. After a few minutes, she sees a snack tray that she'd like for lunch, so I go ahead and let her start eating that in the cart while I continue to shop around and add a few items for myself that I think I'll enjoy. I also find a few things that I could use to make special breakfasts and lunches for me and Libby, as well as a few different teas Marge might like to try. We check out, load up the car, and start the forty-five minute drive to the ranch.

Not even ten minutes in, I look in the rear view mirror and Libby is passed out. I guess all that sugar finally wore off.

I turn the radio down some, and find myself enjoying the quiet while driving back. There's so much to take in and every day, the awe and wonder for this town builds. I think about what I said in the shop about staying, letting my mind drift off to what it would be like if I lived here. How I'd probably be a regular at the coffee shop, where I didn't even have to order. They'd know what to ring in when I walked through the door and I'd hand them a ten dollar bill and say, "Keep the change."

I've loved living in Atlanta. City life has always matched my pace. But something about the quietness of the ranch, the familiarity of the downtown area, and the coziness of the few shops I have been in, has me wondering if maybe I've outgrown my home.

The idea had never occurred to me, because I've always focused on being present where I'm at. I guess I somehow confused the idea of being present somewhere, with needing to stay there forever too. But maybe it's okay to leave somewhere that no longer serves you.

When we pull up to the house, the sky is starting to turn a concerning shade of gray.

I hop out of the car and walk around to the other side, opening the door and lightly rubbing my hand on Libby's arm so as not to startle her awake. She stirs for a second, and then holds her arms up which I assume is her way of asking me to carry her inside. I unbuckle her, lifting her up and out of the booster seat, and into my arms. She wraps herself around me and my heart squeezes so tight, I think it might explode.

I take her straight to her bed, passing Marge who is resting on the couch. I lay Libby down, and pull off her small purple sneakers. She nestles into the sheets as I pull the blanket up and over her frame. Leaving her door cracked, I head back out to the car, whispering to Marge as I pass, "I've got to get the groceries." When I walk back inside, I find Marge waiting for me in the kitchen.

"I'll put things away," she says quietly, taking the bags from me.

We work together until everything is unloaded and I tip-toe down the hall to check on Libby. She's out like a light.

When I come back into the kitchen, I grab one of the empty paper bags, and take off a sticker from one of the bananas we got. Marge watches me curiously and I laugh.

"I have this thing called a junk journal," I explain. "I collect items throughout the day, dedicate a page to what I did, and stick everything on it. So far today, I've saved a napkin and receipt from the coffee shop, I snagged a tag from the boutique, and now I'm grabbing these from the grocery store trip." I wave the bag and sticker in the air.

She clicks her tongue in understanding, walking to the kitchen table and picking up something. She walks back over and hands me the ripped label from her tea bag this morning. "Would you like to add this? To remember our conversation this morning?" She places the paper in my hand and squeezes it shut. I don't know why, but the act makes my eyes burn. It's so thoughtful and accepting, and it pricks at my heart.

"I would love to. That reminds me, I got you a few new teas I thought you might like to try," I say, and she gives me a wide smile.

I thank her for the tea label and am about to head up to the guest room, when I remember what Catherine told me earlier.

"Oh, I'm not going to the store this afternoon. Catherine said it's supposed to storm so she's closing at three when she leaves. Would you like to do something this afternoon since I'll be here?"

"That's alright, dear. You enjoy your afternoon and try to call your friends and family. Sometimes when we get storms like these, it knocks out service for a couple of days. Best to reach out beforehand." She walks back to the couch, sitting down, and picking up a book.

I nod and head up the stairs. When I get into the guest room, I walk over to the nightstand and deposit the few items for my junk journal. I look at all the other things stashed in there, sighing. I have so many days I need to catch up on. But first, I need to take Marge's advice and make a few phone calls.

A soft knock on my door grabs my attention and I open it to find Marge.

"Meant to tell you this was on the table," she says, holding her hand out.

And I grin like a fool when I see what it is.

Dear my best friend who left me for the summer,

I can't believe we've been reduced to snail mail while you're gone. But I guess its good that you're getting to focus on being in the moment. I know that's your thing and all. However! I had to go buy stamps, and oh my gosh, did you know how expensive they are?! Un-freaking-real. But enough whining. I can't wait to hear about how your first few weeks are going. Maybe when you're in town at the shop, you'll be able to sneak in a video call. I miss you bad. Deels. All is well at the store and at your place. I'm enjoying your wardrobe, but wish you were here to help style me. I tried to wear a pair of your heels the other night and they were not comfortable (maybe because they weren't my size, but they matched my outfit SO well) Hmmm... what else. Oh! I've already gone to see Val Pal. We are NOT doing well... and no, I'm not just being ~dramatic~
Anyway, love you bunches and I hope that your service magically gets better so we can text more, but I know you're busy. Okay, that's enough from me. Side note though, I didn't realize how much I would enjoy writing all this out. Is this why you journal? Do I see a new hobby in my future? Okay, now I'll actually stop. Ta-Ta!

Love you bunches.
C. xx

ten

EMOTION SNIFFING BLOODHOUND

GRIFFIN

"Get your ass in the truck, G! The skies are about to open up on us."

I watch Callum make a mad dash for his pickup as a flash of lightning stretches across the sky. Me? I'm still near the fence, trying to figure out exactly how much time I have–and if I can get five more panels of rails nailed in. I'll only have the west perimeter left, if that, and *damn*, does that sound appealing.

Thankfully, Mack warmed up to the idea of Callum helping out more this past week. The two of us have accomplished in seven days what would usually take me about fourteen. I'm sure the change of attitude from the old man has nothing to do with my buddy's actual work, and everything to do with the opinion of his daughter who is his entire world. But I'm not complaining. Well, now I am, because my partner has abandoned me because of a little rain.

Okay, to be fair, we probably should have left an hour ago when the storm clouds first started to roll in. But the sun technically doesn't set until eight, which is five minutes from now and I'm taking advantage of every sliver of daylight.

Another streak of lightning spreads out above me and maybe I'm being a little careless, but I'm at my wits end. I've been up before the sun every day, out here busting my tail so I can finish this before Monday. That'll be two Saturdays I've worked in a row, but if I show up tomorrow, I know without a shadow of a doubt I can wrap this shit up.

I start the walk to my truck which sits near the front of the Kofford house, fully preparing to grab another load of rail boards when a deep voice booms in my direction.

"Aberdeen! You best get off my property, boy. I'll not be paying no damn hospital bill if you get struck by lightning."

Clenching my jaw, I spin around, coming face to face with Mack. I chance a look over his shoulder, Cadence waving apologetically on the porch before mouthing, "Sorry."

"Don't be looking to her to get you out of this. Rumor has it, you're not the one she's actually sweet on," he jeers, cutting a look in Callum's direction—who's trying to act like he's completely unaware of what's going on—staring through his windshield, stiff as a board.

"Sir, respectfully, I'm going to stay and—"

"Like hell you are," he cuts me off and pushes a finger into my chest. That gets Callum's attention and he opens his truck door, stepping out at the same time Cadence starts to walk toward us. If it wasn't for the faint smell of alcohol mixed with Mack's bad breath, I might actually let him get to me. But he's not worth my time.

"Daddy, he's going to go. Right, Griffin?" Cadence grabs her father's arm, in an attempt to re-direct him back to the house.

"Yep," I answer, pressing my lips together so hard they turn into a thin line.

Just as I think the confrontation is over, Mack mutters something under his breath that makes me feel like I've suddenly lost the ability to hear. A ringing fills my ears and it's like time slows down.

"What did you say?" I take a step toward him, Callum running over to me now and pressing his palm against my chest. Cadence has both her hands now wrapped around the back of her dad's arms, desperately trying to pull him away. I heard him the first time, but I'm wondering if he has the balls to say it again.

"G, buddy. Come on." Callum moves in front of me at the same time Mack spits out his next string of words and everything goes as black as the sky above.

"I said you're nothing like your father."

The next flash of lightning rips across the sky, mirroring the tear I feel inside my chest, but before all hell can break loose, the skies decide to finally open up and rain dumps down on us in thick sheets. It must sober up Mack because his face suddenly shifts as if he's realized what he's said, before he turns around and darts into his house.

"He doesn't mean it–it's not–" Cadence starts but I don't wait to hear what bullshit excuse she comes up with. I push past Callum, leaving them both in the rain, closing up my truck bed and getting in. I waste no time starting it up and taking off down their drive.

As rain continues to pour down during the thirty minute drive back to the ranch, the shaking in my hands doesn't stop. I clench my fists around the steering wheel until I start to lose feeling in my fingers.

This is exactly what I was trying to tell Cathy the other day on the phone. These people don't care about us. They don't think about what it's been like trying to carry on in this town and keep our family name afloat even after our lives fell apart.

Hell, Cathy wasn't even around. It was me who showed up.

Me who flipped a switch at nineteen to step up and be everything that Grams and Pop needed. Me who's been letting people walk all over them like a doormat while still getting the job done. Just so when their friends ask who set up their property, they'll say, "It was Griffin Aberdeen. Kid does a damn good job."

Because even though I'm thirty-one now, I'm still a kid in the eyes of most of these old men who order me around their property like I'm their bitch. Because I'll never live up to my father's legacy. I'll never amount to what my Pop started.

Fuck, fuck, fuck! I slam the heel of my hand on the top of the steering wheel with each word. That flicker of anger I felt the other night at the bar comes back with a vengeance burning right under the surface. I roll down my window, the rain pelting my skin but providing me with the cool down I need. I can't break.

Not now. *Not ever.*

I turn the radio up and drive the rest of the way with old country music blaring, water lashing my arm, and my eyes narrowed on the road ahead of me that wouldn't be safe to drive in these conditions if I didn't know it like the back of my hand.

As I pull up to the main house, I glance at the dash. It's a little after nine now, my drive taking over twice as long with the weather. I'm ready to get to my place, shower, and go to sleep so I can end this day. So I can stop feeling. However, I stop my truck when I notice the lights in the kitchen are on. Maybe Cath is still up and a chat with her might help me shake off some of this residual anger. I glance up and for the first time, the guest bedroom light is off leading me to believe the newcomer is asleep.

I cut the engine on my truck and hop out, making a dash for the porch through the rain that refuses to stop falling. Swinging open the screen door, I shake my hair to get some of the water off me, before pushing my key into the lock of the front door and turning it. When I walk in, I don't see anyone but the refrigerator is open.

"Hey, Cath. Can we t–"

The words are sucked right out of my mouth as the fridge door shuts and it's not Cathy behind there. It's not Grams. It's not even Libby.

I don't know who it is and I'm about to go full protector mode when something stops me.

The younger woman is singing quietly to herself and the fact it doesn't sound terrible is what has me pausing. Her headphones sit on top of her head, covering her ears, and making her completely oblivious to me. I use that to my advantage and study her for a second.

Her hair falls in dark wet waves down her back, and for a second I wonder if she was outside in the rain and somehow found her way into the house. It quickly becomes clear though it's wet because she's showered, as her clothes are dry. The faint aroma of citrus and something else I can't quite place but is strangely familiar lingers in the air, and when I take in *what* she's wearing, my mouth also goes dry.

A long T-shirt hangs loosely on her body, hitting at her mid thighs, and making it appear as if she's not wearing any pants. Is she wearing *anything* underneath it? The thought causes a questionable heat to rise up in me, and that's my cue to stop studying and figure out what's going on. I clear my throat before raising my voice a little, hoping to get her attention without startling her and waking everyone else up.

"Who the hell are you?" I call out.

She jumps anyway–*so much for not startling her*–and whirls around. And for the second time tonight, but for completely different reasons, time stands still. It's the yellow sweater girl from the street last Saturday. My mouth falls open and I look around, momentarily wondering if I somehow ended up in the wrong house. Even though I know that's not possible.

"How did you get in here? *Why* are you here?" I ask again, watching the look of panic on her face turn to shock and then... amusement?

She takes off her headphones, setting them on the counter. A smirk plays on her lips and my blood pressure skyrockets.

"Seriously–"

"Well, I live here," she cuts me off, speaking so casually that once again I'm looking around like I'm in the wrong place. She hops up on the counter, picking up a bowl of cereal, *my* cereal, and puts a spoonful in her mouth. The shirt rises up even higher confirming my earlier thoughts about her not wearing any pants and my brain short circuits. "I was starting to think you didn't exist," she says through her chewing.

That's it. My patience from today is not even worn thin, it's non existent at this point, so I don't even try softening my tone with my next words.

"Who. Are. You?"

With each word, I take a step closer to her.

"I'm Delia." She tilts her head looking me up and down, shamelessly, I might add, before meeting my stare head on and smirking again. "But I think you've been calling me Cordelia. Oh, and assuming I'm a grandma. At least, that's what I've been hearing."

I'm never speaking to my sister or my grandmother again.

"You're telling me that you're the nanny. You're helping at the store. You're who my sister hired to live *here* for the summer." Not sure why I'm basically repeating the job listing Cathy posted, but I'd like to chalk it up to being in shock.

"Mhm," she practically sings in response while taking another bite of my cereal.

"Unbelievable," I mutter to myself. "And you knew? You knew that I lived here and that I thought–"

"That I was some old woman? Yeah. And it's not my fault you've been avoiding your family all week." My jaw drops. "I'm twenty-four by the way." She laughs before continuing, "Your sister told me the day I got here about your misunderstanding and how she didn't feel like correcting you because she thought it might be entertaining. Gotta say, she was right."

I don't know whether to laugh, to go wake up my sister right now, or to walk out the front door.

"It's Griffin, right?" The way my name rolls off her tongue is like a balm for the wound left from earlier with Mack. She shovels another spoonful into her mouth, her legs dangling off the counter like she doesn't have a single care in the world. Like she isn't as affected by me as I am her.

I move closer to the counter, still maintaining a bit of distance between us, and get a good look at her. Now that we're closer, without the street between us, I'm able to make out the freckles that sprinkle across her nose and cheeks, as well as the gold hoop in her nose that catches the light and mirrors the gold in her hazel eyes.

"Yeah, that's me." I don't mean for it to come out gruff, but her cheeks flush in response.

"Well, it's nice to officially meet you." She hops off the counter, taking the bowl with her to the sink. As she breezes past me, I get another whiff of whatever scent it is she's carrying, and any anger I had left from earlier dissipates. Odd.

"I'm sorry I'm not what you were expecting," she calls over her shoulder from the sink in a playful tone, and leans down to put the bowl in the dishwasher. I'm not fast enough averting my eyes and catch the very edge of her underwear, as well as a decent glance of her ass. Fuck.

She stands, turning to face me, and I roll my shoulders out as if I can shrug away the heat that's rising in me again. She looks at me, narrowing her eyes as she crosses her arms, and I'm worried that somehow she can read my mind. That somehow she knows I'm picturing what's underneath the T-shirt. But then, her face softens and she tilts her head again like before. Any thoughts of the T-shirt, her, anything really, disappear when she opens her mouth, and the next three words fall out.

"Are you alright?" The sincerity in her voice has alarm bells sounding in my head.

"I'm fine. Why would you ask that?" I take a step away from her, putting distance between us as if to break whatever weird connection she's making with me.

"Just–nothing. Well, actually. This is probably going to sound strange, probably because it is strange," she mutters the last part, "but I'm really perceptive to emotions, and I don't know"–she pauses, heaving out a huge sigh, and continues–"Look, okay. I don't know how else to say this, but I got a feeling something is wrong, so I asked. Sorry. I didn't mean to pry or anything." She looks around the kitchen, and back to me. "Why are *you* here?"

I'm momentarily distracted by her rambling that I don't realize she's asked me a question until a few seconds pass.

"I got back from work and saw the light on. I thought Cathy was up and was going to talk to her about something. But seeing as that's not the case...I'm going to head out now." I run my hand through my hair, my mind a jumbled mess from the last few minutes. Something else registers in my head—I didn't imagine the blonde hair in the window that night.

"Oh, I see." She drops her arms to her sides. "Sorry to disappoint. The storm woke me up and I thought maybe a bowl of cereal would help me fall back asleep. Frosted mini wheats are my favorite so imagine my surprise that your sister eats them too." She tucks a strand of hair behind her ear.

My chest does something strange at the admission that her favorite cereal is my favorite cereal. But instead of telling her it's not Cathy who eats it but me, I grunt out some sort of a response.

"Right. I don't know why I'm telling you all of this. Anyways, goodnight! Maybe I'll see you around. Oh, and now that you know I'm not old, maybe we can even be friends," she says with a soft smile, before taking a step toward me.

My whole body locks up. *Please do not touch me,* I silently plea.

She reaches past my arm though, grabbing a water bottle off the counter behind me, snatching her headphones after, and goes up the stairs.

"Goodnight," I mumble, huffing out a breath of relief.

The walk to my truck, the drive to my place, and the rest of my movements before getting in bed are done on auto pilot. My brain has decided the events of today are too much for it to handle. I don't blame it. I'm not even sure I've truly processed what just happened in the kitchen. The girl from the street is somehow at our ranch and going to be living here for the next two months. I don't even know what to do with that information.

I think most of my annoyance is stemming from the fact that not only did my sister *not* hire an old woman, she hired a young, very attractive woman.

I also can't decide if I'm pissed or impressed that Cathy managed to find the one person to cause my body to react in any sort of way after basically feeling nothing for the last few years. My mind starts to conjure up the image of her bending over at the dishwasher but I quickly shut that down.

Instead, I focus on the fact that she's the girl from the street.

She whistled back at Callum, and boy is he in for a surprise. That is, if I tell him about her. I feel like I'll have to at some point, given how much time he spends over here.

And then I think about how unfazed she seemed during our conversation. How unbothered she was by my presence. Minus the initial moment we met and she checked me out, the rest of the time her demeanor seemed cool and collected. Except for that weird moment at the end, where she asked me if I was alright— said she could feel that I wasn't.

Who says that to someone they just met?

And fuck me, I hope she doesn't think now that we have met, we'll be crossing paths more. But of course she does, or she wouldn't have made that remark I'm hung up on.

Maybe we could even be friends.

I was about to say maybe she could go back to wherever she came from, because I don't do *friends*. New ones at least.

I especially don't need some emotion sniffing bloodhound trying to nose their way into my life.

But it dawns on me, she's not going to be here forever. I heave a sigh of relief, my body slightly relaxing. What the hell was I getting worked up for? Even if she did try to "get to know me", she's leaving in two months time and I'll be able to carry on like she was never here. Even better, I can play off my lack of interest on the fact her time here is temporary. No need to strike up a friendship with someone who won't be around.

With this realization, my semblance of control slowly returns, the remaining tension from the last couple hours leaving me. As I start to doze off, an imaginary countdown forms in my head. 60-something-days until *Delia* will be gone. I can manage that. And life will go back to the way it was, to the way I want it, and the way it's supposed to be.

eleven

"GET WRECKED, DELIA FAIRCHILD"

DELIA

What does one do when they realize that their boss has an extremely attractive younger brother, who will be living in close proximity to them for the next two months, and their heart and *other parts* of their body cannot seem to calm down?

Well, they promptly sprint up to their room and grab their phone like someone who's discovered technology for the first time. I run over to the window and watch said attractive younger brother drive back to his house. Which, did I mention, is not even like two minutes away? I could probably run there in five!

I huff out a breath of air and will myself to calm down. Everything in me feels rattled. Honestly, I deserve an award for how well I kept it together when I laid eyes on Griffin Aberdeen for the first time.

His hair was damp from the rain, shirt clinging to him like a second skin, and honestly thank God for that, because it gave me a glorious view of the abs underneath. And if that didn't already have me feeling like I could combust on the spot, the half sleeve on his forearm did me in.

I don't even care that he caught me checking him out. Hopefully, it distracted him enough and he didn't notice how flustered I was.

I shake my head, getting distracted from what my mission is here.

I don't care that it's almost midnight back home, or that Marge said the service will probably be spotty with the storm, I *have* to call my best friend. The ringing goes through and I peer out the window, hiding behind the curtain as if he could see me—he can't—but here I am anyway... Phone pressed to my ear, peaking out periodically as if I'm a spy or something.

The line picks up and the sound of inconsistent words break through the silence.

"Delia...that you...how are...miss you...much." Clara's voice is garbled and cuts out every few seconds.

Pulling the phone away from my ear, I put it on speaker while walking around, and trying to see if the bars improve at all. There's only one showing, but I'm not going to give up.

"Clara, can you hear me?" I whisper-shout, now that I'm by the bedroom door.

Another bar shows up and my feet stop in their tracks, hoping I can cling to the little bit of service.

"Kinda, is everything okay?"

I let out a sigh of relief. It's not perfect but at least the connection isn't breaking up.

"Catherine, my boss, you know she's my boss, I'm wasting time. She has a very hot younger brother who lives on the property here."

I stare at the phone as if watching my words teleport through the device and hope they make it through time and space or however calls work.

"All I heard was boss and hot brother." Her voice breaks through.

"Ugh! I'll try texting you and if that doesn't work, I'm going to find a way to video call you." I chew on the inside of my cheek, getting more and more worked up. But when Clara speaks again, I'm glad this one part of the phone call didn't get chopped up.

"Yeah, okay. I'm not entirely sure what I'm agreeing to, but okay. I miss you, Deels."

I smile even though she can't see it.

"I miss you too."

Hanging up, I grab a piece of paper and start writing a letter. At least I'll be able to document everything that happened and how I'm feeling in the moment, even if Clara won't be able to read it until days later when I *hopefully* no longer feel like this.

I did not move across the country to meet a guy. I moved for myself. Do I still hope for a little eye candy while I'm here? Absolutely. I'm just a girl after all. But letting any of that eye candy derail me from my plan to figure out what it is I want from life is not on my to-do list.

Curling up in bed, I turn the light off and pick my phone back up. I scroll for a little before going to my music app, putting on one of my favorite groups, Cigarettes After Sex. As one of their songs starts to play, I hum along with it before turning on my side and looking out the window. My humming turns into me singing softly, as I allow myself to forget about everything that's led me to this moment.

I focus on the few stars I can see and how small I really am in this world. But as I marvel at the night sky, I can't help but wish I understood why I am the way I am.

My mind drifts back to the kitchen when I decided to speak on the fact that I could sense something was wrong with Griffin. The look on his face told me that he for sure thought I was a freak and now I'm beating myself up about it. I don't know why I had to mention it. Then of course my incessant rambling had to steal the spotlight.

I groan, trying to stop replaying the events of tonight and all the other instances from my past that haunt me.

I turn onto my back again and stare at the ceiling. So many nights for the last few months have been plagued with unease. I've tossed and turned. I've raked through memories and experiences to try and understand how I got here. How I got settled with this longing for something bigger than myself.

It doesn't help that I'm also cursed with the inability to stop over-thinking. Doesn't matter how hard I try, like so many nights before this one, I find myself in the same position I am now—watching the ceiling fan go round and round, my mind following suit.

With all the thoughts that spin around, I latch onto the same few. The recurring ones that truly spurred this need to search for something outside of the life I'd been used to.

What is my purpose?

Why am I *here?* Not in one place specifically, but on this earth.

What do I contribute to this life that makes mine worthwhile?

I let out another sigh and pull the blankets up over my face, groaning. I'm quite literally convinced I'm one of very few people that think—feel—like this.

It also doesn't help that I feel everything *oh-so-deeply*.

I'm just one big emotional-overthinking-rambling-cocktail.

And I know I shouldn't be so hard on myself, especially because the therapist I met said it's part of being an empath. That

I'm so attune to my emotions and others' that I can't help but view the world differently.

Your empathy is a gift. It allows you to see those in your life in a way others may not. It allows you to love them and understand them in a way most cannot.

If only certain individuals in my past saw it that way too. If only I could fully see that too.

* * *

The next morning, after a night of fitful sleep, I make my way downstairs feeling like I need about twelve more hours in bed.

Once I make sure my little companion is awake, we head toward the kitchen. I turn the corner, Libby in tow, and come to a stop when I see Marge holding the cereal box from last night in her hand. I must have forgotten to put it away after my surprise encounter.

Libby collides with the back of my legs, letting out a small *oof* before pushing past me and climbing into one of the chairs at the kitchen table.

"Griffin must have stopped by," Marge remarks as she moves to put the box away. At the mention of his name, my body stiffens and heat rushes to my cheeks. I press my index and middle finger into my temple, lightly massaging it and letting out a small groan of frustration.

"Have you talked to him?" I ask, curious if he mentioned our meeting last night.

"Oh, no. I must have missed him, but his cereal was on the counter." She turns to face me and must see the shock written all over my face.

His cereal?

"I thought that was Catherine's," I mumble and her eyebrows rise up.

"So, it was *you* who didn't clean up after themselves?" She gives me a playful grin, joining Libby at the table.

"I put my dishes away!" I shoot back, knowing she isn't actually upset. "But now that you mention it, Griffin was here last night. We met," I concede and hope she can't see the redness threatening to take over my cheeks again. But who am I kidding? In the short amount of time I've been here, she hasn't missed anything.

"Oh?" She raises her mug to her lips, no doubt hiding the amused expression that I'm sure is there.

"Griffy was here and I didn't get to see him?" Libby cuts into the conversation and I'm honestly grateful for it because I don't have any desire to be subjected to Marge's psychoanalytical ways.

"You'll get to see him Monday, for the Memorial Day cookout," Marge chimes in and my ears perk up at this information while Libby claps her hands, clearly pleased.

"What's that?" I ask while moving into the kitchen to start breakfast for all of us.

"We host a cookout here every year. Kids, neighbors, anyone and everyone really. It's our way of bringing the community together, in case there's anyone who might be having a hard time with the holiday."

I nod thoughtfully, and she continues.

"Griffin is responsible for the grill, Cathy puts together activities for the kids, and I guess we'll have to find something for you to do." Marge grins.

"Yes, we will." Catherine's voice comes from the hall before she joins us. "The boutique will be closed, so you'll be expected to join us."

"That sounds great. I'm looking forward to it." I finish

preparing the bowls of oatmeal for everyone, with fresh fruit and a little whipped cream for Libby. "Catherine, I'm going to leave a little early for the boutique if that's alright. I wanted to stop by the coffee shop again."

She waves her hand while taking a bite from her bowl. "Of course! Also, this is absolutely delicious. Is this what I've been missing out on during the week?"

"It's nothing, really. My dad used to eat oatmeal like every day, so I picked up a few tricks on how to perfect it." I grin, and head up the stairs to get ready.

This is my first Saturday shift and I'll be working open to close. I offered since I didn't get to work yesterday because of the storm. Plus, 10 AM to 7 PM isn't a terrible shift when I get to take an hour lunch. I also won't be alone. Catherine mentioned a girl who's back for the summer will be getting there around noon.

For a second, I felt like I was back in Atlanta—getting ready to spend the day with customers, working with one of the girls, and being in my element.

I curl my hair, adding soft waves, before sliding into a pair of jeans that hug my body perfectly. It was a little cooler this morning when I woke up, so I opt for a fitted white tank and my butter yellow cardigan, buttoning up all but the top two. I slip on my pink sneakers and already feel more like myself with the splashes of color.

As I head back down stairs, I stop before coming into view, hearing a voice carry through the main floor. *His* voice.

"And you really didn't think to tell me? You thought to play into it? C'mon, Cath." Griffin's words travel up the steps and threaten to tighten around my neck. The words themselves aren't harmful, but they're laced with something akin to annoyance and dislike. And I'm not really sure why, which is the reason I'm about to make myself known when Catherine speaks.

"Yes, Griffin. I played into it. You have to admit it was kind of funny. There's no harm in it. What's the issue? Besides, Libby adores her. Grams has even been more upbeat since she got here. She's been great at the store. I think she's absolutely wonderful."

I hear a scoff, and he speaks again, "Well, I spent maybe ten minutes with her last night, and I think she's weird. She was rambling and…sharing all this stuff with me. She may be great for y'all, but I don't want anything to do with her."

My chest starts to tighten and little whispers of my past start creeping in. But instead of letting them get louder, I force myself to walk down the steps and head right into the kitchen. Their shock is evident as they no doubt try to figure out how much I heard, but I don't give either of them an opportunity to speak.

"Good morning, Griffin. It's nice to see you again. Catherine, I'm heading downtown. Let me know if there's anything you need done. My service hasn't been great but I'm hoping it'll be fine at the boutique once I get on the Wi-Fi." I start toward the front door, turning around when I hear footsteps running up behind me, and then two little arms wrap around my legs.

"Deely, I'm going to miss you today." I peer down at the sweet face glancing up at me. Squatting, I wrap my arms around Libby and squeeze. When I pull away, I tuck some of the hair behind her ears.

"I'll be here all day tomorrow and guess what? Monday too." I cup her face in my hands. "Maybe we can spend time with the horses tomorrow?"

She nods excitedly, and I stand up, grabbing my purse like I'd intended. Libby runs back down the hall to her room as Catherine gives me a misty eyed smile. I don't even bother looking at her brother.

"Thank you," Catherine says. I give her a curt smile, turning on my heels and heading out the front door. Marge is in her rocking chair on the screen porch and as I pass her, she grabs my hand.

"I heard through the window." Her voice sounds unsteady for the first time since I've met her. "Don't listen to him, Delia."

"It's fine. He didn't say anything I haven't heard before." I squeeze her hand before releasing, but she holds tighter.

"I'm going to miss you today as well," she says, before letting go.

When I get into the car, tears spill down my cheeks. I don't know what it is I'm feeling, but I'm aching. The hurtful words from my past combat the hopeful words of my present and it's left me out of sorts. Griffin sounds like my exes. Even down to calling me weird. But Libby and Marge make me feel wanted and valued, Catherine, too.

As I drive to the coffee shop, I try to not let Griffin's words play on a loop in my head. But at the same time, I'm hoping they do. Because the more times I hear it, the less rattled I feel about him. I thought he was attractive, but it seems he has an ugly heart.

Maybe that's unfair of me because I don't know everything about him, or everything he's gone through—assuming maybe that's why he seems so cold. But that's not an excuse. I've been through some shit myself, and I still find a way to keep my heart soft.

It hasn't been easy, and maybe I don't do it perfectly, but I try my hardest. Even if that looks like making myself a doormat sometimes so I can continue making sure someone else feels seen or known. It's dangerous territory, because some might say that's a flaw or a negative behavior, but I stand up for myself if I really need to.

Maybe I'm a walking contradiction.

I zero in my attention back on the road and turn the volume down on the stereo. I don't want to listen to "Griffy's music" today. Instead, I grab my phone and decide I'll settle for it playing through those speakers. Maybe I'll find a store with one of those devices that lets you connect your phone through a radio station or whatever. For now, this will have to do.

I start the playlist that my music app curates for me every day during the morning, afternoon, and evening. This morning is "Emotional Car Anthems Saturday Morning".

How fitting, I think to myself.

They might as well have titled it, "Get Wrecked, Delia Fairchild".

Nevertheless, I start the playlist.

Music is one of those things I pour myself into, probably because it seems to always meet my emotions head on. Sometimes that *also* becomes dangerous territory because I can't articulate which emotions are my own and which ones are being invoked from the music. But it's always there for me, always understands, and never fails to carry me through every season of my life.

A song I'm not familiar with starts playing and I'm immediately smacked in the face with the words. The artist is literally saying what I've been asking for years. Am I hard to love?

Picking up the phone, I quickly save it–"Marble Arch" by Erin LeCount–to my liked songs and continue my drive, letting the lyrics wash over me.

I pull into Boulder Brewing Co., not sure if adding caffeine to the mix is wise, but also knowing the routine of drinking coffee will help.

When I get to the counter, the same barista from yesterday is working.

"Back already?" she asks.

"You'll probably be seeing me a lot over the next two months."

CLARA

CATHERINE'S BROTHER IS SO HOT!!!!
OH MY GOSH.
I JUST MET HIM AND WOW.
okay honestly, he seemed a little rude. BUT!
HOT! LIKE WHOAH. not at all what I was
expecting. woof.
I don't have much else to say other than I
can't believe he's like five minutes away. Oh
and let me give you the highlights. Abs, half
sleeve, little bit of scruff, and a whole lot of
hot.
I will update you if I learn anything else
about him. but do not worry. I haven't forgot
that I'm not letting any guys distract me
during this trip. no if's, and's, or but's.
you'd probably smack me and say "BREAK
THAT RULE."

wish you were here
pp Delia

twelve

LITTLE MISS CHATTERBOX

GRIFFIN

"What the hell is your problem?"

Cathy's voice grates down my back, leaving me uncomfortable like a kid who's being chastised–which checks out. I hate when she goes all mom mode on me.

I hear the creak of the front door and Grams' voice joins her. "I'm with your sister, Griffin. That was absolutely uncalled for."

"I'm sorry, are we assuming she heard what I said?" I cross my arms in front of myself defensively.

"Doesn't matter if she heard you or not. You know what I've always said. It's not what you say about someone in their presence, it's how you speak about them when they're not around." Grams places a hand on my forearm, willing me to uncross them, before she continues, "You don't know anything about her, and somehow you've formed an opinion of her after one conversation?"

"Okay, but she's a lot, right? Like, I'm not imagining that?" I stammer out, feeling like I'm being ganged up on by my sister and grandmother.

"A lot, or more than what you're used to?" Cathy speaks first. "I think you've gotten so comfortable with the people in your everyday life that you don't know what it looks like to meet someone who's perhaps outside of your norm."

Grams nods in agreement.

"Okay, it has nothing to do with that," I start, but Cathy cuts me off again.

"I think it has everything to do with that. Again, you just met the girl last night and *this* is how you're reacting?" She pinches the bridge of her nose before saying something that shifts the conversation entirely. "Griffin, we know that Pop passing was like the final nail in your emotional coffin."

I stiffen at her words, ready to refute them as I have time and time again.

"And we let you have the last couple years, gave you your space to figure out what to do after, but we didn't do that so you could withdraw from everyone and only show me, Grams, and Libby, any sort of affection. Which don't get me wrong, I love that you're soft to us even if you're hard to everyone else, it lets me know you're still in there. But I'd be lying if I said that I don't miss the part of you that isn't so closed off."

And there it is.

"Did it ever occur to you that I'm fine the way I am? That I don't mind keeping most people at an arm's length? Outside of Callum, Fisher, Cadence, and Navy when she's around, there isn't a need for letting people in. Besides, you said it yourself. I have y'all, and I'm more than lucky for that."

Grams sighs, walking over to the couch. "I miss him, too, but keeping yourself guarded like this won't bring him back. It won't bring them back either."

An invisible fist swings into my stomach.

"I can't do this right now. I need to get over to the Kofford Ranch so I can be done with Mack and move on." I turn away from them, starting toward the front door. Had I known I'd run into Delia, I wouldn't have chanced stopping by, but I assumed she was still sleeping. Maybe it would be worth figuring out her schedule so I can make sure what happened this morning doesn't happen again.

"We never talk about it," Cathy calls after me and I hate the small break in her voice. "I wish we did."

"Maybe one day," I respond, not bothering to look back and no doubt see her crying. "I love you, Cath. I love you, Grams. I'm..." I let the words die off because I'm not going to apologize when I'm not sorry for the way I am. I became this version of myself so I could survive.

I don't expect them to understand, but I'm certainly not going to try and explain it now.

On the ride to the Kofford Ranch, my mind is jumbled with the conversation before I left and the interaction before it. I try not to think about how Delia barely acknowledged me when she came into the kitchen.

Her ignoring me told me that she did hear what I said, but part of me didn't want to accept that.

I also tried not to notice the fact she was wearing that same yellow sweater and pink sneakers from that night I first saw her.

I don't think what I said was harsh, mostly the truth. But I guess there's a shred of me that realizes they're right. I don't truly know Delia. Regardless, I stand by what I said. The whole interaction was...weird.

However, there's a part of me that was intrigued observing her with Libby this morning. I haven't seen my niece take to anyone like that.

She does alright with my friends whenever they come around, but somehow in the short time Delia has been here, they've grown close. Libby is smart, too, so when she says that she's going to miss someone, she knows what she's saying.

I also couldn't help but watch through the window as Grams and Delia exchanged words on the porch before she finally left. I don't know what was said, but again, I didn't miss the sincerity in Grams' face.

I don't know why it bothers me that she seems to be getting along with my family so well, but it does.

When I pull up to the Kofford property, Callum is waiting for me and I'm grateful he's willing to help me out on a Saturday again. Although, he told me I owed him, to which I begrudgingly agreed. Who knows when he'll call in that favor.

"You look like shit," he remarks, his eyes moving across my face.

"I didn't get good sleep last night," I mutter. "Spent most of the night tossing and turning, for whatever reason."

"Hey, Griff." Cadence's voice comes from behind me and I turn to see her walking up.

She's wearing a ball cap, her ponytail swinging behind, and clothes that are not made for being out on the ranch–maybe more for a workout class–which lets me know she won't be around today.

I'm half relieved I won't have to witness her and Callum pretending to not be into one another, and half concerned that she won't be here to play mediator if Mack decides to open his mouth again.

As if knowing what I'm thinking, she speaks again. "Daddy's inside. Don't think he wants to face you after what he said. He knows it was out of line."

I snort. "Yeah, well, if your dad wants to be man enough to

come out here and apologize himself, then maybe I'll believe that."

Cadence frowns and quite frankly, I don't feel guilty for the harshness of my words. People like Mack run their mouths, hoping it'll get swept under the rug by someone else in their life.

"Right, okay. Anyways, I'm going for a run near the trails before I head into town. Navy is back at Lasso the Label for the summer and I'm going to see her. I'll probably grab food after. Do either of you want me to bring something back?" She looks at Callum first, but my words tumble out faster than I can stop them.

"You're going to Cathy's store?"

"Yes?" She puts her hands on her hips as if to show she doesn't need my permission. She confirms that with her next few words. "Is that okay with you?"

"Oh, don't start with that. Of course it's okay. It's just..." I lift my cowboy hat off my head with one hand and run the other through my hair, tugging on the ends.

"It's just..." she parrots, her eyebrows raised.

Callum joins in, "Yeah, got to admit I'm a little curious too."

"Nothing. You'll meet the person my sister hired to help for the summer." I place my hat back on my head and stuff my hands in my pockets.

"Oh, hell yeah. The grandma?" Callum adds in, which sends a rush of heat through me. Partly because of the fact I got played by my sister and Grams, but also remembering the moment last night when I realized there was nothing old about Delia.

"Your sister hired a grandma to help?" Cadence asks, her tone dripping with disbelief.

"I thought she did," I start, not exactly sure how to tell this story.

"Wait, what?" Callum steps toward me, his eyes widening and encouraging me to continue.

"I thought the lady was an old woman, okay? Her name is Cordelia, so I assumed she was around my Grams' age. But, I finally met her last night and she's not a grandma. She's not even older. She's twenty-four and goes by Delia."

"Ooh!" Cadence squeals. "She's only a year younger than me! I wonder if she'll want to be friends!"

"Probably," I mutter, more to myself as I think back to how quick Delia was to suggest that she and I become friends.

"Hold on," Callum interrupts. "So there's not some old lady living on the ranch this summer?"

"Nope." I pop the 'p' to emphasize my own shock.

"Okay, well now I *have* to go. I need to meet Delia!" Cadence whirls around, racing toward the older pick up truck she drives, and wastes no time leaving.

"Is she…you know, attractive?" Callum asks hesitantly.

"I wasn't going to say anything in front of Cadence 'cause I don't know what you two have going on, but you remember that girl you whistled at in the street outside of Tombstones?" I watch as Callum's brows furrow and his eyes take on a dreamy look.

"Oh, yeah, how could I forget?" he drawls.

"It's her." I deadpan.

His eyes nearly pop out of his head. "No shit."

"Yeah. Your future wife is living on the ranch for the summer, so imagine my surprise."

"*Your* surprise? You mean there's actually a chance I'll get to see that girl again? And Lord willing, she won't slap the shit out of me for whistling at her when I do."

I shrug. "I don't think she's like that, but yeah. You'll see her again. In fact, I'm pretty sure she'll be at the cookout Monday, or at least I assume so since my family seems to want her included in everything they do." The irritation in my voice is evident, prompting Callum to ask his next question.

"I take it that meeting her was not a good experience?" He walks back over to his truck, getting his tools and reminding me why we're here–to finally get this project done, not spend it talking about little miss chatterbox.

"It was interesting. That's all I'll say. But rest assured, meeting her hasn't changed what I told you the other day at my place. I don't care to get to know her, don't care to interact with her. She's here for my sister, grandma, and niece. Ideally, we won't have to see each other more than maybe once a week."

An unreadable expression washes over Callum's face. He squints like he's trying to assess my words and find hidden meaning in them, but he should know better–I call it like it is. He shakes his head as if clearing off whatever thoughts were starting to come to life in his mind. Taking his phone out, he types something, and promptly stows it back in his truck.

"You ready to finish the fence and get the hell off this property?" He walks past me while I gather the things I need.

"Been ready," I call after him.

The entire day, we hardly talk. Both of us so determined to finish this fence, and also clearly wrapped up in our heads for different reasons. I'm not sure what's got Callum quieter than usual. Normally, I wouldn't be complaining, but as time passes, I start wishing he'd open his mouth.

The first few hours I spent thinking about what Cathy said. How Pop passing shut off that last little bit of my humanity in a way. But she knows that's not true because of how much I love the three of them. She said so herself. And I'll use her words to fight the little bit of guilt that seems to appear every so often when she and I talk about what we've been through.

But it's not just Cathy and I who have suffered great loss, it's Grams too. I know she misses Pop, and that's another thing I try not to think about.

She lost her best friend—the love of her life—after being married for almost seventy years.

That reminder has shame rising in my chest. The realization of how unfair it must be that I've gone on acting like I'm the only one who had someone they loved ripped away from them.

I don't tell Cathy enough what a miracle it was that she ended up pregnant around the same time we lost our grandpa. I know it wasn't an ideal situation, but it gave Grams so much hope. I thought for the first few weeks she might follow after Pop, her own heart literally broken. But when Cathy came home for the funeral, shared she was pregnant—and leaving her dipshit ex-husband to move in with Grams—a flicker of light came back into her eyes.

I remember thinking, what would it take for that flicker to come back into mine? I've questioned if it's even possible for me.

Don't get me wrong, Libby is the light of my life. Being an uncle to that little girl has brought out parts of me that I didn't know existed, and in some ways, has healed me. But it isn't akin to how I saw Grams choose to persist and remain optimistic. That's where we differ.

The next couple of hours, I again think about my conversation with Delia. More so, what irked me. That she, a stranger, could somehow sense something was wrong. Maybe I hadn't schooled my expressions as well as I thought, or maybe she took a wild guess. Either way, it felt like I was suddenly standing before her bare and vulnerable.

If I'm being honest, it unnerved me because it reminded me of my dad.

He always had a way of knowing how I was feeling, even when sometimes I didn't. He saw me and understood me in a way not a lot of people did.

It made for an interesting teenage life 'cause there wasn't

much I could hide from him, but when I look back, I don't view those years of my life with embarrassment. Instead, I carry them with reverence. My dad—and my mom—loved me for me, I never questioned that. I never had to wonder if they really knew who I was. There were no secrets. Not that I was a huge trouble-maker or anything, but I had a little fun toward the end of my senior year. Fun that slipped away after I graduated and very quickly had to grow up—in more ways than one.

I knew for most of high school I would end up working with Dad and Pop, but I was also interested in working at Wesland Ridge Resort, similar to what Callum does. I thought it would be a cool way to meet a bunch of people. I chuckle at the thought, given that now you couldn't pay me to try and entertain that many people, especially ones I don't know.

Cathy's words ring true in my head about Delia. Maybe she *is* out of my norm and it makes me uncomfortable. But why does that mean I have to try and fight that? Shouldn't I be allowed to carry on like always? They may want to form lasting relationships with her, but I don't need to. Besides, have they forgotten that she's leaving at the end of the summer?

A wave of dread washes over me as a new thought dawns on me. One that has my palms becoming clammy, my stomach drop-ping, and my eyes nearly popping out of my head.

What if they want her to stay? What if she does?

I didn't once consider the thought and now I feel so stupid for thinking this, *she,* was an easily solved problem.

"Hey. You good?" Callum breaks the hours-long silence, and at the perfect time.

"Yeah, great. I think we're about done." I try to hide my face from him, but it's too late.

"You sure? You look like you're gonna be sick," he continues.

"Maybe a little hungry. Which reminds me, should we ask

Cadence to bring us back something?" I'm not telling the whole truth, but also not really lying either. I haven't eaten since breakfast.

"Yeah, I already texted her, but she said she wouldn't be back 'til closer to five."

I look down at my watch. Damn. We've been out here since a little after ten, and it's already three. While time is moving quickly, I don't know if I can wait two more hours to eat. I'm also curious as to what turned her quick visit into being gone for so long, and hope it has nothing to do with *her*.

"I've got some protein bars we can have 'til then," he offers, interrupting my thoughts.

"That'll work. If we stop now to take a break and eat those, I figure we'll be done right around five when she gets back." I set down my tools and walk over to his truck with him. He reaches inside and hands me one, and gets one for himself.

"Hey, I thought of how you can pay me back for coming out today," he casually says as we open the bars.

"Alright, let's hear it," I mumble over the bite I take.

"Come out to Tombstones tomorrow night with me again."

I stop chewing and narrow my eyes.

"You don't have stay for long. You don't even have to drink if you don't want to. Fisher texted that he's working and I think it'll be fun. So, there. That's my request." His rambling reminds me of someone else and maybe that's why my guard flies up so quickly.

"I don't know," I start. Taking another bite, I mull over the ask. It's really not that big of one. And again, it'll give me an opportunity to stay away from the ranch. "I still have to get up fairly early on Monday to help get things ready for the cookout, but I guess I could go for an hour or so."

"I can work with that," he says with a devilish grin.

"What're you up to?" I point at him.

"I don't know what you're talking about." He scoffs.

"Sure you don't. Whatever, I'll go." I relent and he finishes the rest of his protein bar, dusting off his hands like he's accomplished more than finishing his food. "But we're keeping it chill."

"When do I ever not?" He shoots me a wink and while I'd probably be wise to ask what that means, once again, the more time we stand here talking, the more time we have ahead of us working. I wave him off and head back to work.

Two more hours pass, and the damn fence is done.

I lost Callum about thirty minutes ago, but when I walk back over to our trucks, I see him eating with Cadence on the porch. There's a take out bag on the hood of my car and I don't bother interrupting them. Instead, I load up my truck, grab the bag, and holler, "Thanks!" before getting in and making my way straight to my place. There will be no stopping at the main house tonight. Not until I learn the schedule of a certain nanny-caretaker-boutique-helper.

Now I need to find a way to ask without making it seem like I care. Because, really, I don't. But I know Grams or Cath will try and spin it, and I'd rather not admit that I'm only asking so I can make sure I never have to run into Delia again. Which is already proving hard to do, given we're likely going to be around one another most of Monday... Great.

thirteen

FAMILY BREAKFAST

DELIA

When I wake up Sunday morning, I feel like I'm lingering in the oddest form of déjà vu.

I glance around the room, reminding myself once again that I'm not back in Atlanta, before rolling over and closing my eyes for a few more minutes, playing back the events of yesterday in my head.

I got to Lasso the Label right before ten, counted the drawer, and opened for the day. Around noon, a girl walked in with her head down, searching for something in her purse and the red hair made me think for a second I was back home at work and Clara was clocking in. She looked up, no doubt catching me staring, and gave me a bright smile.

"Hi, there, I'm Navy! You must be Delia." She made it to the cash wrap and placed her purse into one of the cabinets.

"Hi, yes. That's me. Sorry, you look almost exactly like my best friend back home. She also works with me, so when you walked in–for a second–I was back in Atlanta. But obviously, we're not. We're in

Jackson Hole. And you're not Clara, you're Navy." I tucked my hair behind my ears and shamed myself for already rambling with her.

"That's so sweet! Hopefully it'll be comforting then, having a reminder of home around. I'm so excited to be back." She began to recount to me where she'd been and the whole time I had to stop myself from staring too long at how similar she is to Clara–physically, at least. Other than that, they're quite different.

Navy recently graduated with her Masters in Social Work and is here for the summer while she figures out what job she wants to take. Apparently she'd got a few offers, but isn't in a rush to settle into one. She'd been helping at the shop since she was in high school, and a part of me wanted to ask if that meant she's close with Griffin, but I held my tongue.

We talked for maybe fifteen minutes before I heard a loud scream echo through the shop, and a blur of a person barreled toward Navy, wrapping her up in a bear hug.

"I missed you so much!" The unknown person squawked before pulling back, and when she did, my breath caught.

I'd like to think that I'm attractive, but this girl could stop traffic. She hardly had any makeup on, clearly just got done with a work out, and yet looked like she could be getting ready to go model. Her soft brown hair was pulled back, not a single piece out of place.

"Hi," I butted in, not liking how I felt left out, but also not sure what else to say.

She turned and gave me her full attention and another squawk came from her.

"You're Delia! Oh my gosh, you're Delia?" Her mouth hung open a little before she smirked. "Oh, this is actually so good."

"I'm sorry?" I scrunched up my face, trying to understand her words.

"Griffin conveniently left out the part that you're drop dead gorgeous." She said it so nonchalantly, I'm almost positive I misheard her. "I'm Cadence, by the way."

"You saw Griffin today?" Navy asked, and the inflection in her voice answered the question I didn't want to ask earlier. She definitely knows him.

"Yeah, he's working on our ranch. Well, was. No doubt he's finished up after today," Cadence responded.

"Hm," was all Navy said before turning the conversation back to me. "What's the deal with you and him?"

I also didn't miss the inflection this time, the one that's tainted with jealousy.

"No deal," I answered quickly. "I'm not sure what she's talking about."

"Oh, he told me and Callum, our friend, about his little misunderstanding." She grinned again, and while it made me want to ask more about the conversation, I thought better of it.

"Misunderstanding?" Navy glanced between the two of us, clearly not liking she was on the outside of whatever was going on.

Cadence gave her the brief summary of what happened and Navy had lost any semblance of jealousy and was now doubled over in laughter.

"No, because, I can only imagine how he probably reacted when he found out." She spoke in between her laughs.

I awkwardly smiled, and decided to speak the truth. "He was actually kinda rude."

Both girls turned and looked at me, their mouths taking on an O-shape.

"Well, well, well," Cadence drawled. "Where have you been hiding?"

"Um, Atlanta?" I tried to joke in response, not entirely sure what she meant.

"It's about time someone else showed up here and doesn't put up with Griffin's shit." She crossed her arms.

"Cadence," Navy started, "You know–"

The brunette held up a hand, cutting off her friend's words, and shocking me when she said almost exactly what I had been thinking in the car.

"People go through shit all the time, Navy. He isn't the only person alive who's been dealt a fucked up hand." She glanced over at me, continuing, "Pardon my french."

I held up my hands to show I took no offense.

"Anyways, he's had all of us walking on eggshells for far too long. And now we have the perfect person to help shake things up." She honed her golden eyes on me. "You, miss Delia, are exactly what we've been needing."

I shrugged, not sure what to say to that. Navy, on the other hand, looked a little irritated, and I'd have to see if I could figure out somehow what the deal is there.

I left Navy and Cadence to catch up as customers came in. I didn't mind running things on my own for a little, it's exactly what I was used to.

Once the store was empty again, I found Navy and Cadence wrapping up their conversation. Cadence locked eyes with me across the store and called out, "Delia, you're coming out with us tomorrow night!"

I froze.

"No if's, and's, or but's," she continued.

I stalked over to where they stood and Navy chimed in. "Yes, you have to. We need another girl to deal with the guys."

The guys.

"I don't think Griffin will like me being there," I muttered.

"And I don't give a rat's ass what Griffin will or won't like," Cadence answered with a grin plastered on her face. "You're coming with us, end of discussion. Let me see your phone."

I reached under the counter and grabbed it, handing it to her.

"I'm texting myself now, and I'll make a chat with us three. Do you have cowgirl boots?"

I nodded, watching as she typed on my phone.

"Perfect. Wear those and something hot and flirty. I want to test something." Cadence snickered as she handed me back my phone.

"Cadence…" Navy mumbled.

"Let me live," she remarked out of the side of her mouth to her friend. "Actually, Delia, have you had lunch yet? It's, what, a little after one? How about you take your break and get a bite with me somewhere and we can chat more. Think you can survive without her?" She winked at Navy who rolled her eyes.

I'm stunned into submission by the way Cadence commands the people around her, so effortlessly too. It wasn't rude, either.

After confirming with Navy that it actually was okay if I took my break, I left with Cadence and we spent the next forty-five minutes talking. I was shocked that I didn't feel like I was rambling, probably because Cadence didn't stop asking me questions, which prompted me to continue sharing.

She told me a little about herself, too, but not a ton. The biggest thing that stuck out was how she loves to bake. So much so, that she'd love to own a bakery one day.

And by the time we finished eating, I made a promise to her that we'd do this again so I could hear more about her and that bakery idea of hers. It seemed to take her by surprise that someone was interested to know more than what she offered up.

She dropped be back off at the store and Navy and I worked in tandem as if this wasn't our first shift together, but our hundredth.

When we closed, I swore there was still a piece of me confused that I was at Lasso the Label and not my store back home.

A knock on my door breaks me from my sleepy thinking. I sit up, pulling the comforter up to my waist, and rubbing my eyes.

"Come in," I call out.

The door creaks open, and I see Catherine first, followed by a little body that scrambles toward me and up on the bed. Libby clambers into my lap, wrapping her small arms around me.

"Good morning, Deely." She looks up at me and I don't know when she decided to give me a nickname, but it makes my heart clench every time. I glance past her at Catherine who mouths, "Sorry," and I shake my head to show her that there's no need for apologies.

"Are you ready to make breakfast and then go see the horses?" I redirect my attention to Libby, who's playing with the ends of my hair, twirling it between her fingers.

She nods furiously, stopping abruptly, and tilts her head to the side. She reaches up to my nose and bops the ring there before blurting out, "Why do you have that?"

"Libby," Catherine calls from the door. "That is not polite."

I laugh. "It's fine. I got it because it's pretty."

"Did it hurt?" she asks and I reach for her chubby forearm with my thumb and pointer finger.

"That much," I say, pinching her softly.

She giggles before rolling out of my lap and climbing back off the bed. Catherine picks her up and smiles. "We'll see you downstairs, but no rush. Someone was excited to see you this morning."

She shuts the door again, her footsteps growing fainter. I push back the covers and start walking toward the en suite bathroom, when I catch a glimpse of someone out the window and freeze.

Why is *he* here?

As if he can sense my eyes on him, his gaze darts up to the window and I rush toward the bathroom out of sight.

After washing my face and brushing my teeth, I decide to braid my hair again since we'll be with the horses and not bother with makeup. I head back into the room to slip on a pair of older jeans and one of my dad's old shirts. I pause for a second, realizing I need to maybe invest in a pair of boots to wear around the ranch, my tennis shoes already starting to see better days. Maybe Catherine has an extra pair I could borrow in the meantime.

I head downstairs, hesitating when I see Griffin standing at the kitchen island talking to Marge. But like all the times in my past when someone else's presence threatened to make me feel small or act differently, I choose to ignore them and be myself anyways.

I breeze past Griffin, stopping to give Marge a side hug, and open the fridge, grabbing some of the ingredients I need for breakfast.

I'm excited to cook for everyone. All week I've been hyping up my French toast to Libby, who told her mom, and now I've got an audience ready to try it. And while it's my day off, I don't feel like I'm working. Probably because there's not a second that passes where Catherine, Marge, or Libby don't ooze gratefulness.

Libby, in her own way of squealing and hugging me, telling me every meal is the best she's ever had. Catherine will leave me a Post-it note here and there, or send me a text along the lines of, "Can't say thank you enough" or "Thank you again". Marge shows it when she stops me, takes a hold of my hand, and looks me in my eyes as if staring right into my soul and whispers, "It's so nice to have you here."

This morning feels like, well, family breakfast. My heart squeezes at that concept.

I get to work mixing my wet ingredients together, my secret

being adding a little syrup to the egg wash to really get that maple flavor into the bread.

"Catherine, do you have an old pair of boots I could borrow for today? I still need to pick up a pair for myself," I ask, while dipping the thick cut bread I picked up at the store for this exact meal.

"Actually, I do. A few pairs. You don't have any cowgirl boots?" she responds while sitting at the table, coloring with Libby.

"My friends got me a pair before I left, but they're more fashionable than practical. Is there a local shop here you recommend?" I drop the butter into the skillet and lay down the first piece of bread.

"Yes, I'll text you the names. What size are you?" she asks.

"Like a seven and a half." I continue the process of dipping the bread, and cooking it until it's golden. I've got a decent sized stack already accumulating on a plate and while my back is to everyone, I can sense multiple pairs of eyes on me.

"Oh, perfect! I've got a pair that's an eight, but I think it should be fine for now." Catherine's voice floats through the kitchen, mixing with the sound of sizzling, Libby's laughter, and the soft chatter between Marge and Griffin.

I start to hum to myself, something I naturally do when I'm in a flow state. I peel a few bananas and slice them up, before assembling everyone's plates. I place Libby's in front of her first, making a show of sprinkling the powdered sugar over the plate and a swirl of syrup. Her eyes grow about three sizes. Once Marge and Catherine have their plates, I place Griffin's in front of him. The look of shock on his face tells me he didn't expect me to prepare anything for him, but I can't not.

"Do you want powdered sugar and syrup too?" I ask over my shoulder as I grab the two items for my own plate.

"Uh...sure." His voice is low, and I add the toppings to his before doing the same to mine. "Thanks."

I nod, moving to sit at the table with the rest of the girls, leaving him at the kitchen island.

"Delia, this is truly amazing. I think we might have to make this a Sunday tradition," Catherine says, and Libby nods with her mouth full, cheeks stuffed like a chipmunk.

"We might have to keep you around for longer than the summer if you've got more recipes like this up your sleeve," Marge adds in and a clatter rings out behind us.

I turn to see Griffin has dropped his fork and knife, quickly picking them back up while clearing his throat. "I'll meet y'all at the stable when you're done," is all he says before getting up, washing his plate off, and putting it in the dishwasher. He's out the door before anyone can speak.

"He's joining us?" I ask no one in particular.

"Yes," Catherine answers. "He leads Libby's lessons, not to mention the horses have been his responsibility for the last six years."

"Griffy said I could ride on Bowen today." Libby picks up her plate to lick off some of the syrup and Marge chuckles. "I wanna go get my shoes, Momma."

She wiggles out of her chair, before coming to my side, laying her sticky cheek on my arm, and giving me a hug. "Thank you, Deely." She bolts down the hallway disappearing into her room.

"Wash your hands, Libs!" Catherine calls after her before facing me. "And yes, thank you again for making breakfast, this was a treat." She pushes away from the table and gathers everyone's plates. Once she sets them in the sink, she turns down the hallway. I pick up my mug of coffee and take a few sips when she comes back and sets a pair of old, faded brown cowgirl boots in front of me. "Try these."

I slip my feet into them and they fit perfectly. "They're amazing!" I look up at her and she gives me one of those misty eyed smiles of hers.

"They were my mother's." She reaches out and tugs on the bottom of my braid. "You remind me of her in some ways, at least how I remember her when I was about Libby's age. The braids, now the boots. It's uncanny in a way. Sorry, I hope that doesn't make you uncomfortable."

I clear my throat, my chest tightening at the emotions I can sense in the air. The empath in me rising to the surface, wanting to claw it's way out, but instead, I find my voice and respond. "Marge mentioned to me the other day when I had my hair in braids that your mom wore it like this sometimes. I hope it doesn't upset you in any way."

"It doesn't," Catherine starts to say, when Marge interjects.

"It's refreshing. For so long, it's been as if we aren't supposed to remember what they were like. As if they didn't spend time here and these walls don't carry memories of them."

I'm finally about to ask for the whole story when Libby barrels around the corner, straight for me. "Let's go, Deely! I wanna see the horsies."

Both women give me a smile, signaling the end of the conversation, so I stand, take Libby's hand, and start toward the door.

"Oh, wait, Delia," Catherine calls. "This came for you yesterday, I forgot to give it to you."

My darling daughter,

It brought me great joy to get your letter in the mail yesterday. I am so glad that you are settling in and enjoying the company of Margaret and Catherine.
I know that it's been hard without your grandmothers, but maybe you will find a similar comfort from Margaret the more time you spend with her.
Are you enjoying the views? Have you and Libby gone on any more adventures? She really sounds like such a precious girl. I'm sure she is having a great time with you, I know you were worried about that.
I was thinking about you the other morning while having coffee on my porch. Do you remember when you decided to move to Atlanta? I said, "Delia, why do you want to move downtown?" And you said, "I just have a feeling."
   You're always listening to your heart, and I love that about you. You've always been so special, and I'm sorry that life has not always been kind to you. I admire that you have not let it harden you. My dreamer girl. I look forward to your next letter or call and I hope you are enjoying your Polaroid. Send me one if you feel so inclined. I love you, Delia Rose.

                              Keep dreaming,
                              Mom

fourteen

"I WAS FEELING."

DELIA

After tucking my mail away in my room and a small detour to check on the chickens, Libby and I finally make it to the stable.

When we walk in, I spot Griffin shoveling a stall. I look at the three horses I've only gotten to pet since I arrived here as I wait for him to notice us, and when he finally does, I let Libby run over to him. He scoops her up effortlessly.

"Who let you in here?" He speaks so softly to her, tickling her side, causing the bubbliest giggle to erupt from her.

"Deely!" She squeals and he presses little kisses all over her cheek. The entire interaction has me frozen in place. How is this the same guy?

Once again, my empath radar is flying off the charts and something in me feels drawn to Griffin. Of course there's more to him than the bristly guy I encountered in the kitchen, I'm not naive. But I didn't expect *this*.

He clears his throat, setting Libby back down before focusing his attention on me. The action causes my cheeks to warm and I really hope he doesn't notice. But there isn't any possible way he could, because his eyes are glued to my feet and my stomach turns into a pit.

"Where did you get those," he clips out.

"Your sister gave them to me," I force myself to say as evenly as possible.

A tick in his jaw forms, before he turns to Libby and ignores me completely. "C'mon, Libs, let's get Bowen ready for you."

I stand there, feeling like a complete idiot. Except, I'm not. I haven't done anything wrong, and I refuse to let him, once again, make me want to tuck my tail between my legs and cower away.

He picks Libby back up and they walk over to the stall where Bowen, a salt and pepper horse, pokes his face out of the window opening. Libby told me all the horses' names when we went out to the pasture a few days ago for a walk, so I head to the stall where Maven, a chestnut colored horse, is also poking her nose out.

"Hey, pretty girl," I whisper, before using the back of my knuckles to rub up and down her muzzle, paying extra attention right above her nostrils. She pushes into my hand and I can't stop myself from resting my forehead against hers.

"I'll bring her out for you." Catherine's voice startles me, causing me to jump back a little.

"That would be great."

I move out of the way, focusing on where Griffin has brought Bowen out and gotten him ready for Libby, who's put a helmet on now. I can't help the laugh that escapes me when I realize it's pink and sparkly like her rain boots.

I watch as he picks her up, places her in the saddle, before taking the reins, and walking Bowen out into the pasture. Libby looks like she belongs up there and it reminds me of the comfort I used to feel when I rode.

A few seconds pass and Catherine has Maven out of the stall, handing me her reins. "I remember you mentioned in your initial interview call that you used to take lessons, let's see how much you remember."

Muscle memory takes over as I move to find a brush and sweep off Maven's back to ensure there's no dirt or debris that could get trapped under the saddle pad. Once I've done that, I stop and give her reassuring rubs. Not necessarily part of the steps, but something I can't help doing. I place the saddle pad down, then the saddle, and tighten the cinches. When I'm done, I nuzzle into the side of Maven's face and turn to face Catherine who smiles approvingly.

She gives me a nod and I guide Maven out to the pasture as well, where I note Griffin is now leading Bowen in a slow trot.

"If you feel comfortable mounting, I feel comfortable letting you ride her at the walk gait."

I can't help the giddiness that overcomes me, but I don't want my excitement to transfer to Maven and cause her to be jumpy. I take a deep breath as I place my left foot in the stirrup and grab hold of the pommel, swinging my other leg over and situating myself in the saddle. I take hold of the reins again, clicking my tongue and giving a light tap on Maven's side with my heel. She starts to walk and Catherine follows alongside, but doesn't seem to be worried.

"You're a natural, Delia," she comments after a few minutes pass.

"I've missed this so much," is all I can say in a dreamy-like voice. "It was so healing for me when I was younger, but I didn't understand it then the way I do now."

"How do you mean?" Catherine asks.

"When I was younger, I often felt uneasy or anxious, but I didn't understand why. I know now it's because my parents weren't getting along, but I was too young to pick up on that. My body, however, could, and it left me with all these emotions I couldn't process. The only relief I found was always after my lessons. I'd leave feeling more at peace, almost lighter. I later learned it's because horses are perceptive of emotions, and that's why I love them." I stroke down Maven's mane. "They're empaths, like me."

Catherine smiles as she comes to a halt, leaning against the fence. "If you want to trot with her, go ahead."

Maven and I move on, picking up the pace a little. We follow the perimeter of the fence and I'm careful not to encroach on Bowen and disturb Libby. I do my best to keep my gaze forward and not wonder what Griffin is thinking.

At one point, the sun peeks out from behind the clouds and kisses my face. I crane my neck toward the light and the warmth on my cheeks mixed with the light breeze in the air causes me to pause. I pull on Maven's reins, bringing her to a stop, and sit there in the saddle with my eyes closed and bask in the sun.

There's something so healing and serene about the moment, yet tears start welling up behind my eyelids. My mind drifts back to when I was in the coffee shop with Clara. How out of place I felt. How lost... And somehow in two weeks, I've managed to catch glimpses of what I think I'm looking for. I don't know if that means Wyoming, or more so connecting with the things from my past that once gave me solace.

Maybe that's what I've been missing–doing something that I not only enjoy, but fills my cup. It sounds so easily put, but when you find yourself wrapped up in the everyday routine of your life, the simple pleasures are usually the first thing to slip away from you.

Perhaps when I get back to Atlanta, I'll find an equestrian center and start riding again. I'll actually wake up and make breakfast for myself like I have here, and I'll make more time to enjoy things like walks outside or sitting on my balcony to journal.

Hope spreads through my veins as I start to reconnect with a version of myself I didn't realize had been stowed away. When I blink open my eyes, the tears falling down my cheeks, I immediately find Griffin staring at me–no, studying me. His head is tilted and the way his eyes are narrowed, I'm sure he's reading me to filth in his mind. I'm probably not doing myself any favors by wearing my emotions on my sleeve like this, adding another example to his list of "Reasons Why Delia is Weird" or whatever he thinks of me.

But I don't care. I need this moment. It's been awhile since I've left myself truly sit with my emotions. *We won't count the plane ride here*, I think to myself. But before that, like the night I said bye to my mom, I didn't want to *feel*. I thought I could acknowledge the emotions and move on, but I don't know why I fight myself on that sometimes. Well, I kind of do know… It can be so overwhelming, but there has to be a balance somewhere. Right?

I tap Maven's side and trot back over to where Catherine stands by the gate connecting the pasture with the stable. I dismount, and to my shock, hear Griffin call after me. "You can untack her and put everything away, but leave her to graze in the pasture."

I give him a curt nod and do exactly that. As I'm finishing up, I stop and peek into the stall where the last horse, Rally, is resting. He's a beautiful ivory color, and his gaze reminds me of how it feels when Marge looks at me. Like they're not just seeing me, but through me.

I hear footsteps coming up behind me and I spin on my heels assuming it's Catherine, but lose my footing when I see it's Griffin. I straighten myself and regain my composure, dusting my hands off on my jeans then meeting his attention.

"Is there anything else I can–"

"What were you doing out there?" Griffin cuts me off and the coldness in his voice is a contrast to the warmth I felt from the sun mere minutes ago.

"Um–I–" I start to say, peering over his shoulder to see Catherine and Libby aren't far away. At least they didn't leave me alone with him. I meet his gaze again and he's got the same expression as when I opened my eyes. "I was…feeling," I finally respond.

"Feeling?" He repeats the word but it drips with disgust when he says it. I don't know what comes over me, but I cross my arms and lift my chin up.

"Yes, Griffin. I was feeling. I'm not sure if you know what that is–honestly, I don't think you do. But that's what I was doing. You should try it sometime." I give him a fake smile, starting to walk past him toward Catherine and Libby, but a strong grip around my upper arm halts me in place. The second I register his fingers on my bare skin, chills erupt.

With us facing opposite directions, he pulls me closer into his side, before tilting his head and whispering, "Trust me when I say that I'm the last person you want to push to feel something."

I slowly turn my head before meeting his gaze. Clenching my teeth, I suck in a large breath of air in through my nose, slowly blowing it out through my lips. My hope is it will diffuse the frustration and anger that's starting to seep out of me so I don't snap. Griffin's stare on me doesn't falter and I know this is a challenge to him, a power move. He must recognize the breathing pattern and know that he's rattled me, because he chuckles. But it only makes me double down.

"I feel sorry for people like you," I say in a hushed voice.

140

His grip on my arm loosens and I know I've shocked him.

"People like me?" he challenges. "And what does that mean?"

"You think that by turning off the part of you that feels something, it makes you stronger than everyone else. But really, it makes you weak."

I shake his hand off of me, pushing past him for good this time. His voice calls after me, "You don't know what you're talking about."

I turn to face him one more time. "I know enough."

fifteen

BRIGHT CRIMSON BOOTS

GRIFFIN

A cold shower is not enough to extinguish the flames that are consuming me from my interaction with Delia. The nerve of that girl to show up here and suddenly act like she knows everything.

She may have my sister, grandma, and niece wrapped around her finger, but I won't be falling victim to whatever spell she's got them under.

I close my eyes as I stand under the shower head, the icy water cascading down my still tense body. When she finally left with Catherine and Libby, my body was vibrating with anger. I don't know what she's heard or how she came to the conclusion that I've turned off my emotions, but it was enough to make me charge straight to the main house and find Grams immediately.

Thankfully, Libs and Cath walked over to the dock with Delia, and I found Grams alone on the porch. Before I could even open my mouth, she spoke without glancing in my direction.

"You better find a way to calm down before you speak to me."

I shouldn't be surprised that she could sense my anger, but

that only wound me up more because it left me feeling the way I have the last few times I've been around Delia. As if the years I've worked to put all these different stones in place to build a wall around myself, were merely flecks of sand waiting to be blown away.

I tried to ask Grams if she'd spoken to Delia about me, but she wouldn't entertain it. Told me if I wanted to know what Delia thought of me, I needed to ask her myself. Like hell I'd be doing that.

I'm left to assume that in a conversation with either Navy or Cadence, someone let something slip. Now I need to find out exactly *what*.

I run a hand down my face, pulling myself from my thoughts. Balling my hand into a fist, I pound it once against the shower wall, and shut it off before grabbing a towel, wrapping it around my waist. As I move to my room, I consider bailing on Tombstones tonight with Callum. Another part of me feels compelled to storm out of here and find Delia, demanding she tell me what she's heard.

I pick my phone up and my eye catches on Navy's contact. I was wondering when I'd hear from her since she got back, but didn't know if I would. I've known her longer than everyone in our friend group, mainly because she started working at the boutique with my mom when we were in high school.

We dated for a few months of my senior year and into the summer after graduation, but when my life fell apart, she was the first person I kicked to the curb. And that's putting it lightly.

She came back to town a few times and tried to be there for me, but to put it simply, I told her to fuck off. On more than one occasion.

It's not something I'm proud of and I've since apologized for, countless times. But I still feel like there's a part of her that struggles to see me as the man I am now, and not the boy I was those few years after graduation.

I click on her message and frown.

NAVY

I'm apologizing in advance

My eyebrows come together as I try to understand what she's talking about, when another notification comes through.

* You have been added to a group chat *

CALLUM

Tombstones at 8, dinner before?

You want to pick where, ranch princess?

CADENCE

Fuck off Callum

I have plans already with Navy

FISHER

I'm going in at 4 but bring me something

CALLUM

Excuse me? Plans before that I'm not invited to?

NAVY

Girls only

FISHER

So why wasn't he invited?

CALLUM

Ha ha ha

FISHER

I think we broke G's phone

CADENCE

Or he's ignoring us as usual

Not sure what I need to contribute to this.

CALLUM

He lives

FISHER

It speaks

CADENCE

Omg hi Griffin! So nice of you to come out into the sun and play!

* You have left the group chat *
* You have been added to a group chat *

CALLUM

Just for that G, I'm making you meet me early at Smokey's. Since everyone else is conveniently busy

FISHER

Dude it's my job

CADENCE

Hey Callum

If I wear something low cut tonight, will you quit whining?

CALLUM

Done

NAVY

I can't believe y'all

I'll meet you for dinner, Cal. 7?

Yeah, welcome back, Navy.

I set my phone down and glance at the clock. It's a little after three now, which means I need something to do for the next four hours. I should probably go through my emails and make sure I have all my projects lined up for the next couple weeks.

I throw on a pair of jeans and a plain white T-shirt, before sitting on my couch and opening my laptop. My first order of business is to send the final invoice to Mack so I can mentally strike off Kofford Ranch and hope I don't have to step foot back on that property unless absolutely necessary. I don't care what Cathy said about us helping our community. If he wants more contract work done, I'm sending Callum by himself, or Mack can find someone else.

The next few projects I have lined up are smaller ones that shouldn't take me but a couple days each. They're maintenance jobs on structures like stables, barns, and a bigger one right around the third week of June. Cathy has a customer who wants a custom screened-in porch added to the front of her house, similar to the one we have. Hopefully I can get Callum to help me out with that as well.

Once I have everything organized in my calendar, follow up emails sent with estimates and quotes, I shut my laptop and set it beside me. I lean my head back on my couch, closing my eyes for a few seconds, but no part of me wants to slow down. Picking my head back up, I shoot off a text to Callum asking if he wants to meet up now for food, and head to Tombstones early to play a few rounds of pool before it gets crowded.

"That's another ten bucks right there, Griffy boy. Pay up," Callum jeers as I fish out another ten dollar bill and slap it in his hand. I

ELLE F. SUN

don't know why I let him hustle me every time we play pool together, but the last hour has been no different.

After we met at Smokey's to grab some barbecue and talked about bullshit for a good hour, we headed to Tombstones and played pool, waiting for the girls to get here.

We put the pool sticks up and head over to sit at one of the high tops when I notice Callum's attention drawn to the door. Assuming Cadence and Navy are who've piqued his interest, I turn my head as well and I think my eyes deceive me for a second. Because it looks like the last person I expected–or wanted–to be here is somehow walking up to our table with two girls who are wearing the most devilish grins.

I can't stop myself, it feels like the first time I saw Delia in the street. My eyes rake over her body and absorb her appearance.

She's wearing jean shorts and a fitted black tank top which also happens to be very low cut... Shit. Why am I even looking? I quickly glance away, not wanting her to notice my gaze lingering *there*.

But as the three of them get closer, I chance a look back her way, my eyes immediately drawn to the cowgirl boots she's wearing. Of course she'd have a pair that are a bright crimson shade that calls the attention of everyone. One glance around Tombstones has an odd burning sensation forming in my chest, because *yeah*, every guy is staring.

I'm shocked as it's usually Cadence who commands the crowds, and even though she looks good tonight, it's Delia who has everyone's attention. I can't even lie. She's a total smoke-show, and something tells me she knows it. Or maybe she's still on her high horse from earlier.

At the memory of our conversation today, I'm pulled from whatever lustful haze took over and reminded that I do not want her here. But, more importantly, she shouldn't be here. Which only makes my blood boil more, because that means...

"What is *she* doing here?" I grit out.

"Well, I invited her of course." Cadence shimmies past me, pulling behind her the personification of a thorn in my side, while Callum cough-laughs into his beer bottle.

Navy stops in front of me, gives me an awkward hug, and continues on toward the bar.

I cut a look in Callum's direction. "Did you know about this?"

He raises both his hands to show he's innocent, but I don't believe him for a damn second. And I'm not going to sit here and entertain this. The chair squeaks as I push it back, rising to my feet and getting ready to relocate to the bar, catch up with Navy— literally do anything but be here. But I'm stopped when Delia speaks again.

"Hey, I recognize you!" She points her finger in Callum's face. "You're the guy who whistled at me."

Cadence raises her eyebrows, looking between the two of them. And I wish, more than anything, I'd bailed on coming out tonight. Although, I guess this moment was bound to happen at the cookout, so may as well see how it plays out now.

Callum laughs. "Well, shit. I was hoping maybe you wouldn't recognize me."

"Wait a minute..." Delia turns her attention to me now. *Here we go.* "You were there, too. I thought you looked familiar."

I shake my head. "I wish I hadn't been."

Cadence interrupts, putting her hands up in the air to halt the conversation. "I'm sorry, can someone explain to me what happened?"

"The night G here stole you from me on the dance floor?" Callum starts, and I swear, if he wasn't my best friend, I'd consider punching him in the mouth. Actually, because he *is* my best friend, I should do it.

It's now Delia who looks between Cadence and myself.

My loud-mouthed friend continues. "Before we came in, we were outside and I saw Griffy here looking at something, *someone*, I realized."

He's really asking for that punch now.

"When I saw her," he points at Delia, "I thought it would be fun to whistle. I mean, can you blame me? She's easy on the eyes."

Cadence scoffs and I stand there, stiff as a board, while Callum digs my metaphorical grave. I can feel Delia watching me, no doubt curious to why I was looking at her in the first place, so I quickly speak up.

"She was wandering down the street with her phone up in the air. I'm sure everyone around noticed her."

"Oh, that's right," Delia adds. "I was on a video call with my best friend. I wanted to show her the restaurant and stuff."

"You haven't let me tell you the best part," Callum butts back in.

"Please continue," Cadence deadpans.

"She whistled *back*." He clicks his tongue and smirks.

"My kinda girl," Cadence quips, before leaning into Callum's side and reaching up to grab his chin, angling his face toward her. "You're lucky I didn't know about this before that night or I might not have wanted to dance with you."

Delia turns to me, eyebrows raised, and mouths, "Are they?"

I shrug her off and shake my head, because I don't know. And I'm also over this entire situation. Navy comes back to the table with a drink for herself and a shot of tequila for Cadence.

"No lime?" Delia asks when Cadence takes it.

"Never," she says.

"I didn't know what you wanted and it felt like a bad time to ask," Navy says, looking at Delia.

I take this as my opportunity to *finally* make my move toward the bar, but, surprise, Delia is hot on my trail. When we get to the counter top, Fisher notices me and holds his pointer finger up, letting me know he'll be with me in a second.

"Do you need something?" I ask Delia without looking at her. The same scent from the night in the kitchen is starting to waft into my nose, making my chest tight.

"A drink?" She motions to the liquor behind the counter.

I hum in response.

"But while we're waiting, I am curious. Why didn't you tell me that was you in the street?" I can sense she's turned her body to face me but I keep my gaze locked ahead, as if the torn wallpaper is the most interesting thing in the world.

"Because it wasn't me. I didn't whistle, I was just there," I clip out.

"And you didn't think to mention it?" she presses.

"It wasn't a memorable moment."

I chance a look out of the corner of my eye, watching as she scrunches her face up before shaking her head. I shouldn't be startled by her next statement, given how I'm acting, but I still don't expect her to call me out so bluntly.

"God, you really are a jerk," she declares, before walking back to our–*my*–friends. Before I can think more on her remark, Fisher knocks on the hard top in front of me, garnering my attention.

"Who is that?" His voice carries a dreamy-like tone and I swear, are all my friends enamored with her? But then I have an idea. Callum and Cadence may be doing *whatever*, but Fisher...

"Delia, the person Cathy hired to help out for the summer. And as far as I'm aware, she's single."

"Interesting," he mutters. "What'd you say her name is, Delia?"

"Yep. Can I get a—"

"Delia!" Fisher shouts over me, making multiple heads turn, including the one mentioned. Her eyes dart between me and him before she walks back over.

"Yes?" She rests her hands on the bar top, Fisher picking one up and kissing the top of it.

"What're you drinking, pretty girl? It's on the house."

sixteen

HOT MALE ATTENTION

DELIA

If I'd known that all I needed to do in order to receive some innocent male attention was visit Wyoming, I would have booked my flight a lot sooner. Because it's not just male attention, it's *hot* male attention.

The sexy bartender who I now know is Fisher–and also a part of this friend group I've been roped into–has been wooing me all night. A free drink here. A dedicated song there. A compliment here. A slow dance there. My heart is fluttering and my cheeks are burning, but that could also be from the tequila shot I took with Cadence.

Which, did I mention, I'm obsessed with her? Seriously. I thought I didn't take shit from people, but she really marches to the beat of her own drum. I couldn't be more grateful that she took me under her wing and brought me out tonight, because I'm having the most fun I've had in a while.

She and Callum keep passing me off to one another on the dance floor when Fisher goes back behind the bar. They twirl me, kiss me on my cheek, and act like we've known each other for years.

There's a lightness in my chest that I wish I could bottle up and save for later.

Wandering back over to the bar where Griffin and Navy have been posted up for the last, *who knows how long*, Fisher quickly comes up to the counter when he spots me.

"I think I might have to cut you off," he says playfully, taking the empty cup from me.

"I've only had two, three drinks," I whine, pressing both palms on the wooden surface and rising up on my tippy toes to get closer to his eye level.

"And two shots," Navy interjects from where she stands, leaning against the edge facing away from us.

I cut her a look, snarling before giggling. "So, I'm a light-weight? Sue me."

Griffin scoffs from his place on the other side of Navy and I cut him a look next.

"Yes?" I ask, pushing off the counter to glare at him. "Do you have something to say?"

I can see his jaw clench and I huff out a breath before setting my sights back on Fisher. Leaning forward on the bar again, I prop my arms under my chest this time, knowing it's putting my cleavage on full display. The blush creeping up Fisher's neck tells me I'm successful in my tactics.

"You're playing dirty," he speaks in a low voice.

Griffin leans back, glancing to the side at his friend's words and his eyes also land where Fisher's were, before he snaps his gaze back up and looks at Navy. "I'm going over to Callum and Cadence."

I can't help myself. A laugh bubbles out of me.

"Something *you* want to say?" Griffin jeers at me. I don't bother giving him my attention.

"Yeah," I huff. "Could you be any more obvious about not wanting to be around me?"

He doesn't respond, looking at Navy who shows she has no plans to follow him. As he heads back to the table, she breaks the silence.

"I gotta say, you're really good at getting under his skin." She spins around so she's also facing Fisher and he smirks at her words.

"I don't want to get under his skin. I want to understand him." The words escape me before I have a chance to stop them and both Fisher and Navy look at me like I've grown a second head.

"Understand Griffin?" Navy scoffs. "Yeah. Good luck with that." She taps the counter top and walks over to the table, leaving me alone.

I follow her with my eyes, my gaze catching on Griffin. Once again, this imaginary force tugs on me. As if he's the magnet and I'm the metal, forced to collide together. He meets my gaze and holds it for a few seconds and it's like all the noise around us fades out. He narrows his stare and turns away, breaking contact. The music rushes back into my ears and at the same time, I hear Fisher clear his throat behind me.

I spin around and he reaches over the bar, tucking a piece of hair behind my ear. The touch is delicate and soft, and I find my gaze wandering to his lips. I tilt my head to the side, considering what it might be like to kiss him. Maybe I *am* a little drunk. Clara would be delighted as all get out right now because a-few-drinks Delia is a flirty Delia.

"Fisher," I whisper, my eyes now back on his.

"Delia," he says, his voice low again.

"I think you were right about cutting me off." I gaze back to his lips, licking mine in the process. I've also started to rise up on my toes, leaning over the counter and closer to him.

"Yeah? Why's that, pretty girl?" The hand that was tucking my hair behind my ear comes back to the side of my face. His thumb moves in soft circles on the apple of my cheek.

"Because I think it might be fun to kiss you," I confess, and one corner of his mouth pulls up in a soft grin. His hand stills on my face and he leans closer until his lips are against the shell of my ear.

"If you still feel that way when you're sober, I'll take you up on it." He draws back and softly kisses my cheek, murmuring, "but I have a feeling the universe didn't bring you here for me."

Embarrassment and confusion wash over me at the same time.

"You're right," I quickly recover. "I get flirty when I drink. Well, flirty at first, then sleepy. Actually, you'd be doing me a favor if you let me have one more drink, because I'll curb the flirty and get to the sleepy. And I'm rambling. Sorry. And I'm sorry for trying to kiss–"

"Delia," Fisher stops me and places a hand over mine. "You don't need to apologize. I'm flattered, because don't get me wrong, you're exactly my type."

"Which is what? Female?" Cadence's voice makes me jump and Fisher rolls his eyes before he walks away to help another patron.

"Hi." I give her a lazy smile, and then pout. "Fisher won't let me have another drink."

"Boys, they ruin everything, don't they?" She turns and gets the attention of another bartender. "Lucky for us, he isn't the only one working right now."

Cadence and I take another shot of tequila before she whisks me back to the dance floor.

After a few more songs and an attempt to teach me a line

dance to one of them, we wander back over to the table where Callum, Navy, and Griffin are still sitting and engaging in some sort of heated conversation. The giveaway is the flush of Navy's cheeks and Griffin's pinched brows. Callum, however, is leaning back, as if holding an imaginary carton of popcorn and watching it all unfold.

As we get closer to the table, I catch the last sentence from Navy.

"You know, I tried standing up for you earlier, but maybe they're right. You certainly have become more of a jackass since the last time I was here."

My eyes widen and I turn around, running smack into Cadence.

"I don't think I want to be a part of this conversation," I say in a hushed tone.

"I got this," she whispers before spinning me back around and pushing me into Callum's lap while she takes the empty seat next to Griffin. I awkwardly try to adjust myself while I watch Callum and Cadence engage in some sort of silent conversation with their eyes before Callum turns to face me and gives me a goofy smile.

"Having fun?" he asks before looking back to the group, clearly moving past the fact I'm sitting in his lap. He even wraps an arm around my waist, tucking me into his side. I chance a look over at Griffin and I don't know why I'm surprised when I find him glaring at me.

"So, Delia," Cadence starts the conversation and pulls my attention back to her. "What do you think of Wyoming so far? How does it compare to Georgia?"

"How do you know she's from Georgia?"

Everyone whips their head to Griffin, clearly shocked by his contribution to the conversation, but Cadence waves him off.

"We had lunch yesterday," I say before Cadence can. Griffin

huffs before looking around the room like he's bored again. I tilt my head, really taking him in, and come to the realization that while I may think he's insanely hot, his attitude and personality certainly make him unattractive.

Then the empath in me argues with that thought and tells me there's likely a reason he is the way he is. Yet, I argue back using the thought I had in the car and what Cadence said the other day as well.

We all go through shit, but it doesn't give you a green light to treat people poorly. It seems Navy is picking up on that as well.

"So, Georgia?" Callum quietly asks behind me and I realize I've zoned out, *while* staring at Griffin.

"Right," I quickly answer, redirecting my gaze once again to Cadence. "I mean, it's all I know. I've never been out west, mainly traveled along the east coast, but I've always wanted to come out here. Like something was tugging on my soul, if that makes sense? Probably not. Anyways, I thought maybe Montana, except I wasn't having any luck finding a job there. My best friend suggested expanding the location and that's when Catherine's listing popped up. You'll meet her, Clara, my best friend. She's going to come visit, not that you asked." I bite down on my bottom lip, willing the words to stop spilling out. "Sorry–"

"Well, I've never been to the east coast, so maybe we'll have to come visit you after the summer!" Cadence suggests before I can apologize for rambling again.

Navy starts to talk about a trip she took one summer to Carolina Beach and I shift on Callum's lap trying to get more comfortable. I'm in the process of wriggling my hips when Callum leans forward and whispers into my ear, "Not sure what you're doing, but I think you might want to stop. I'm still a guy, and you're a very attractive girl, sitting in my lap."

I stiffen when I realize what he's implying, a blush creeping into my cheeks. I turn my face to the side, whispering back, "Sorry, I'm trying to get comfortable."

"That's fine, I'm just letting you know if you don't stop moving your ass on my dick, you're *really* not going to be comfortable."

I choke down a laugh as I lift myself up slightly, shifting until I'm on his lower thigh, and lean forward to rest my arms on the table. My body seems to relax with the distance, and while I know I'm not stepping on any toes since Cadence herself threw me into his lap, I still feel strange knowing there might be something going on between them.

That, and I have to keep reminding myself I don't really know any of them. No matter how welcome I feel, the truth is I just met them.

I'm not naive to the fact that I have an uncanny ability to get close to people quickly and that's mostly credited to once again, the empath in me that seems to draw people in.

"Isn't Georgia's state fruit like a peach or something?" Callum suddenly asks.

"It is," Griffin clips out, and it's clear he's annoyed with the conversation, but I don't know why. Unless he dislikes me *so* much that even talking about something as random as peaches unnerves him, for being remotely associated with me. I'm still not sure I understand how he can form such a quick opinion of me.

"Yeah, it is," I echo his words as Callum wraps an arm around my shoulder and gives me a light squeeze.

"So, I can call you my Georgia peach then?" He nudges into me and Cadence narrows her eyes at him.

Okay, that's it.

I don't care anymore if she put me in his lap so I didn't have to sit by Griffin, this is too much. I spring up and grab her hand, pulling her toward Callum, and taking her seat.

A playful squeal comes from Cadence as Callum wraps his arms around her waist and pulls her into him. Yeah, that's definitely how things should be. I settle into the chair next to Griffin and don't bother looking in his direction.

Navy snorts at the entire interaction before setting her sights back on me. "Why did you want to move away?"

I consider her question. I could give some blasé answer, but I've never shied away from being honest about how I feel, so why start now? Because Griffin is at this table?

"To be honest, I felt really lost," I start, pinning my focus on my hands instead of the group, before picking my head up and sharing my heart with them. "I've been in the same job for like four years now and I used to love it. I mean, really love it. I woke up excited and ready to get to work, but over the last few months something in me started to shift. I felt out of place in my own life. I don't know how to explain it, but…" I pause, biting on the inside of my cheek, before continuing, "I've experienced a lot of loss in my life—various forms—and to feel like I was beginning to lose myself? Well, that terrified me enough to decide I needed to make a change, even if it was temporary."

Silence stretches between the table. I can tell Griffin has gone rigid next to me, Navy has gone quiet, her lips pressed together, and Callum sits there rubbing Cadence's arm. She breaks the silence, reaching a hand out to me and taking one of mine.

"I'm really glad you ended up here," she says with a slight crack in her voice and my empathy comes to life, picking up on what feels to be grief as it wafts off of her like a perfume only I can smell.

"I didn't mean to upset you," I say quietly, squeezing her hand back. "I'm sorry. It's hard for me not to overshare."

"No, no, no," Cadence rushes out. "It's honestly refreshing."

"Agreed," Navy chimes in and I look over to find her giving me a soft and comforting smile.

"I think it's bad ass that you picked up your life for the summer," Callum adds on, and that leaves Griffin, who's still stiff next to me.

"Thanks," I offer, weakly. A yawn escapes me and the sleepiness I mentioned earlier creeps up. I blink a few times, looking at Cadence who must see the weary expression on my face.

"Well, I think we can call it a night, especially since we'll see each other tomorrow at the cookout." Cadence kicks Griffin's boot with hers, grabbing his attention. "Think you can get *my* peach home?"

"Oh, that's—"

"Excuse me?"

Griffin and I speak over one another and Callum butts in. "Oh, she can be your peach, but I can't say it?"

She rolls her eyes before continuing. "Griffin, you can give her a ride back to the ranch. You're going to the same place, there's literally no reason you can't."

If the tension wasn't noticeable before, it is palpable now.

"I can call a car, it's really not a big deal," I quickly say, pulling my phone out of my boot when Griffin's voice breaks through and stuns us all.

"It's fine. Let me close my tab." He pushes away from the table, leaving everyone with wide eyes, except for Cadence who has a smirk on her face. We say our goodbyes, and I find myself trailing after one grumpy, broody Griffin.

"Seriously, I can get a ride-share," I start, but he cuts me off with the same phrase as earlier.

"It's fine." He doesn't even turn to look at me.

"Is it?" I call after him, picking up my pace and letting another long yawn slip out. "Because it sure doesn't seem like it.

Which I get, honestly. I know you think I'm weird, or whatever you said that morning."

Griffin freezes and finally gives me his attention. "Do you make it a habit to eavesdrop?"

I scoff, drawing back as if he's physically slapped me. "Eavesdrop? I was coming downstairs to leave and happened to catch the tail end of your conversation."

"Sure," he clips out, closing the distance to his truck. He reaches for the passenger door, opening it, and motioning with his hand for me to get in.

"Oh, wow. How chivalrous."

I don't care how rude I'm coming across right now. There's no reason for him to be acting this way toward me and I've had enough of it. I'm slightly drunk, exhausted, yet once again, my empathy for him is flying off the charts for some reason. It's draining.

I push past him into the front seat and he slams the door before rounding the hood and getting in himself. When he puts the key into the ignition, he stops for a second and places both hands on the wheel.

It's like there's a hum filling the cabin of his truck and I can't help myself from reaching out and touching his arm. The second I do, I swear my fingertips absorb some sort of strange sadness radiating off him, before it's quickly replaced with anger.

He glances down at my hand, and then back up at me before shrugging my touch away. Redirecting his gaze forward, he turns the key and the engine roars to life.

I should leave it. I should keep my mouth shut. And I know I'm not helping my case with him, but I have alcohol and exhaustion to blame if need be, so I let the next few words leave my lips.

"I'm sorry you're hurting."

My voice is so soft, I'm not sure why I even spoke if it wasn't meant to be heard. But Griffin heard me alright, because he stops all his movements and looks me dead in the eyes. For a moment, a second, there's a flicker in his eyes that makes the gray suddenly appear blue, but then it's back to storm clouds.

"Look, I don't care what you think you know about me, what feeling you might have or whatever the hell you said the other night in the kitchen. Stop acting like you know anything about me, or understand me for that matter." He shifts the truck into gear, pulling out of the parking lot, and dismissing my statement. And because I can't seem to help myself, I double down like earlier in the stable.

"I don't have to know you to fully understand you." I buckle the seatbelt and lean my head against the window, my words now coming in lazy but short statements as sleep begins to encroach on me.

"What does that even mean?" He grits out, and I don't have to even look to know he's clenching his teeth.

"Let me guess? Something really rocked your world. Made you see life differently. And it hardened you." Another yawn escapes, and I continue. "Now you keep everyone at an arm's length, except for Catherine, Libby, and Marge. You hang out with your friends enough so they stay off your back. And well, you don't like me because I haven't been around for you to convince that everything is grand and you're doing absolutely peachy." I pop the "p" and close my eyes, my head starting to lull in rhythm with the truck's movements. "But what do I know? I've probably had too much to drink and I'm the *weird* emotional chick. Whatever."

Silence stretches between us and before I give into the comfort of my alcohol induced slumber, I mumble one last thing, not a care left to give.

"I'll figure you out, Griffin..."

seventeen

"THEIR LOSS."

GRIFFIN

"Figure me out?" I repeat her words, but it's no use. She's out cold.

When I hit a stop light, I glance over, observing her under the cast of the red glow. She's resting her head against the window and it's strange how still and quiet she is. Every moment with her in the brief three days since we met has been charged, and something about being near her like this...I can't ignore the calmness radiating off her.

To say I don't understand this girl would be the understatement of my life.

More often than not, when I meet someone, I form my opinion of them within the first few minutes. And I don't allow a lot, *if any*, margin for that opinion to change. But I find myself surprised by her, mostly from her challenging me or calling me out for my shit. Oh, and the rambling and over sharing.

All that to say, I'm not entirely sure what to think of Delia, which gives me another reason to be so apprehensive of her.

When she called me out for saying she was weird, Grams' remark about being mindful of how you speak about someone damn near smacked me across the face. Do I think she's weird? Yeah, she's certainly different, but I didn't know why I felt the need to say it. Well, now I do.

I don't like that she's here.

She's already disrupting everything and asking questions that I've worked hard to avoid, and it's only been three. Fucking. Days.

Contrary to the frustration I feel though, I don't disagree with what Cadence said about Delia's openness and transparency being refreshing—not that I would ever admit that out loud.

I don't know many people who wear their heart *and* emotions so boldly on their sleeve. Which is why I was so caught off guard in the pasture earlier when she suddenly stopped Maven and sat in the sun.

But then she had to take that moment and turn it into challenging me. Making some bold claim that she feels sorry for me? That I'm weak because I've shut off parts of myself?

A small bit of anger threatens to flare up again at the mere thought of that heated moment, but it's quickly snubbed when Delia shifts, leaning to rest her head on the console, her hair spilling over the side and onto my lap.

I'm seconds from bumping her back to her side, when I realize waking her could very well result in more talking. Hard pass.

When we pull up to the main house, I nudge her gently hoping she'll wake, but she hardly stirs.

I'm going to have to carry her inside.

The realization slams into me and I'm ready to let out a long wind of curse words when she reaches for my hand, squeezing it lightly.

"Can you take me to bed?" Her voice comes out in a whine, her thumb skimming across the top of my knuckles, reminding me that she's holding my hand.

I quickly pull it out of her grasp and get out of the truck, rounding the hood to open her door. She turns her body slightly before leaning into me, and I maneuver one hand behind her back and the other under her knees, hoisting her out and into my arms. She snuggles into my chest and *fuck*, the scent of her is everywhere.

I groan, and try to tell myself that this is no different than having to carry my niece to bed. It's a means to an end. Except, who am I kidding? This is nothing like that, one glance down at the freckle dusted nose confronting me with my unfortunate reality.

Leaving the truck door open, not wanting to make more noise than I have to, I walk to the screen porch and thank God that I'm able to quietly open it. Having kept my keys in my right hand, I work to unlock the front door, and step inside. But I freeze when I notice Grams on the couch. I wait, trying to see if she's awake through what little light there is, but she doesn't stir or speak, so she must have dozed off out here reading.

I quietly work my way toward the steps and Delia moves to wrap her arms around my neck, pulling herself even closer to me. The warmth of her body against mine has my heart racing for some strange reason, and now more than ever I want to get her to the guest room and get the hell out of the house.

When I finally make it to the room, I lay her down as gently as I can, turning to leave, but she reaches for my wrist and stops me.

"Griff," she whispers, and all the air whooshes out of my lungs. She tightens her grip, and I slowly turn to face her. She's lying on her side, blinking slowly, a sheen of tears illuminating her hazel eyes. And something in me cracks. It's so visceral that I swear it makes a sound you can hear. I don't know if it's the look she's giving me or the way she's shortened my name, but some part of the wall I've curated to keep me safe, cracks. A tear slips down her cheek as she speaks again. "You think like them, don't you?"

And for the first time in maybe the last ten years, I'm caught off guard with no clue how to respond.

"Get some sleep, Delia," I choose to say, but that clearly wasn't the right response because a soft whimper escapes her. This is not how I pictured the rest of the night going.

"You do think like them," she says again, and I don't try to talk my way out of it this time. Maybe if I entertain the conversation, she'll let it go. She'll let *me* go.

Hell, I don't even know if she'll remember this.

"Think like who?" I try to hide the exasperation in my voice.

She closes her eyes again and winces, as if remembering something that physically hurts her, and that strikes up an odd sensation in my chest.

"My exes," she finally answers. If she had her eyes open, she'd see the shock on my face right now.

"Think like them, how?" I ask, not sure if I really want the answer, but also not understanding. She opens her eyes again, pinning me with a look that is somehow both stoic and pitiful.

"That I'm too much. Too emotional. Too…everything." The last word is so quiet, I barely hear it. I'm contemplating my response when she continues. "It's why they all left. It's why you think I'm weird. And it makes me sad." Her voice cracks with the last word as more tears escape.

Oh, fuck me. Now I really feel like the jerk she called me earlier.

"Delia, I shouldn't–"

She interrupts me, her eyes narrowing, determination now covering her face. "Because I think it makes me special. But they never seem to see it that way. Or stick around long enough to find out." She lets go of my wrist, rolling on her side to face away from me, but not before mumbling out, "Their loss."

I stand there at the edge of the bed, hovering over her. And once again, words fail me. For someone who has planned out the last handful of years and made an effort to never be surprised by what comes across my path, I'm feeling like it's my first day of life.

I shake my head, trying to regain my senses, but the uncertainty lingers. This girl laying in front of me, this stranger essentially, is quickly intertwining herself into the lives of everyone around me. And what's worse is she's making it clear that she intends to do the same with me.

I don't waste another second, exiting the guest room and heading downstairs. I'm almost to the front door when the lamp next to the couch switches on and I whirl to face Grams who's sitting there with an unreadable expression. But then she says, "You get her into bed?"

I freeze. No thoughts, no sentences appear. I have nothing to say, my mouth gaping open instead. Another beat passes, still no response from me. Grams gets up, walks toward me, and places one hand on my shoulder.

"Don't worry, your secret is safe with me."

She starts to walk toward her room when she abruptly stops, turning to face me again.

"Do you remember what your mother used to say?"

"Grams, I don't…" I trail off because I can't have this conversation right now. Not after everything else that's happened today.

She sighs, speaking anyway. "Life loves to surprise us when we least expect it, but need it most."

I see her mouth say the words, but I hear my mom's voice in my head. The memory threatens to take me out right there in the living room as my ears start to ring and my chest tightens.

I don't wait for Grams to say anything else. I bolt for my truck, tearing down the path to my house, and rushing inside.

I need to make a phone call, now.

But when I dial the number, instead of the familiar beep, I'm met with an automated message that sends another crack through me, but for an entirely different reason.

"Voice mailbox full."

I slam my phone down on the nightstand and roll over, hoping when I wake up tomorrow, everything will feel somewhat normal again.

* * *

My alarm starts to go off, but I'm already awake having barely slept. Today is going to probably feel like one of the longest days of my life.

I don't waste any more time in bed, getting up and ready for the day. I've got a few chores to do around the ranch before heading over to the house. My stomach knots at the mere thought. I really don't want to see Delia again after last night, but I need to talk to Cathy, so I'll have to suck it up. I make myself a cup of coffee and leave so I can knock out my to-do list.

Around nine, I finally make my way up to the house. When I walk in, Grams eyes me from her spot on the couch with Libby next to her, glancing over at the kitchen before looking back down at the coloring sheet Libby has. I follow her gaze and see Delia sitting at the table, hunched over a notebook and what looks like...trash? I take a few steps closer, checking out the messy bun on her head completed with a sweatshirt and boxer shorts. It looks so natural for her to be at the table, and that thought instantly makes me want to turn back around.

But before I can, she peers over her shoulder and a soft smile graces her lips when she sees me. One that I'm not entirely sure I deserve. I don't smile back but nod, walking over to the table and assessing what's covering it. Receipts, wrappers, napkins, and other things I can't identify are grouped together in small piles. There's also glue, tape, stickers, and markers. I'm not sure if this is some craft she has planned for her and Libby, but I'm curious either way.

"What're you doing?" My words come out scratchy, having not spoken yet this morning. She quirks an eyebrow up at me, whether in question at the sound of my voice or the fact I'm speaking to her. Maybe even both.

"I'm working on my junk journal." She reaches for one of the napkins and tapes it down before picking up some of the other items.

"Your *what*?" I don't mean for it to come out condescending, but it does, and she picks her head back up, scrunching her face into the same expression as last night before she called me a jerk.

She holds my gaze for a second before saying, "It's nothing."

"Certainly doesn't look like nothing," I push back.

"Fine," she relents. "It's basically like a scrapbook and diary combined. I collect things throughout the day, like keepsakes almost, and then create a page to remember it. My mom got me a Polaroid camera before I left to add pictures in, but I keep forgetting to use it. I need to set a reminder on my phone or something. Maybe put it on the dresser so I remember to grab it. Oh! Maybe, I'll keep it in my bag. Anyways, I'm behind from traveling and trying to get settled into my routine, so I'm playing catch up. I took the napkin from Tombstones, but I wish I had something else from last night."

Her rambling really is something else, I think to myself.

A small smile sneaks onto my face at the thought and that's when Delia's eyes go so wide, they look like saucers.

"Are you smiling? At me?" She presses her palm to her chest.

I don't give her an answer, instead rounding the table, picking up the half eaten Pop-Tart sitting in front of her, and waving it in the air. "You know these are terrible for you?"

She narrows her eyes. "You know what else is terrible for *you*?"

"What?" I cross my arms, and I don't miss the subtle shift of her gaze to my forearms and tattoos, before her eyes slide back up to mine.

"That attitude of yours you seem to always have." She raises her eyebrows like she's won the conversation then directs her attention back to the journal.

A snort resounds in the room and I glance over to see Grams pressing a hand to cover her mouth. Little late for that.

"Here." I fish my wallet from my pocket, taking out the receipt I put there after closing my tab. I slide it across the table and Delia reaches for it, our fingers brushing for just a second like in the truck. I pause, wondering if she remembers last night, but she snatches it away.

"Is this a peace offering?" She quips, looking over the paper before placing it down onto the open page. I don't know why I'm being nice to her. Maybe it has to do with her remark about me being like her exes. I certainly didn't appreciate that.

"Sure, Delia. It's whatever you want it to be."

She nods, focusing back on her task at hand.

I take that as my cue to leave and turn on my heel to head down the hall. When I reach Cathy's office, I can see through the cracked door that her attention is glued to her computer. I rap my knuckles twice on the wood.

"Bad time?" I ask, stepping into her space.

"No," she sighs. "I'm trying to finish up some paperwork for the store and figure out what the schedule will look like come August. I know Delia basically just got here, but she'll be leaving before we know it and I want to make sure I have everything figured out before that happens."

"If there's anything I can do, let me know, yeah?" I run a hand through my hair and tug on the ends before spitting out the question I came here to ask.

"Do you have Dad's phone somewhere?"

She pushes back from her desk, crossing her legs before tilting her head.

"His phone?" she repeats the words. "From nearly ten years ago?"

"Yeah, I know how crazy it sounds. But do you have it, yes or no?" I sit in one of the chairs opposite her desk.

"I think so, yes. Do you need it right this second? Or do I have time to find it?" Her voice takes on a more playful tone and I'm grateful for it because that means she won't ask any more questions.

"Whenever you have a chance..." I pause, considering what I'm about to ask next. I've been going back and forth, wondering if even putting the idea into her mind would stir up some sort of trouble for me.

But like a few moments ago, I spit out the other question.

"Did you hear anything last night?"

"No," she starts, tilting her head the other direction. "Should I have?"

"Nah, only wanted to make sure Delia didn't wake you up or anything when she got back." And before Delia becomes the topic of conversation, I quickly pivot. "Is everything for the grill in the fridge? Do I need to get anything last minute?"

My sister narrows her eyes, seeing right through my distraction tactics, but she chooses to ignore them. "We have everything."

I rise to my feet, ready to head out of the room and do a few more chores around the ranch before the cookout, but Cathy clears her throat.

"Also, not that it's any of my business," she starts, and my heart drops into my ass, "but Delia wasn't irresponsible by any means? She doesn't seem hungover to me, again, not that it's any of my business, but I've been wondering, maybe even hoping a little, that she has at least one flaw. Seems too good to be true."

Annoyance and anger war under my skin again.

This idea that Delia is the best thing ever, not to mention how fascinated everyone seems to be with her, doesn't sit well with me. I consider telling Cathy that she was basically drunk, maybe putting a dent in Delia's shiny exterior, but a strange twinge of guilt flares in me. Not wanting to analyze what that could be about, I quickly answer Cathy's original question.

"She wasn't irresponsible."

"Well, damn." Cathy chuckles.

"Damn," I echo her as I walk back toward the kitchen. Delia's at the table still, with Libby in her lap this time. She's flipping through some of the pages, telling Libby what the items are or the memories that come with them. I have no intention of listening, but my footsteps are halted as my ears catch the end of her sentence.

"...last day with my best friend's dad."

My mind drifts back to last night when she was answering Cadence's question and said she'd experienced a lot of loss. I didn't put too much weight into the statement, but now questions are starting to rise up in me. I shake my head, coming back to the moment, and push on to head outside.

"Hey, Griffin," Delia calls after me and I still. "I was planning on riding a little before the cookout, will you be working in the stables? I don't want to get in your way."

"You're good, but people will be here around three," I shoot back. And now I'm thinking about yesterday again, and the confrontation we had at the stalls. I need to get out of this house and for my friends to get here so I can focus on something, *anything,* else.

eighteen
THOSE DAMN BRAIDS

GRIFFIN

"You're burning the burgers," Grams says behind me.

I look down at the grill, quickly flipping the patty before picking my head back up. Everyone's been here for about two hours now, and nothing is going as planned.

Cadence, Callum, and Fisher, showed up together, except when they got here, they didn't come to me. No, they went looking for Delia. Navy showed up by herself a few minutes after, and even she didn't pay much attention to me—which never happens.

Delia. Delia. Delia.

She's all everyone seems to be thinking about.

Now, I'm watching Fisher carry her around bridal style because, well, I'm not really sure why. Her head is thrown back, her hair in those damn braids. I'm annoyed that she's wearing my mom's boots again with her jean shorts and tank top, but what's really got my attention is how she isn't fighting Fisher on being in his arms.

I can't say I'm surprised though. I saw them at the bar last night, the way Fisher whispered into her ear. His eyes were locked with mine during the whole exchange, as if to make it obvious he was calling dibs. Not that there was ever any need for that.

The flush that lingered in Delia's cheeks was also a tell that *something* had gone down between them. But I didn't consider the fact until this very moment that if they do start dating, that's another reason for her to not go back to Georgia.

And fuck me. Because why didn't it cross my mind sooner that if *any* of her relationships somehow get really strong here, she may end up hanging around. That's the last thing I want.

A sharp jab into my back rips me from my thoughts, Grams snatching the spatula from me and turning over the few hamburgers that are now almost black.

"I think if you stare any harder, you might burn holes into her," she mumbles.

I go to open my mouth and respond when Delia's eyes catch mine. She gives me a soft smile and a small wave before Fisher bounces her in his arms, throwing her over his shoulder, and carrying her to the picnic tables. Her laugh is so loud, dancing through the air. I'm shocked when a smile graces my lips.

Cathy walks up to us, her eyebrows raised. "Looks like Delia's found herself an admirer."

"Absolutely not," I quickly reply, my smile falling. "I hardly know her."

"I was referring to Fisher," she says with a smirk, reaching for the tray of cooked hot dogs.

"Right, yeah. Of course." I scoff.

"But that's interesting..." She lets her words trail off, exchanging a look with Grams before heading over to where the rest of the food is. I hear a snort of laughter behind me and I don't bother looking back at the source.

"Don't start," I huff, returning to the grill and finishing up the last couple burgers.

"Oh, I have nothing to say. Your secret is safe with me, remember? But, Griffin dear, do try and be a little more discreet with the staring," she remarks, patting me on the back as she walks over to join everyone else.

"I wasn't staring," I call after her, but Grams keeps walking.

I let out a sigh, scrubbing a hand down my face.

I glance over at the picnic tables, my eyes unintentionally landing on Delia again. She's wearing that damn smile she seems to always have, sitting with Libby in her lap. She takes a bite from a hot dog she's holding in one hand and with the other, she holds a corn on the cob for Libby to take bites of.

Grams sits down next to her, motioning to the table, and I watch as they exchange words before Delia turns and pins her gaze on me. Panic ricochets through me at what Grams could have said, but Delia holds up her hot dog in my direction and mouths, "Thank you!"

I nod, closing the grill and making my way toward Callum and Fisher who are over by the fire pit. I collapse into one of the Adirondack chairs and let out a sigh that seems to have been sitting in the depths of my body. Immediately Callum gives me a look of question, but Fisher beats him to it.

"You good, G?" He takes a sip of his beer and waits for my reply.

"Yeah," I huff out. "Got a lot on my mind."

"Anything that would have to do with a certain nanny?" Callum supplies and I wince.

"What's going on with you and her?" I direct my attention to Fisher, ignoring Callum altogether.

Fisher sets his bottle on one of the chair arms, but before he can say anything, Cadence comes over and surprises everyone when she sits down on *my* thighs.

"What're we talking about?" She takes a sip from the cup in her hand and glances around the fire pit at all of us. Callum is still staring at *where* she's sitting while Fisher picks up his beer and takes another sip. "Oh, don't get shy on me now, boys." She pushes out her bottom lip into a dramatic pout, feigning sadness. She sighs when still, nobody speaks. "Ugh, you're no fun."

"Cadence, what are you doing?" I break the silence.

She turns to face me, looking over my shoulder to smile at something or someone, and directs her gaze back to me. "Interesting," she murmurs. "Griffin, can we talk?"

Callum's eyebrows shoot up before he shakes his head.

I don't know what game she's playing, but I don't want any part of it, especially if it's at the expense of my best friend.

Before I can say exactly that, she stands back up, extending her hand out to me.

"The dock?" she presses, and I don't miss the shift in her tone from playful to insistent—urgent even.

With a sigh, I take her hand as I rise to my feet. I chance a look at Callum and he must have also caught on to the change in her voice, because he nods at me, no longer wearing an expression of jealousy or irritation.

Cadence leads me the distance from the fire pit to the dock, and when we finally are out of earshot, she pulls her hand from mine, shaking it as if to get rid of my touch. I really don't understand her sometimes.

"We need to talk about Delia," she says, while moving to sit on the edge of the dock, letting her legs dangle off the edge.

I'm so surprised by her words that I don't move at first. I stand there, looking at the top of her head now that she's sitting down. She glances back up, rolls her eyes, and pats the wood next to her. My brain and body connect again and I sit beside her.

"What about her?" I ask, exasperation lacing with my words.

"Something happened between you two. I can tell. And I want to know what," she replies, her gaze fixed on the water beneath her toes.

Oh, for fuck's sake.

"Nothing happened, Cadence. Is this really what you dragged me over here to ask? C'mon now. That's not like you. Spit out what you really want to say," I respond.

"Fine. Since we got here, I've noticed you watching her. I don't think you even realize you're doing it, but I saw you. I saw the way you were looking at her when Fisher had her in his arms. I tried to ask Delia"–I stiffen–"but she didn't tell me anything. I pushed about last night after you guys left and she did mention how she wished she didn't say something in the car, but that's it."

"Did she clarify what she wished she hadn't said?" I chance asking. I try not to get hung up on the other part that maybe Grams was right and I *was* staring.

Cadence turns her head so quickly, her ponytail smacks the side of my arm. "So something *did* happen."

I run a hand through my hair, pulling on the ends and starting to feel on edge. "Are you forgetting that we all literally just met her?"

Cadence frowns. "Okay, and?"

"*And* why is everyone acting like she's been around for ages?"

"Maybe because somehow it feels like she has?" Cadence retorts, her answer making my stomach drop. But I don't want to go back and forth on this anymore, so I get back to her original question.

"I don't know what to tell you, Cady. Yeah, Delia said some things last night, but it's not my place to talk about it. I also don't really want to talk about it, much less think about it. But nothing happened between us."

And that's the God honest truth. Maybe I see Delia a little differently, but I still want nothing to do with her.

Cadence pouts, for real this time, casting her gaze back onto the lake, and stuns me with her next sentence.

"If there's anyone to get through to you, to bring you back from wherever it is you've lost yourself, I think it's her."

"What the hell does that mean?" I shoot back, my defenses immediately rising. What is with everyone lately trying to talk about my damn feelings?

"That!" she says, raising her voice and using her hands to gesture at me. "That right there! You're so quick to shut down anyone who voices even the faintest bit of concern for you. Anyone who hints that you're not the guy we knew before–"

"Before my world fell apart? Before I lost everything?" I cut her off, my temper starting to flare. This is not the turn I expected this conversation to take.

"Look around, Griffin!" Cadence chokes out. "You didn't lose everything! You have all these people around you, who still love you, who want to be your friend, some maybe even more than your friend. Here. Right now. Not gone. And I'm thinking that Delia is the only person who might be able to help you realize that, because she hasn't been around long enough for you to push away. But if you're going to act like this, continue to be like this, stop looking at her and Fisher like you wish it was you."

"You've lost your damn mind," I say through gritted teeth.

"I'm serious, Griffin. You forget how long I've known you, and also I am not stupid. So you leave her alone, you quit giving her a hard time, and you let Fisher and her get on if they want."

"That's exactly what I want, Cadence! I don't want anything to do with her!" I try to keep my voice even, but I'm losing this battle. I don't know where she got the idea that I've taken up some sort of interest in Delia, but that's the most absurd thing I've heard.

"You're an idiot." She scoffs.

Pressing her hands onto the dock, she stands back up. I don't even bother looking her direction. The anger radiating through my body has all of my attention, but I feel the light squeeze of her hand on my shoulder.

"I...I saw something different in your eyes earlier. Something I haven't seen before. It gave me hope," she whispers, turning and leaving me to stew on her words. I'm sure she's gone, but I hear her say one more thing. "Would it really be that bad? To let someone in? To feel something?"

The movement of the dock lets me know this time, she's gone.

I clench my teeth so hard, I'm worried I might break a tooth. She has no idea what she's talking about. Because yes, it would be that bad. Because I wouldn't just be feeling something. I'd be feeling everything from the last decade of my life and the truth is, I don't know if I can survive that.

"Fuck this," I mutter to myself, rising to my feet and heading back toward everyone. I'm going to tell Cath or Grams that I'm not feeling well and go back to my house. I can't be around all these people when my anger is this potent. When it's consuming me like this.

I'm steps away from my sister, when a hand wraps around my bicep that withdraws itself as quickly as it got there. I don't have to guess who it is. I know from the half second touch.

I spin to face Delia, who looks at her hand perplexed, a small frown on her face. She studies her palm, then glances up to me and says, "You're burning up."

"Yeah, I'm going back to my house," I deadpan, starting to turn around again when I hear her suck in a breath, and feel her grip onto me again. I look down at where her fingers hold onto me, her hand trembling.

What is happening right now?

"Okay, I'll walk with you," she states and I whip my gaze up to meet her hazel eyes. There's a fiery determination to them that makes the gold flare. It mirrors the blaze licking up inside of me.

"Like hell you will," I scoff, trying to shake her hand off of me, but she squeezes tighter. As her grip intensifies, it's like the anger is moving through me toward her touch. As if she's leeching the feeling from me. The way her hand shakes, I start to question if somehow she's doing just that.

"You're not okay," she fights back, but I recognize she's kept her voice low, and I'm grateful for that. The last thing I need is an audience.

"Delia, I say this with the utmost respect. I do not want your help, I want you to leave me alone. Go back to Fisher."

I shake her hand free this time and the instant her touch leaves me, my body is flooded with anger again. Delia opens her mouth, promptly clamping it shut, and does the last thing I expect her to. She steps forward and wraps her arms around my waist, hugging me. Her cheek rests on my chest for a split second as she squeezes me in the embrace, before she steps back and nods as if completing some sort of task.

"I hope you feel better," she says, and starts to walk away, leaving me stunned, for more than one reason.

Like earlier with Cadence, I'm sure the conversation is done, but she turns around, gives me a soft but sad smile, and speaks again. "I'm sorry that I thought..." She trails off, her eyebrows pinching together as if wrestling with her thoughts. She shakes her head and huffs out a breath. "I won't... I'll leave you alone."

I watch her walk away.

I watch her slip into Fisher's lap.

I watch Cadence find me with her eyes, shake her head, and turn back to our friends.

I watch them all talk and laugh, *as if I don't exist.*

At that moment, I realize the implications of what Cadence said on the dock. I glance around at everyone here–my family, my friends.

Am I really pushing everyone away? Even my family?

Then another sickening thought takes over.

What if Grams and Cath choose Delia over me? Could I be replaced as the person who's always around to help out? What if they feel like they don't need me anymore?

I head back to my house with a new fear and a new realization.

Delia must leave at the end of the summer, and I will do anything to make that happen.

I won't lose my family again.

my dearest clara,

sigh. this is a waste of paper and stamp, but i'm here to let you know that catherine's brother, Griffin, is a grade-A jerk.

do my empathy spidery senses go off around him? yes

but do I think it's worth me ignoring his heinous attitude to figure out what's bothering him? undecided

all this to say, his hotness has been canceled out by his assholeness. that's not a word, but it is now.

however...he does have a really HOT friend who seems to be interested in me. so we will pivot our attention there.

reporting live from hot guy land,
Delia Rose(cheeked) Fairchild

nineteen

A LITTLE HOMESICK

DELIA

True to my word, the next two weeks pass and I stay out of Griffin's way.

I've made it a point to look for his truck in the morning, and when I get back from the boutique. Even if I don't see it, I still wait a few minutes before going down the stairs or coming into the house. Always listening for his voice, in case he walked over.

He's probably trying just as hard to stay out of my way, though, since our paths haven't crossed. Maybe he finally figured out what my schedule is. Regardless, I've been carrying on just fine. Out of sight, out of mind.

Kind of…

I may or may not have had a dream (or two) about him, but I'm sure it's only because I don't know how he's doing.

Catherine nor Marge have brought him up—not that I thought they would—but no mention at all has put me a tad on edge. I'm not sure if they know something happened, or have picked up on the subtle shift in behavior from us both.

So in the meantime, I've been spending more time with Cadence; going on runs, trying her latest baked goods, and making regular visits to the coffee shop together. It seems she's also avoiding a certain someone.

I don't know what happened between her and Griffin at the cookout, but I saw them talking on the dock. I saw the way he reacted to something she said and the look of utter defeat on her face as she walked away. I don't think they've talked much since.

It's all radio silence. Except for the one place where I need it most—my mind. I'm can't stop thinking about what happened between him and I, the things he said to me.

I don't know why I thought I'd be able to help him, but the second I grabbed his arm and felt the pure rage coursing through him, I couldn't stop myself.

I wasn't even going to try and make him talk about it. I just wanted to be there for him, walk with him back to his house so he knew wasn't alone. But he made it crystal clear that he wants nothing to do with me, and I've been pushed away enough in my life to know when to fight back and when to accept defeat.

I'd lost this time.

I wish my empathy would stop trying to argue with me on my decision, though. It's like dealing with an actual person I can't get rid of, always chiming in and telling me why I shouldn't give up on Griffin.

"Hurt people, hurt people," it reminds me.

But I shoo it away, because let's be real–I hurt, and I don't go around hurting other people, so there will be no budging on leaving him alone.

Cadence also keeps trying to get me to go back to Tombstones with her. And I keep declining. She promises that there will be "no assholes", but I don't want to take the chance.

The only person who doesn't seem to pick up on the stalemate between me and Griffin is Libby, of course, who keeps asking why I'm not joining them during her riding lessons—not that I would ever tell her what's going on. However, yesterday in her own words, she put together some sort of idea about what's happened when she asked if 'Griffy' and I are not friends.

I chose to be honest and said yes. Followed with, not everyone can be friends.

She gave me one of those thoughtful Libby nods, and handed me Kyle, *the bear*, and said he would be my friend. *Kids.*

The only other person that I've been making time to see is Fisher. I wouldn't say we're dating, because we're not exclusive and nothing has happened between us sexually, but we've gone out a couple times. I'm still standing firm on my conviction, though. I did not move out west to be distracted by a guy. Fisher is nice and we get along well. That's it, plain and simple. *For now.*

I found out he lives not far from Tombstones, in a studio apartment. I was shocked the first time I met him there and saw the dozen or so paintings covering the place. Apparently he went to school for art but couldn't find a job after he graduated, so he took up bartending and paints as a hobby now.

I'd texted Clara that little bit of info and buckled over with laughter when she finally replied, "So, what you're saying is he's good with his hands?"

With him on my mind, I glance at my phone checking the time. It's Taco Tuesday, and I said that I'd meet him for dinner after I got off. There's only one woman in the boutique, but we closed five minutes ago and it doesn't look like she has any plans to leave soon.

Navy saunters over and leans against the counter, glancing beyond me at the customer.

"I can close by myself, you know?" she says, not so quietly, and I'm wondering if she's hoping the lady will hear her.

"It's alright." I put my phone into my pocket. "Fisher can wait a little," I say with a laugh.

"So, what's going on there? Any developments?" She arches an eyebrow.

"None," I reply. "We're hanging out and getting to know each other. Which honestly feels kind of nice. Not having any pressure, I mean."

She nods thoughtfully, pursing her lips and contemplating her next words.

"What?" I prod.

"I didn't want to say anything," she starts, and my stomach immediately pitches.

"What…" I say, this time lowering my voice.

"Callum may have mentioned to Cadence, who mentioned to me, that a certain someone tried to nonchalantly ask him if you and Fisher are dating." She closes her eyes with a wince, as if bracing for impact.

"Oh," is all I respond with. I was expecting something much worse, but I'm not surprised he asked about that. Well, maybe a little.

"Oh?" she quips, popping her eyes back open. "That's it?"

"Yeah, Navy. I don't really care. Fisher and Griffin are friends after all, so I assumed it would come up at some point."

"See, that's the thing," her voice comes out in a whine. "Griffin hasn't talked to Fisher about it. He hasn't really talked to him at all."

"Okay…" I gesture for her to continue.

"So, Callum spoke for Fisher and said that, yeah, he thinks y'all are dating." She gives me an uncomfortable smile, once again gauging my response.

"That's fine. I don't blame Callum for assuming that. And as far as Griffin goes, well, he can think whatever he wants, honestly." I glance over my shoulder when the door bell chimes and the customer finally leaves. I look back at Navy and continue. "It's really none of my concern. *He's* none of my concern. He made that very clear a few weeks ago."

"I know, I know," she drawls. "I still can't believe he said that stuff to you. Well, actually, I can, considering he's told me the same thing, but antics, these are antics." She flares her hands out and I can't help but laugh.

Over the last few weeks, we've gotten closer from working so much together, and I'm learning that Navy is comically dramatic. Sometimes she talks like we're in a period drama, but I welcome the semantics. She genuinely makes me laugh and it keeps things light between us. Which is why I still haven't pressed on what happened between her and Griffin, but I'm sure it will come up eventually. Maybe if I'm lucky, it won't. I don't need anything else to overthink.

All of this turmoil has left me with a dull ache, making me feel a bit lost again. Which has turned into feeling a little homesick.

I miss Clara. I miss my parents. The texts and letters haven't been enough lately.

Yes, I can talk to Marge and Catherine. Yes, I have enjoyed my time with Cadence, Navy, and Fisher, but it's not quite the same.

There's also the fact that my birthday is next week and I can't help but wonder what I'd do if I were back home.

I don't have to wonder what I'll be doing here though, because Cadence somehow found out about it and has told me we're going out. No more excuses. Even though my birthday isn't for another week, Cadence insists we have to go out this

Saturday because she'll be out of town during my actual birthday weekend.

All I really want is to spend this weekend junk journaling, and next weekend eating Coca Cola cake.

"Hey, are you sure there's no getting out of going to Tombstones this weekend?" I call out to Navy who's now across the store, checking to make sure the fitting rooms are empty.

"No chance in hell," she shouts back.

"Ugh," I groan. The whole idea making me nauseous.

The last time I went to Tombstones, it ended with Griffin driving me back to the house, and me admitting some things I wish I hadn't. The next morning I acted like I didn't remember, and he did exactly what I suspected he would and didn't bring it up.

"Look," Navy says as she makes her way back to the cash wrap, "Griffin isn't going to show up. Why would he?"

"Um, maybe because all his friends are going out?" I retort.

She laughs. "Yeah, and that hasn't made a difference in the past, so...I don't know why it would now."

I let out an exasperated sigh, my emotions slipping. Grasping the edges of the counter, I turn to face her and blurt out, "I really think he wants me gone. Like sooner rather than later, if possible. And maybe if he came to the bar, he'd—"

"Delia, babe. I'm going to stop you right there. Griffin may be an asshole, but he's not a malicious asshole," Navy cuts in.

I frown, running my hands through my hair before dragging them down my face.

"You're right. You're absolutely right. It's..."

It's, what? What am I going to tell Navy? That I haven't been able to stop thinking about what I felt when I grabbed his arm at the cookout? That the pull toward him is stronger now more than ever?

"I get it. You're drawn to him," she offers, and I cut her a look of alarm. "Relax," she continues. "I'm not going to make things weird. It's pretty obvious. Well, to me, at least. Especially when you said you wanted to understand him, and from the rest of our conversations. Let me guess, you're an empath?"

I quirk up a brow. "Maybe."

"Uh huh," she says, reaching past me to grab the key from the cash drawer and drop it into the safe.

"Yes, I'm an empath, but you say it like it's a secret super-power or something." I grab my bag and we walk together around the store, making sure everything else is done from the closing tasks.

"I mean, in some ways it can be. I took a decent amount of psych classes while working toward my Masters, and one of them spent a great deal of time talking about empaths. It varies with each person, but some people can actually absorb the energy and feelings of those around them. Emotional, and physical."

I've always been aware that I'm perceptive of people's emotions. My therapist often said that being an empath is like being an emotional sponge, but actually *absorbing* someone else's feelings?

My mind flits back to the few times I've been around Griffin. The few times I've touched him and how it *did* feel like that. Like I was syphoning away his emotions, and taking them on myself.

"Holy shit," I mutter under my breath.

"Yeah, and to someone like Griffin, you're basically his kryp-tonite." She walks past me to the front door, setting the alarm.

"Okay, now *that's* a bit dramatic," I say, following her out into the parking lot.

"I'm being serious, Delia." She stops and squares her shoul-ders, facing me head on. "Griffin has worked to build some of the most impenetrable walls, but they don't work with you because you can literally feel through them. It doesn't matter what he says or how he acts, you can tell how he really feels. And even if he did try to mask his emotions, all you'd have to do is touch him and you'd know the truth. Which I've gotta be honest, I'm a little curious. What do you sense from him?"

I chew on the inside of my cheek and give her the short answer. "Sadness, and a whole lot of anger."

"Eh, checks out," she says, shrugging her shoulders. "Look, I say all of this to let you know that no matter what Griffin does, even if he shows up this weekend, you'll always have the upper hand."

She blows me a kiss, walking to her car and leaving me to contemplate her words.

I'm walking toward the 4Runner to exchange my work bag for my purse before I walk to the restaurant when I hear a whistle. I stall, my mind conjuring up the memory of being in the street when Callum whistled at me. I spin around and see Fisher jogging up. He stops in front of me, gives me a hug, and kisses the side of my cheek.

"How was work, pretty girl?"

"What are you doing here? I thought I was meeting you?" I ask, confused but happy to see him.

"When I didn't hear from you around six, I figured you must have gotten caught up at the store, so I thought I'd come here and we can walk together. I like your pink sneakers," he says while dragging his eyes up and down my body. I'm wearing a denim romper that looks more like a dress, but Fisher seems to approve.

"I like your band tee," I quip back, and he winks.

"Ripped jeans and a band tee, can't beat it," he says.

I give him a soft smile, before opening the car door, switching bags, and shutting it. He holds his hand out to me and I lace our fingers together. We walk down the sidewalk, talking about our days until we reach Cowboy Cantina. The place is busy, which isn't surprising given the two-dollar taco special they're running today.

Since there's a wait, we walk up to the bar, ordering drinks–a margarita for me and a beer for him–and head to the back patio to find a standing table.

Not long passes before we get our drinks and our table is ready. We don't waste time ordering, spending the next thirty or so minutes eating. I tell Fisher about Clara and how I hope she can visit soon because I'm missing her a lot lately. He suggests that she should come around the Fourth of July, and I tuck that away for later to bring up with Catherine.

When we're done, Fisher politely pays, and we start the walk back to the store.

"It must be nice that you live down here and can walk every-where," I say when we get to the parking lot.

He hums his agreement and stops when we're next to the driver's door. I turn to face him, resting against the car and trying not to notice how close we are.

Fisher pins his gaze on me and my cheeks flush.

He really is hot, I think to myself. Like panty dropping hot, with his messy dark hair and light eyes. Not to mention all the tattoos he has. Okay, maybe I *could* bend my no-distraction rule a little…

"So, I wanted to talk to you about something," he starts to say, and I feel my stomach drop.

"Okay," I respond, my voice wavering. "What's up?"

"Do you remember what I said at Tombstones the night we met?"

"You said a few things," I say, laughing a little. "Can you be a tad more specific?"

"About you wanting to kiss me."

My eyes widen. "What about that?"

"I've been wondering if you've thought about it again, sober." His gaze flicks to my mouth for a second.

"Um." I pause, heat creeping into my cheeks. "I mean, yes…"

"It's not a trick question, I'm just curious. I've really enjoyed spending time with you these last couple of weeks. I also think you're ridiculously attractive, but I wasn't sure where things stood past that." He reaches out and tucks a strand of hair behind my ear and I bite the corner of my lip.

"I kinda promised myself that I wasn't going to be distracted by any guys this summer," I whisper.

He takes a step closer to me, placing his hands against the window and caging me in.

"I would be a distraction for you?" he taunts, voice husky.

"I mean, maybe." I don't intend for my words to come out breathy, but they do.

"Maybe," he repeats my words just above a whisper. I notice he's been leaning closer to me and I'm not stopping him.

"I think…" My voice trails off as his lips hover in front of mine and he moves a hand to the back of my neck, tangling his fingers into my hair. And then, we're kissing.

At first, it's soft and tentative, but he lightly pulls on my hair, my lips parting with a gasp. His tongue slides into my mouth and I lift my hands to the sides of his face, deepening the kiss. A couple seconds pass before he pulls away, his lips swollen and puffy. He pushes off the window, putting some space between us again, and runs the hand that was in my hair through his own.

My mind is spinning, and I'm trying to think of what to say when he lets out a breath and shocks me.

"Anything?"

I answer truthfully–consequences be damned–and shake my

head side to side. My stomach knots in anticipation at what his response will be.

"Oh, thank fuck. I was worried it was just me," Fisher exclaims with a chuckle.

I can't help but laugh as relief washes over me. "Holy shit, I was really worried there for a second."

"Yeah, it's all good. I think we're meant to be friends," he says lightheartedly.

"I guess it would seem that way. So what now?"

"We keep on doing our thing. Nothing has to change, but now there won't be this question of 'what's next?' looming over us."

"Good, because I like spending time with you." I step forward and wrapping my arms around his waist to hug him.

He rests his arms on my lower back, giving me a squeeze. "Am I allowed to say that I'm still ridiculously attracted to you, but I think maybe that's it?"

I tilt my head back, resting my chin on his chest and looking up at him. "Are you saying you're in lust with me, Fisher?"

He leans back to peer down at me. "Don't tell me you wouldn't kiss me again too, now that we don't have to worry about feelings."

I swat at him playfully, but he catches my wrist.

"I have a favor to ask, though," he says, a mischievous glint in his eyes.

I narrow my gaze. "I'm listening."

"Can we keep flirting? In public? When we're around Gr–"

"I'm gonna stop you right there," I cut him off and break our hug. "I'm not sure if you've been living under a rock, but I am not trying to be *around* Griffin."

"Yeah, but if we are–"

"No," I clip.

"Aww, come on, Deels. I think it gets under his skin and it's funny as hell watching him squirm."

"Isn't he supposed to be your best friend? That doesn't sound like something a best friend is supposed to do." I raise my eyebrows and playfully push him away.

"Please," he scoffs, "it's exactly what best friends are supposed to do."

"I'll consider it." I turn to open the car door, getting in, and giving him one last glance. "See you Saturday?"

"Saturday, pretty girl," he agrees before turning on his heels and walking away.

A LEVEL PLAYING FIELD

GRIFFIN

Something I will never get used to is that no matter how much time passes, no matter how hard I try to ignore it or act like it doesn't exist, I will always carry my grief with me.

And I hate it.

I hate putting a name to the feeling I've stuffed down and don't want to admit is there.

But I know at the core of it all, that's what it is. Grief.

I stare at the old cellphone in my hands, finally lit up after sitting on the charger overnight, and I'm glad I live alone so no one can see my hands shaking.

Cathy found our dad's phone yesterday and I was thankful knowing that I'd have Saturday–today–to take my time figuring this out since I'm not working.

What I didn't plan for was how difficult it would actually be. I've worked hard to push down and avoid anything and every-thing that reminds me of the worst day of my life. But now, I'm here, with a physical representation of what I've been trying to outrun, and I feel sick.

It's not just the phone, though. Something in me has shifted since the cookout.

I haven't been able to stop thinking about what Cadence said. And if I thought I was going to try and talk to her about it, I'm shit out of luck. She's iced me out since.

I also haven't seen Delia once.

Yes, I'm the one who told her to leave me alone, but after realizing it's not that I dislike Delia, but more so that I'm worried she might replace me in my life, I feel like maybe I shouldn't have been so harsh with her. It's clear that she wants, or at least wanted, to try and be my friend. I think it's fair to say she might even care about me in some capacity. But there's still something about her that unnerves me to my core. I feel like she sees through me and my walls, and it's unsettling. I also can't quite figure out the whole her hugging me thing.

So while I've been wrestling with those thoughts, I've also been stuck on how Cadence made it a point to mention that the people in my life have accepted that I've pushed them away. While I've known that might be the case with my friends, I convinced myself that wasn't true with Cathy and Grams. But now that two weeks have passed, giving me plenty of time to sit with my thoughts and Cadence's words, I realize maybe it is.

I won't let them talk about certain things. I won't tell them how I'm angry all the time. So maybe it is fair to say that I keep them at an arm's length, too. And if I want to make sure that my fear of not being needed by the two women who mean the most to me comes true, I have to do something differently.

It's why once I summon up the courage to deal with the phone, I'm heading to the house and spending the day with Cath, Grams, and Libs.

Delia will be at Lasso and she's going straight to Tombstones after, giving me all day to be at the house.

Callum is the one who let it slip that they were going out tonight. I guess Delia's birthday is next week or something, but they're going out early because Cadence won't be in town. And while I wasn't necessarily *not* not-invited, I know I'm not welcome. Callum doesn't seem to have a clue what's going on, however, which shocked me. I for sure thought Cadence would have told him, but maybe they're not close like I thought, or maybe they had their fun and it fizzled out.

The older model iPhone lights up in my hand again, alerts and notifications beginning to come through, ripping me from my thoughts.

I stare down at the screen, the logo of our family business peeking out from behind all the chaos popping up. Swiping to unlock it, I'm reminded how good of a man and husband he was. He never had a password—for much of anything, because he never had anything to hide.

The outdated home screen shows apps with notifications well into the thousands, however, I don't let my mind get distracted by, and go straight to his voice mailbox.

I start selecting as many as I can, including any spam calls or random numbers. But most of them are from me, the dates ranging from a few weeks, a couple months, and then years. I knew there had to be a limit so I tried to make the calls sparingly, but it's strange seeing all of them together.

While I don't talk about my shit with anyone, I find it easy to rattle off what's on my mind in a voicemail I know will never be listened to. But sometimes, I let myself believe that maybe my dad hears them. I can't think on that for too long though because of the wave of emotion that tries to accompany it.

Making the decision to keep paying his phone bill might be

the craziest thing I've ever done, but I don't care. No one else knows, except for the worker at the phone store who gave me access so I could keep it open. And it will stay my secret.

There's no rulebook on how to cope with loss or grief. I found something that helps, and I'm sticking with it. I found a way to hold onto a means of communication with my dad.

Once I get to about four years back, I hit delete, watching the voicemails disappear, and a weight lifting off my chest. I can talk to my dad again.

Even more relief floods me knowing that I'll have the phone on hand if this happens again.

I shut it back off and stow it away in my night stand, taking a deep breath and making my way toward the house. On the walk there, I notice something feels off, the relief I just felt starting to waver. I'm not as confident that I've resolved things. Instead, I feel like I opened myself up to something and I'm not sure how to deal with that.

By the time I'm done walking to the house, I've decided that maybe I can try to talk through this with Cathy and Grams. I have to find a way to do it without opening myself up too much, but enough to show them that I'm not pushing them away.

I walk through the front door and come to a halt when I spot Delia on the couch. She glances over and scrambles to her feet, clearly not expecting to see me.

The feeling is mutual.

"You're not supposed to be here," I blurt out.

Her face pales as she turns, likely to dart upstairs.

"Wait, that's not what I meant," I quickly say. "I wasn't expecting to see you here."

She stops, still not facing me fully, and finally says something.

"I'm going in late today."

I think this is the first conversation I've had with her where she isn't rambling. I don't know why, but it feels wrong.

"Gotcha. Are my sister and Grams not here?" I realize I didn't even check to see if the cars were here, much less ask if they'd be around today. I assumed, since they usually are.

"They should be back soon," she says as she subtly inches toward the stairs. "The three of them went to the grocery store. Catherine told me last night to go in at noon since I've been working so much lately."

I glance over at the clock on the oven, it's half past ten. When I look back at her, she's going up the first couple steps and I take a deep breath.

"Delia, can we talk?"

She stiffens. Honest to God, freezes with her hand on the rail and everything. It's so unlike her to shy away like this. Granted, I told the girl to leave me alone, but still. She's never backed down before in the–now almost–month I've known her.

"I've been thinking about what happened and I shouldn't have spoken that way to you. You were trying to help–"

She cuts me off, turning back around to face me. "We don't have to do this. It's fine. You've made it clear that you want nothing to do with me and I should have respected that from the start."

"It's not," I pause.

What am I about to say to her? I don't want her to think that I'm turning over a new leaf and want to be buddy-buddy, but I also recognize that I don't have to be such a dick. Damn, this morning with the phone really messed with me. I rub at my chest and don't know why I'm surprised when Delia tilts her head and speaks up.

"What's wrong." It comes out more like a statement rather

than a question. Because she doesn't have to actually ask, she already knows. She somehow *always* knows.

"Nothing, I had a weird morning. But I don't want to talk about me, I want to tell you that I shouldn't have treated you the way I did at the cookout. I'm not used to…" I let my words trail off and she comes back down the steps, moving closer but still keeping her distance.

"Someone who won't let you push them away?" She scrunches up her face, before pinning me with that determined look of hers. "Someone who calls you out on your shit?

"Alright, I get it," I clip, but I have to hide a smile because *that's* the Delia I want to talk to.

"If it makes you happy, I don't really want to be here anymore," she says quietly, and the smile is ripped from my face as I snap my gaze to hers. "So, you win, I guess."

The defeat in her voice makes the ache in my chest deepen.

"Wait, what?"

"I don't want to do this. Exist in a space with someone where I can physically feel their annoyance with my presence. I've been around enough–" She stops talking and pinches the bridge of her nose. "Look, I remember the night you brought me home from the bar."

My stomach drops.

"I know what I said to you. And I don't regret that I said it because it's all true. But the thing is, I've dealt with so many people like that in my life. Who make it very obvious that I'm not their cup of tea, because I'm maybe a little more emotional than the average person. And the truth is, I don't usually stick around those people. Because why would I surround myself with those who make it so obvious they don't want me? Yet I don't really have that option here, Griffin. I'm just trying to do *my job*, figure some things out for myself, and I'll be out of your hair.

Until then, I will respect what you asked and stay out of your way."

On the one hand, it's nice to hear more than one sentence from her. On the other, I don't know what to do with everything she said.

Before I have a chance to respond, she speaks up again. "Sometimes I think you believe I came here to mess with your life. When reality is, I didn't even know you existed. It was also a surprise for me that you were going to be around this summer."

I consider her words, wondering if maybe there is some truth to them. That maybe I have been carrying on as if she's here to bother me, when that's not even logical. Like she said, this is literally her job. And I don't know why this is now clicking for me.

"You're right," I admit and her jaw falls open. "We both were surprised and I've taken it personally since. But you're here to work and help my sister out, and at the end of the day it has nothing to do with me."

"Well, at least we can agree on that," she scoffs.

"But it's good you're staying," I say.

"Is it?" she challenges, and I laugh.

"Yeah, my sister really does need your help. You also get on really well with Libby and Grams," I say, and then for some unknown reason, I blurt out my next few words. "And Fisher. Y'all are…"

I hesitate. Why am I bringing this up?

"Are what?" She puts her hands on her hips and tilts her head, raising her eyebrows.

"Dating? Or at least that's what Callum said," I quickly clarify.

"Hm, did he now?" She pauses, pursing her lips, before continuing. "We've been on a few dates."

"Nice," is all I'm able to say, and I feel like an idiot.

She laughs a little and we stand there, in some sort of silent stand off.

But then there's a shift in the air, and I think maybe we're *finally* on a level playing field—in a neutral zone. But like usual, she catches me off guard with her next few words.

"I'm sorry you had a weird morning. You deserve to have one day where something isn't bothering you. I hope that you can talk to your sister or grandmother about it. I'm going to go get ready," she finishes her sentence, spins on her socked foot, and heads up the stairs for good this time.

My mouth falls as if I want to say something, but the door opens, Libby barreling toward me with my sister and Grams behind her. The words–the moment is lost.

"Hey, Griff. Everything okay?" Cathy calls out as she sets down some grocery bags on the counter. Her gaze drifts to the stairs then to me, and I know what she's really asking.

"Yeah–was talking to Delia about something," I answer nonchalantly as I walk over to help unload the items.

Libby snakes around my leg and takes a few things from me, putting them away, or at least as best she can.

Grams takes a seat at the dining table and flicks through some mail. I notice her set aside a few envelopes and they must be for Delia. I know she's been writing letters since she got here, having intercepted a few of them myself when checking the mailbox.

After a few minutes when everything is neatly put into the cabinets or fridge, Cath sends Libby to her room for some quiet time and pins her gaze on me.

"What?" I say, putting my hands up in the air.

"Were you kind to Delia?" she asks, throwing me completely off guard.

"Wh-wha?" I splutter. "Was I *kind*? What kind of question is that?"

"One worth asking," Grams interjects, also giving me a sharp look.

"Why wouldn't I be kind to Delia?" I scoff, sitting at the table too. Cathy comes to join us as well with a mug of tea in hand, setting it down in front of Grams.

"Well," my sister starts, "there's the fact that you haven't spoken kindly of her before. You were acting a little shifty at the cookout. And, well, let's be honest. You two have been avoiding each other since."

"Okay, and…" I stop myself from saying what I really want—that it's none of their business—trying for once to not immediately get defensive.

"And I'm sorry, Griff, but I don't see Delia being the one to cause something like that to happen." Cathy shrugs.

"We want to make sure you aren't giving her a hard time is all," Grams adds on. "We really like her being here and, like we said before, just because she's a little out of your norm, doesn't mean that you have to be unkind to her."

I scowl, looking between the two of them, trying to work over how to respond in this situation. I recognize this is a moment that could serve as a chance to open up to them a little. That's the goal, after all, and I need to keep reminding myself of that.

"Fine, alright. I can understand why you'd think that," I say, and both of their eyebrows shoot up to their hairlines. "She *has* gotten under my skin, but if you must know, that was what our chat was about before you guys got back. And she reminded me that she's here to work, and I was never supposed to be a part of that equation."

It's Cathy's turn to look sheepish.

"Well, I didn't really think about that," she says with a hint of guilt in her tone. "I was amused that you thought she was a grandma, but I didn't think about how it might have caught her off guard as well. It didn't come up in our initial conversations because they were so focused on Lib and Grams."

She twists her lips to the side, a contemplative look taking over her face.

"I guess maybe in hindsight, I definitely should have mentioned it. Although, I did say our family lived on the ranch, but didn't think to–"

"Catherine, it's okay," Grams stops her. "We can't undo what's happened, but yes, maybe a conversation with Delia herself is in order so we can ask how she actually feels about the situation instead of trying to put Griffin here in the middle. I'm sure he doesn't fully know the extent of her feelings regarding the situation anyways."

I grunt out some sort of laugh before schooling my expressions again.

"Yeah, I'd rather not be the middle man. Besides, I'm sure she would be more than happy to talk to someone about her feelings, since that's like her thing or whatever," I joke.

"Griffin," both women say in unison, reaching out at the same time to give a light smack on my arms.

"Okay, ouch?" I draw away from them. "Don't act like it isn't true."

"We don't know why you need to poke fun at it," Cathy argues and gives Grams a look that says, *"back me up here"*.

"Griffin, what is it that you have against feelings? We know that you're reserved and we try not to talk about it, but are you really that bothered by someone else having such big ones?" Grams gives me a thoughtful look, continuing, "We love you as you are, but we also wish that you didn't believe you have to be so closed off."

I let out a deep breath, pinching the bridge of my nose with my free hand. Grams squeezes my fingers and I know this is definitely the moment. This is my chance to finally share something with them, so I steel my nerves and try.

"I don't know how to navigate them," I admit with a small twinge of defeat in my voice. "I don't know how to face them, so instead, I've shoved them down."

I look between my sister and Grams, their eyes both starting to well with tears, and my stomach drops.

"Did I say the wrong thing?" I quickly rush out.

"No, no," Cathy chokes. "It's nice to hear that it's not that you don't want to feel, it's that you're scared to."

"Okay, well I wouldn't–"

"Did something prompt this sudden willingness to share with us?" Grams cuts me off, ever the intuitive.

I contemplate how to answer her question. I don't want to give away everything, especially not the phone thing. My eyes dart back and forth on the table as if an answer will appear in the wood.

"I had a talk with Cadence at the cookout that kind of left me thinking about some things. And this morning, having Dad's phone made me reflect a little."

I wait for them to respond, feeling like that is a safe-ish answer.

"I didn't want to ask what you needed the phone for, but is everything okay?" Cathy tilts her head.

I scramble for an answer. "Oh, yeah. I was trying to find some, err, old records for work."

Grams gives me a look from the side of her eyes that screams, "*I call BS",* but to my surprise, doesn't call me out. Instead she asks, "Let's go back to the other part, your conversation with Cadence?"

I hum in response, when I hear the creak of wood behind me. I look over my shoulder to find Delia trying to make her way downstairs as quietly as possible. I swear if she could make herself invisible, she probably would. Except, it's hard *not* to notice her right now.

She's curled her hair and has on a short but flowy white dress with what looks like blue flowers on it. Her signature crimson boots are in her hand making it even more evident that she didn't want to be heard coming down the stairs. And to finish it off, she's wearing that damn yellow sweater with the buttons open so it's more like a jacket. She looks like a warm summer day.

What the hell am I even talking about?

"Pretty!" Cathy calls out from the table and I blink quickly, realizing I've been staring off into the distance.

"Thanks," Delia says, a shy smile on her face. "I'm not sure if I'll change before tonight, I might get something from the store. I'm not sure what the girls are wearing. Not that you asked."

She sits on the bottom step now that her presence has been made known, and slips her feet into the cowgirl boots. When she stands, she makes her way to the door, stopping to give Grams a hug around her shoulders. It's the most natural movement, as if they've been in this routine for years.

I watch Grams close her eyes as if absorbing something Delia is giving her and it reminds me of how it felt when Delia hugged me. My whole body was overcome with this sensation of warmth and peace. It was fleeting, though, because she stepped away as quickly as she'd hugged me, but I still felt it. And now that I think about it, maybe that's what I felt the night I carried her in my arms.

"Thanks again for letting me head in late, Cathy," Delia says as she breaks the hug and walks over to the coat hanger by the door, grabbing her purse. "You'll text if you need anything?"

"Of course," my sister says, donning a bright smile like Delia just offered her a million dollars.

My instinct is to roll my eyes, but I stop myself when I realize why my sister is smiling like that. I think that's the first time Delia hasn't referred to my sister as Catherine and when the hell did that change?

"Sounds good," Delia says, a step from the door. I think I'm in the clear, that I can breathe again, but she calls out, "See you tomorrow, Libby-Loo!"

The crack of a door announces the incoming presence of said little girl and my niece barrels into Delia's legs, giving her a tight hug. Me? I'm slack jawed at her using the nickname I gave Libby. Did she hear me say it or come up with it herself? Granted, it's not an uncommon nickname. But still, it gives me a similar feeling to when Delia said that her favorite cereal is my favorite cereal.

It bothers me that we could maybe be more alike than I'd like to believe.

Delia darts out the front door, Libby heading back to her room, and I start to push away from the table. This has been a weird morning for me, and I think I'm at my limit for "feelings" or whatever is trying to kick around in my chest.

I'm also stuck on her calling my sister Cathy.

It seems in the last couple weeks that I haven't been around, she's grown closer with all of them. I do my best to not let that realization make me resort back to wanting to send her packing.

"Wait," Cathy says before I can make my escape. "Are you going to Tombstones tonight for Delia's birthday?"

I huff out a laugh, but realize she's being serious. "Oh, no. I didn't have plans to. I wasn't exactly invited," I share, running a hand through my hair.

"Nonsense," Grams says. "All of your friends will be there."

"Yeah…" I hesitate. "I think it will be better if I hang back tonight."

"I think it would be good if you went, Griffin. Especially if you really did talk to Delia this morning about trying to be amicable. I'm still not entirely sure what happened between you two, but either way, this could be an opportunity to extend the olive branch." Cathy claps her hands as if she solved all my problems.

"I don't know," I say with a sigh.

"Please," Cathy says, putting her hands together in front of her chest in a praying position. "For me and Grams! Go and try to have fun."

Okay, well, how the hell am I supposed to say no to that, especially when the whole point of coming here today was to try and show them both that I'm willing to put some effort forward?

"Fine," I say, trying not to clench my jaw.

"That's my boy," Grams says. "Besides, it's the least we can do for her. She won't have her family around and I feel terrible about it. Oh, and the Coca Cola cake…" Grams' words trail off and Cathy shares my same look of confusion.

"The *what*?" she asks.

"Heavens if I know. She told me during one of our conversations that her father makes her a Coca Cola cake every year for her birthday." Grams waves a hand in the air to dismiss the thought.

"Interesting," Cathy says. "Maybe it's a Georgia thing."

"Anyways, you need to go tonight," Grams says. "It'll be great."

And I don't know why, but as I walk down the hall to spend some time with Libby, I have the strangest feeling it will be the farthest thing from great. I still can't shake the feeling that I've opened up something in me that I'm not sure I know to close back up.

Maybe it's all in my head.

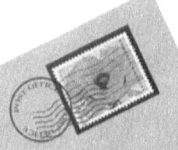

Delia Pie,

I can't believe you've already been gone for almost a month. I'm so proud of you and I know that your mother is too. I'm sorry to hear that you've been homesick. I was shocked when you sent me the letter saying you wanted to come home early, but I hope that you have worked through that. The day you spent with Cadence and Navy on the lake sounded like fun. I'm glad you've found some friends while you're there. I saw Clara's mom last weekend, she said she's glad Clara is living in the city. Have you thought about if you're going to renew your lease when you get back or find somewhere else to live? Just something on my mind. I want to make sure you're where you're happy. I'm always here for you. Your biggest fan.

Love,
Dad

LIKE A FREAKING EGG

DELIA

"So you lied to him?" Navy about shrieks into the store.

"Shh!" I wave my hands in the air as if anyone in here actually cares about what I'm saying.

I've been at the store for all of thirty minutes and was immediately interrogated. Apparently, it's evident that I'm scatter brained and flustered.

Which is a royal understatement.

I've been nothing but a ball of nervous energy since Griffin found me on the couch in the house. I swore he was going to be with Callum today, but I also had no real confirmation of that. I was betting on the fact that the last two Saturdays he'd avoided the house. How could I know today he would suddenly change that?

The morning keeps replaying on a loop and I haven't stopped beating myself up about how I shrank. In that moment, I didn't want to be anything to Griffin. Which broke one of my biggest

ELLE F. SUN

promises I made to myself: I will never let someone make me feel small.

When he blurted out that I wasn't supposed to be there, that feeling of being unwanted took me out like a tidal wave.

Not that it mattered for too long, because of course, *of course*, I cracked. Like a freaking egg. The second I sensed something was wrong with him, I folded. I couldn't help it.

However, I also recognized that the second I let my empathy take over, the feeling of being small faded. I felt strong and bold again. But surprise, I detoured and ended up sharing something with him that I'd never planned to.

I didn't want him to know he'd gotten to me so badly that I considered leaving early. But I'm glad I told him, because the look of shock on his face was worth it. I think I actually got through to him about the whole "this is my job and I'm not here to ruin your life" thing, too.

"Delia!" Navy claps her hands and I shake my head, coming back to the moment. "I need you to focus."

"Right, sorry. I didn't want him to know why I actually came in late. So, yeah, I lied to Griffin," I say, nibbling on my bottom lip.

And I did it again when I left out the fact that there's nothing between Fisher and I, other than the mischievous plan he's concocted to continue messing with Griffin.

But I don't tell Navy about that lie because, well, I actually haven't told anyone about what happened after the kiss. I also haven't told anyone about the kiss either.

There's a little part of me that wouldn't mind keeping him on retainer for a possible friends with benefits situation. But I'm definitely keeping *that* to myself.

I've also been considering his mischievous plan of keeping up our little flirting game, and the more time that passes, the more curious I am about playing it.

"Which is?" Navy pushes, pulling me from my thoughts once again.

"Cathy and I were up late talking, it got emotional, and she told me I could take the morning," I say, and it's true. I just don't want to tell Navy exactly what we talked about.

"Oh… Well, I don't blame you then for not telling him, because that's basically like giving Griffin free ammo to use against you," she says. "Or he'd get defensive and start asking what exactly you talked about because when there's emotions involved he's always concerned he might somehow be brought up."

I snort out a laugh.

"That is true," I say, walking over to the fitting rooms when I notice some clothes on a rack needing to be put back out.

As I idle on the sales floor, doing small tasks, straightening the hangers, my mind wanders to last night. To the depth of my and Cathy's conversation.

It was a little after ten and I'd come downstairs after not being able to sleep. I found Cathy at the kitchen table, with a mug of tea and a distraught look on her face.

"Mind if I join you?" I move slowly toward the table.

Catherine looks up at me, freezing for a second as if she's seen a ghost, and then blinks a few times, giving me a tired smile.

"Delia, hi. No, I don't mind at all."

I pad my way over to the fridge, grabbing a juice before sitting down across from her at the table.

"Can't sleep?" she asks, her tone laced with that motherly concern I know from my own.

"Not really," I answer truthfully. "Everything okay with you?"

She lets out a sarcastic laugh, a single tear running down her cheek. In that moment, I don't see Catherine as a mom anymore, but as someone only a little older than me, who clearly has a lot on her shoulders.

"That's a loaded question, but I'm sure you already gathered that."

"My empath senses are maybe tingling," I say with a light laugh and she smiles. "But if you'd like to talk about it, I'm happy to listen. In fact, it would be kind of nice. I'm so used to playing therapist for my best friend, Clara, and while we've exchanged texts and letters, it's not the same."

Catherine nods and takes a small sip of her tea.

"I don't know how to say this, but–" her voice cracks, "I really miss my dad." She stifles a cry with the sleeve of her sweater that she's wrapped around her fist.

A lump forms in my throat, my eyes suddenly burning, but I try to push it away so I can be here for her. I also don't know what to say.

"Were you close?" I ask, hoping that's good enough.

"The closest," she says, in a voice that makes me feel like I'm speaking with the younger version of Catherine that existed when her dad was around. Then she takes the breath out of my lungs when in a tone laced with sorrow, she says, "They died. My mom and dad."

I'd gathered this from my conversation with Grams, but the way she says it, it's like hearing it for the first time.

"I'm so sorry, Catherine," I'm quick to say as I move my hand on instinct to cover hers.

"It comes in waves, you know?" She rolls her lips as if contemplating something, so I fill in the silence.

"I do, actually. I've lost all my grandparents, my best friend's dad who was like a dad to me, and a friend right after I

graduated high school. I've learned that it never really goes away."

She nods thoughtfully, reminding me of Libby which makes one corner of my lips tug up into a soft smile.

"It sucks," she blurts out. "Like, there's really no other way to describe it, other than it just sucks."

I laugh at her words, but there is so much truth to them.

"Yeah, it really does. I'll have stretches of time where I'm cruising, living my life, but one day I'll see or hear something, smell something, and it's like I'm having to face it all over again. It's maybe not as difficult, but it still hurts." I take my hand off hers and swipe it across my cheeks where a few tears of my own have fallen.

"That's exactly what happened tonight. I was putting Libby to sleep and she made a comment about how she's glad I'm her mommy. Which isn't strange by any means, but then she said she isn't sad that she doesn't have a daddy. I was so caught off guard, but I pushed past it and told her I'm glad she isn't sad and that we have each other. And she looked at me, with that sweet little face of hers, and asked if I'm sad that I don't have my daddy, and I almost lost it."

She pauses to sniffle, but continues. "It was such a simple question, but it knocked me off my feet because it's not something I really ever consider anymore. I was twenty-three when my parents died, so now after thirteen years, it's something I've come to live with. But to stop and consider if it makes me sad? Well, yeah. It does, actually. It makes me really sad."

I sit there for a few seconds as more tears fall down her cheeks and I start to wonder if there is a bigger reason I was brought to this ranch.

While last week, I'd let Griffin's actions make me consider going home early, this conversation is pushing me to consider that there's a bigger picture than I can see. That the universe didn't bring me here only to be a caregiver, nanny, and sales associate. But maybe, to help a family heal from the things that they've gone silent about.

"Do you ever talk about it? With Marge or your brother?" I ask as I finish my thought.

"Sometimes with my grandmother, but it seems selfish to bring it up. She's carrying her own grief. She lost her son and daughter-in-law, who she loved like her own, and then her husband. We've shared some moments but I mostly keep to myself. There's a few moms I'm close to from Libby's school, but I think everyone in this town feels like they'll always be walking on eggshells around us because of the accident." Catherine sighs.

"And what about Gr—"

"Griffin? Yeah, right. He's boarded and locked up basically any part of him that doesn't require affection for me, Libby, or Grams."

"Yeah, I kinda gathered that." I try to stifle a laugh, but Catherine suddenly pins me with a look I can't quite read.

"You challenge him, you know? I can tell. Yes, he said what he did that morning in the kitchen, and I'm not excusing it, but it's because you're one of the only people who hasn't been around to know that we don't ask certain questions or talk about specifics with him anymore. And here you are, saying things to him that he hasn't heard in a while, maybe not ever."

I chew on the inside of my cheek and decide to fess up.

"We shared a moment. That Sunday night before the cookout. He drove me home from the bar and I basically told him that I was going to figure him out. I don't think he liked that very much."

Catherine snorts. "I'd pay to have been a fly on the wall for that."

I give her a half-smile before continuing. "Just wait, it didn't stop there. I decided I should tell him that I know he thinks I'm weird or too emotional, whatever. And that he isn't the first person. Basically all my exes ended things with me because they said I was too much. It's something I've heard a lot, actually, and at first, it hurt so badly that I tried to shut off parts of myself. I tried not to feel and pushed things down. But that only made things worse for me, so I chose to accept those parts—that I'm an empath. And I realized that it isn't this massive flaw. I still struggle sometimes to believe that, especially when someone says something like Griffin did, but for the most part, it's an honor to be someone who feels so deeply."

The tears falling from Catherine's eyes have slowed and she reaches out with both hands, clasping them around mine.

"Do you know how badly we needed someone like you to come here?"

I shake my head because the lump in my throat is so big now, I can't speak.

"You should *be proud to be an empath. It's a beautiful thing to experience emotions so deeply, and I'm sorry that anyone has ever made you think differently. I hope you never change and you continue to embrace the depths of your feelings. You have the power to heal people, and don't ever let anyone make you forget that."*

A drop of something slides down my cheek ripping me from my thoughts and I realize I've started crying at work. I quickly pat my cheeks, hoping to press the tear into my makeup and not smudge it off.

I don't know how long I've been standing in this one spot, so I quickly turn to find Navy busy with a customer and none the wiser of my little *moment*.

I'm seconds away from going to the bathroom now that I

know she's got things handled, when the door bell chimes and I hear the familiar voice of one sassy brunette.

"Where's my birthday bit–girl?"

I laugh at her last minute word change as she scans the store and notes the customers who would likely not appreciate the profanity.

She darts my way and gives me a kiss on my cheek, taking my hand to twirl me, my white dress fluttering out around me.

"Cute, but not hot. I thought we were going for hot tonight," she says with a pout.

"I'm going to buy something from the store," I respond, smirking.

"Oh?" Cadence widens her eyes. "Well, I can't wait to see. I'm coming back here right at seven, okay? We can do touch ups and you can change, and we'll head over to Tombstones together. Fisher told me they're doing karaoke tonight which is perfect!"

A bittersweet feeling washes over me. Clara and I used to go to karaoke bars all the time in Atlanta, even though she always gave me shit because of my go-to song. I can hear her voice now; "Who sings sad songs at karaoke?"

But maybe it'll remind me of Clara, of home, and I'll feel more comfortable. Maybe the night won't be so bad after all.

STUPID TEQUILA

DELIA

Tombstones is buzzing, the voices of those singing karaoke filling the space and the people in the crowd echoing the words.

We've been here for about an hour and I've already taken two birthday shots of tequila with Cadence, and Fisher has been kind enough to sneak me water for all the other shots people have been buying me after Cadence announced to all the patrons that it's my birthday. I will be pacing myself tonight, in an attempt to avoid a repeat of the last time I got tipsy. I don't need to spill any more secrets to anyone.

"My lady," Callum says, holding his hand out to me to help me off the bar stool. I snort in response, taking it, and hopping down.

Navy, Cadence, and I wander over to where the small dance section is and start twirling each other. Laughter bubbles up and spills out of me, my cheeks beginning to hurt from how much I'm smiling.

"Are you having fun?" Navy calls over the music and the off-tune singer who's trying to master "Don't Stop Believin'" by Journey yet failing miserably.

"I am! I'm glad we came out," I shout back, meaning it too.

"Good!" Cadence chimes in, giving me a big smile.

We keep dancing and I glance over at the bar where Fisher is handing Callum another beer and shoots me a wink.

"So, what's going on there?" Cadence says, gesturing toward the guys with her head.

I bite the inside of my cheek and decide maybe I'll let one secret slip tonight.

"We kissed after we went to Cowboy Cantina," I fess up.

"What?!" Both girls exclaim so loud that a few heads turn to look at us.

"And you're just now telling us?" Cadence barks.

"It's just, ugh," I groan and step closer to them, as if anyone could actually hear me over the music and off-pitch singing.

"Just *what*, ma'am? Spill!" Navy pokes me in the arm.

"There was no spark," I say with a wince.

"Ooooh," Cadence says, rolling her lips together before smacking them.

"Damn," Navy echoes, giving me an awkward smile.

I quickly fill in the missing details. "He didn't feel one either, so it was fine, actually. But he did ask me something I wanted to get y'all's opinion on."

"Oh?" Cadence stops dancing and pops a hip out, her eyebrows raising and eyes lighting with mischief.

"He asked if he and I could keep up with the flirting stuff around Griffin. He said it gets under his skin and it's entertaining, I guess." I let out a sigh.

They share a look with each other before a laugh bursts from them.

"What?" I gawk.

"PLEASE do that," Cadence says. "He's not wrong. And even though Griffy and I had a little chat this afternoon and made up, I still want to keep him on his toes."

My eyebrows pinch together. This is news to me.

"Yeah, I mean, it's all in good fun," Navy agrees.

"I don't know," I admit. "Feels like poking the bear to me."

Cadence shrugs. "Griffin isn't supposed to care about anything, remember? So if you and Fisher flirting gets a rise out of him, which let's be honest, it does, then I find that rather interesting. Don't you, Navy?"

The red head hums her agreement and twists her lips to the side, giving Cadence a strange look. It's like they're communicating with their eyes or something as they nod and shrug, speaking without words.

"Yes? Would someone like to fill me in?" I interrupt their moment.

"Okay, I feel like this girl chat is long overdue," Navy speaks first. "I know we've tiptoed around certain things, but I think we need to skip past any awkwardness and talk about this."

"Agreed," Cadence says.

"Besides, if it wasn't obvious before, I'll make it clear now. You're one of us for the summer," Navy states with a thoughtful look while Cadence nods emphatically.

"I'll come back to that sentiment later, but first, talk about what?" I raise my eyebrows, clearly missing something.

"About you and Griffin!" Cadence practically shouts.

I can't help it, my jaw falls open. Then I laugh. I laugh loud and hard, but both girls just look at me like my reaction isn't warranted.

"There is no me and Griffin," I say through breaths while I try to rein in my laughing.

"I don't know about that. I didn't want to say anything because I wasn't sure what was going on with you and Fisher, but now that we know there isn't anything. Well…" Cadence trails off and starts to bite her nail.

"Well?" I grab her hand, dragging her over to the wall where it's quieter and there aren't as many people. Navy follows behind and we press into a small huddle.

"Okay, so you know how the cookout is when everything kind of went to shit?" she starts.

"Yes?"

"So, before you and Griffin had that stand off moment, he and I talked on the dock. And, well, it had to do with you." She scratches the side of her cheek and looks around avoiding my gaze.

"I'm sorry, what?" I can't believe what I'm hearing right now.

"It's why I asked you if something happened between y'all after he drove you home. I noticed he was keeping his eye on you basically the whole time at the cookout," Cadence says.

"It's true," Navy butts in. "We all noticed."

"*We* did not!" I say, my voice rising.

Cadence groans, pointing to her and Navy, and in the direction of the guys at the bar. "*We* did. So… I asked him what happened and, tale as old as time, he got so defensive. Especially when I mentioned that I caught him watching you and that it looked like maybe he had taken up an interest in you."

I can't help but laugh again, because there's just no way.

"I'm not sure if you forgot, but he told me to leave him alone, and go back to Fisher. I'm pretty sure there's no interest there at all." I run a hand through my hair and try to think back through the events of the cookout. I try to think if there is any validity at all to what they're saying. There were a few times where I did look at him to find he was already looking at me, but that was purely coincidental. Right?

"Yeah, I might have told him to do exactly that," Cadence says in a whiney voice. "Because there's no reason for him to be such a jerk to you, and if he isn't going to be kind, he can leave you alone and let you have your fun."

Navy nods, the truth finally coming out when she says, "Griffin and I dated our senior year of high school. I'm sure you put two and two together but let me just give you some more context here. The Griffin you've met and been around, is not really him. I know we've talked about it here and there, that he's changed, and we've all made remarks about it. And you've figured some of it out too, but when…" Her words trail off.

"I know about James and Paige," I admit. "Cathy told me."

Cadence and Navy exchange another look, but Navy speaks again, "What we're trying to say is, you bring out a side of Griffin that we haven't seen in a long time, maybe ever."

"People change with grief," I say, feeling a strange need to defend him, but quickly deflect. "I mean, people change in general. Nobody should want to stay the same forever, right?"

Cadence rolls her eyes. "This is what I'm saying. You just… get him."

"You're right though, people do change. But this is like, past the point of change. This is like, self destruction in some ways. And we know you're only here for the summer, but we're all just excited that maybe some of his harsh edges could be softened before you head back to Georgia," Navy says with a timid smile.

"So, essentially I come here and leave him better than I found him?" I joke.

"Pretty much," Cadence deadpans.

"Well, I've tried to be his friend and he wanted nothing to do with that. So if anything is going to change, it's on him," I say with a finality in my voice that has both the girls sighing.

"We get it." Navy reaches out and squeezes my arm. "But it's his loss. You're a pretty great friend."

"Damn straight," Cadence says. "I'm trying to figure out how I made it so many years without someone like you in my life."

My heart squeezes and a bittersweet feeling accompanies it. I won't be here forever and for the first time, I feel a bit of sadness about that. But in the same second, I think about if I did live here, I wouldn't be close to Clara.

Damn. What's with the universe letting you become best friends with people that you're separated from by a plane ride?

"What an odd place to have such a deep conversation," I say with a chuckle.

"Um, not at all," Cadence tuts. "Don't you know some of the best conversations are had in dive bars?"

"This is true," Navy agrees.

We laugh and walk back onto the dance area. My attention is on the stage where the next karaoke victim is full on laying down while trying to perform some country ballad. Cadence and Navy are in front of me dancing again, and when I come back to meet their gaze, something has snagged their attention behind me.

I go to look over my shoulder when Cadence takes my hand and pulls me into her, spinning me out so fast that I let out a squeal and close my eyes. Probably not my best decision, as I collide into a hard something–someone.

Fingers squeeze my hips, steadying me, and my hands meet the soft fabric of a T-shirt. When I pop my eyes open, my stomach dips so low, it might as well be on the floor.

"Griffin!" My voice comes out high and pitchy. I cut a look over my shoulder at Cadence, who gives me one of her shit eating smirks, before she and Navy continue dancing with each other, not paying me an ounce of attention.

It's at that moment I realize my hands are still on Griffin's chest, *his very hard, muscular chest*. Not just that, but his hands are still resting around my waist.

I quickly clear my throat and push myself away from him. He must realize what I have and shoves his hands into his pockets. I smooth down the front of my dress and chance a look up at him again. He still hasn't said anything, so I do what I do best. I fill the silence.

"Hi, um, you're here! I didn't know you were–I'm sorry that I just–you're here!" I laugh nervously, tucking my hair behind my ears. I'm not sure if it's the conversation I just had with the girls and the little bit of insight they gave me, but there's a crackle between him and I, making me feel out of sorts. I open my mouth again, but ultimately clamp it shut. I do this a few more times, probably looking like a damn goldfish.

"Hi, Delia," he says, making up for my inability to string together a coherent thought. I don't know why, but the way he says my name makes my cheeks flush. Stupid tequila.

"I'm sorry. I didn't mean to smack into you like that," I blurt out, lifting my hands to gesture to his chest. "Cadence must not have seen you walking up, or she wouldn't have spun me so hard."

"Oh, I think Cadence knew exactly what she was doing," he answers, taking a hand out of his pocket and running it through his hair. "I hope it's okay that I'm here. Cathy and Grams thought it would be nice of me to come, so here I am."

I let my jaw fall dramatically.

"You? Doing something nice? That seems suspicious," I tease.

"Yeah, well, I wouldn't get used to it," he says with a laugh, but that defensive edge to his voice is back.

I roll my eyes in response and he huffs out another laugh. He nods at the girls behind me before turning and heading toward the bar. Fisher gives me a look and I already know he's about to stir the pot.

And maybe, I'll let him.

BOUTIQUE BABES

Janie

What is this I'm hearing about
a hot brother? And does he
have any friends?

Clara

Yes, Delia. Tell us more about
the HOT man you're going to
be living with for the summer

> Thank you Clara for informing
> the masses. And yes, actually.
> He does have friends. Hot ones

Lola (ASM)

You lucky bitch. You mean to tell
me you're spending your summer
with a bunch of hot guys?

> Okay, first of all. I'm not here just
> frolicking around with hot guys.
> I'm actually working. But maybe
> you and Clara should flip a coin
> to see who gets to take PTO and
> visit me

Clara

You're HILARIOUS. Wow. Tears
streaming down my face. Flip a
coin? I will Dudley Death Drop
you. Don't even

> Uhhh.... Been watching a lot of WWE
> again have we, Clara bug?

Janie

Literally every day

twenty-three

DOCK TALK 2.0

GRIFFIN

I don't know what I'm doing and that rarely happens.

The only other time I've felt like this in a while, was a few weeks ago when I drove Delia to the house. I'm starting to sense a pattern here.

Where Delia is involved, uncertainty follows.

And I don't like that.

I also don't like the general unease that has been lingering from this morning, even after my time with Libby, and some more talking with Grams and Cathy. If I had to put a word to it, I'd say I feel vulnerable. And that is the absolute last way I want to feel. Ever. But especially right now, when I'm about to be around the one person who seems to be able to see right through me.

I clench and unclench my fists as I walk toward the entrance of Tombstones. I didn't tell anyone I was coming tonight and maybe that was a stupid decision, but I was worried I'd be told not to come and I didn't want to hear that. Even if maybe I deserved it.

I thought about telling Cadence I was coming when she called me earlier, but the conversation had been good and I didn't want to mess it up. I'm making progress with this project of mine, slowly letting people see that they shouldn't push me away, and I'm worth keeping around.

I take a deep breath and run my fingers through my hair, wondering if I should have left my cowboy hat on to stop myself from the nervous habit. I look down at my blue jeans and brown boots. I paired it with a faded green T-shirt and laugh at myself for even being concerned with what I look like. But I have my mother and sister to thank for that.

I pull open the door and scan the crowd. I'm only a few steps in, weaving through the people that are dancing in the small as shit space, when I notice Cadence and Navy. More like, they notice me. I head in their direction when Cadence quickly grabs who I realize is Delia and pulls her in, spinning her out right toward me.

Delia squeals and–for fuck's sake–closes her eyes, slamming into me. I can't stop myself from grabbing her waist to steady her. I'm not going to just let her eat shit in front of all these people. Her palms land on my chest and when she finally opens her eyes, it's written all over her face that I'm the last person she expected to have caught her, let alone be here.

"Griffin!" she says, her voice lilting and confirming my thoughts. She quickly withdraws her hands from my chest and I notice mine are still on her hips. I remove them and watch as she rights herself. I find myself taking in her appearance as she does so.

She's wearing a short black and white dress that has a bow right in between her cleavage where it dips low. Just like the other time when she had on that black top, I find myself having to look away before I give myself up. The girl may be a thorn in my side, but I can't deny the way she gets my blood boiling–in more ways than one.

She finally looks at me and rambles like she always does, but she's not really making sense. I decide to cut her a break and speak up.

"Hi, Delia."

And maybe I'm seeing things, but I swear her cheeks flush a little. She blurts out an apology and I let her know that she wasn't to blame. I run a hand through my hair again before asking if it's okay that I showed up tonight. I use the Grams and sister card for support, and I don't know why I'm surprised when Delia still gives me a hard time.

After a minute, I realize things feel a little too comfortable, and I reel it back in and reinforce the walls. I nod at Navy and Cadence before turning to head toward Callum and Fisher who I spot at the bar.

"Well, well, well. Look who it is," Callum drawls and I don't give him my attention. Instead I direct it at Fisher.

"She drinking a lot?"

Fisher's eyes widen a little before he schools his expression. "I'm not sure who you mean. There's lot of ladies here tonight."

"Cut the shit, man. Delia–has she already had a few drinks?" I settle into one of the bar stools next to Callum as someone gets up and walks away.

"Why are you asking?" Callum interjects.

"Because I'm not driving her home like last time," I answer quickly.

"Ah, of course. Can't have Griffy here doing anything nice for someone. For a second I thought maybe you cared," Fisher dead-pans while sliding me a beer. "Don't worry. I'll get her home or take her back to my place."

I pull the bottle to my lips and tilt it, letting the cold liquid wash down and soothe a strange burn in me that flares at his words.

"Nice," I clip.

A moment of silence stretches between the three of us before Callum lets out a breath. He sets his drink down, getting up and heading toward the girls, leaving me alone with Fisher. Fucker.

"What's the deal with you two? We never got to finish that conversation at the cookout." I turn my attention back to Fisher.

"Yeah, or any other conversations since then. What's it to you, G?" he says, resting his elbows on the bar top and tilting his head.

"I don't know, maybe the fact that she's leaving in like a month? I'm just wondering why you'd want to start up something with someone who's not going to be around," I answer, taking another swig of my drink.

He hums thoughtfully at that, and pushes back up to stand. "Sure," is all he says, as he moves out from behind the counter and heads toward the stage. He takes the mic and cuts everyone in line, standing in front of the crowd.

"This one goes out to the birthday girl," Fisher speaks into the mic and points at Delia. I shake my head and let out a breath, walking over to join my friends.

A song called "Fool" by Djo pops up on the monitor before Fisher starts to goofily sing to Delia, about how he's a fool for her, and her cheeks match the crimson boots on her feet.

When he's done, he comes into the crowd and grabs Delia's hand, spinning her, and kissing her on the top of her head. I grimace at the interaction and that's when I feel Cadence's eyes on me. I give her a *"what?"* look and she gives back her own *"you know what"* look.

No, I actually don't know.

"You have to sing!" I hear Navy shout to Delia over the

person who's taken Fisher's place on stage and definitely should have the mic taken from them.

At her suggestion, my mind drifts back to when I found Delia that night in the kitchen. She had been singing and it's what halted me from immediately asking who she was. I also noticed the morning she made everyone French toast that she hums or sings to herself when she seems to be in a groove.

"I will!" Delia says loud enough for everyone to hear. "I just might wait a little, my song is kind of slow and doesn't really seem like the vibe right now."

I arch an eyebrow at that, wondering what the song could be, but think less of it and head back to the bar to get some water. After making small talk with the other bartender, I feel Cadence saddling up to me. She bumps her hip into mine and nods toward the back door that leads to a small outdoor area–if you can even call it that. It's just a few older picnic tables and a spot for people to get some air or take a smoke.

I start to move in the direction of the door, glancing over my shoulder for some reason to place eyes on Delia before we leave. She's sandwiched between Callum and Fisher, the two of them spinning her back and forth. I don't see Navy anywhere, though.

Cadence's fingers interlock with mine as she drags me toward the door, ripping my gaze away from them.

"Come on!" she shouts over the music.

Once we're outside, the worst type of déjà vu hits me and I immediately speak up.

"This isn't going to be like the dock talk 2.0, is it?"

Cadence snorts and walks to sit on one of the picnic table tops, placing her feet on the bench. I stand in front of her and cross my arms, narrowing my eyes.

"You're so dramatic, Griffin," she scoffs, pulling a cigarette from her bra with a lighter. My eyebrows raise and she rolls her eyes. "Don't give me that judgey look."

"I just didn't know you smoked," I say, honestly.

"I don't," she counters. "But sometimes a cigarette just hits differently when you've had a few drinks, so I keep some in the truck and bring them with me. But that's not why I brought you out here."

"Right," I say, looking over at the door, and back to her again.

"Hoping someone specific is going to come out here?" she drawls, lighting the cigarette and bringing it to her lips.

"Where did Navy go?" I snatch the cigarette and take a drag myself. Cadence snickers as I let the smoke out and hand it back to her.

"Delia wanted to go get her Polaroid camera from the car, but Navy said she'd do it cause we're all parked at Lasso and she wanted to grab something from her car, too."

I hum in response as Cadence starts to speak again. "Hey, I'm glad you showed up tonight and don't want to dampen the mood, but I need to talk to you about something serious."

I watch the cherry flicker, casting an ominous light over Cadence's face as she takes a long pull from the cigarette. That's when I notice the tension in her body.

"What's wrong?" I say quickly, stepping closer.

She takes another long drag, tapping her boot on the bench. As she exhales, blowing out a stream of smoke, a vacant look takes over her eyes. Her voice is low when she asks, "What do you know about property ownership?"

I tilt my head, my eyebrows pinching together. "What do you mean?"

"When Pop passed, I'm assuming the ranch and family business naturally defaulted to Grams?"

I take a deep breath, trying to steady the flicker of anger that accompanies talking about this, but I tell myself this is Cadence wanting to talk about professional things, not asking me to open up.

"My parents had ownership of the company, since they antici-pated being..." My words trail off and I run a hand through my hair. "It defaulted back to Pop and Grams, and when Pop died, it defaulted to her. Now everything in relation to Aberdeen Crook & Co. sits under Grams' name, but Cathy and I have paperwork drawn up. If something happens to her, it goes to me. We have paperwork for the ranch, too. It's always been Pop's and Grams', but they wanted it to pass on generationally."

She hums, putting the cigarette out on the table.

"What's going on? Why are you asking about this?" I press.

"I was going through some stuff the other day. I've been trying to clean up the house, and I came across some paperwork. It has to do with our ranch and the property. My dad apparently had it changed after my mom died and there's–" She stops speaking abruptly, dragging her palm down her face before slap-ping her hands on her thighs. "There's something written in there now that says I can't inherit the property if I'm not married."

I rear back, my eyes nearly popping out of my head.

"What the fuck?"

"I know," she says in a serious tone. "I tried to ask him about it and, you can guess how that went. So, what I'm asking is, is there any way around that? For me to still get our family ranch if something happens to my dad and I'm not married yet?"

"I mean...I don't know. It's probably not likely, but why are you even worried about this? You probably have years and you could meet someone by then."

"He's dying," she deadpans, staring off into the distance

again. "Found out last week he maybe has a year left before his liver finally gives in to all that alcohol."

I blink rapidly, trying to process the information I'm getting right now—it being the last thing I expected to hear from her, and also hitting me in a strange way. Cadence is going to lose her dad. She's already lost her mom.

The ache that started this morning starts to rise back up in me at the realization that I know exactly how she feels, except I have Grams and Cathy. She has no one.

"Who knows?" I quickly ask.

"Just me. But that's why I'm going out of town next weekend. There's a lawyer I found a few hours away that deals with stuff like this, and I'm going to see if there's any way around it. Because I don't think I'm getting married in the next twelve months." The lack of sass in her voice feels so wrong.

"I'll look into it. Talk to some of the lawyers we've worked with, see what they say," I offer.

"Thank you," she says, meeting my gaze again and forcing a smile back on her face. "We should go back inside. I'm pretty sure Delia is going to be singing soon and I don't want to miss that."

"I mean," I start, and she smacks me on the arm.

"Don't even," she snaps back and I'm just relieved that her attitude has returned.

"I'm just going to the bathroom and I'll find you after. We'll figure this out, Cadence."

She nods and heads inside, me trailing after her but ducking off into the bathroom.

I take a little longer than planned, pulling my phone out and already sending a text off to one of our lawyers even though it's almost nine. The distress I saw in Cadence made me feel the way I do with Cathy whenever something's wrong. I let myself have the moment of pride that I'm already doing better with trying to show up more for the people around me.

Moving to the sink, I start washing my hands when I hear the faint sound of the next karaoke song starting and it sounds like…

No. There's no way.

I direct my attention back down to my hands while I wash them. I'm hearing things. This morning just put me on edge, it opened up parts of my memory that I've worked to shut off, and now I'm imagining things. And then, the conversation with Cadence brought up more shit. Damn, I need to get a grip.

But then the smooth voice of a girl starting to sing becomes clear, as it seems the bar has quieted down, the crowd captivated. I would be one of those people lost to the beauty of her voice if my heart wasn't suddenly pounding in my chest, my body going rigid.

I quickly finish washing my hands, needing to get the hell out of here. I can't breathe.

I push out the bathroom door and my stomach plummets as I hear the lyrics of "Fade Into You" by Mazzy Star even clearer now, filling the space, and coming from none other than *Delia.*

I start to shove through the crowd, but it's like I'm not really here. The room feels distorted as her voice and the song continues to press into my brain. At the same time, it feels like something in my chest is trying to claw its way out. Cut me open. Tear me apart.

Pushing through all the people who are standing there awestruck, my friends included, I cut one glare at the girl who's been fucking with my head since the moment we met. Our eyes meet and the look of anger I give her must say enough, because she immediately stops singing, watching me as I don't waste another second and storm toward the door.

The song keeps playing, a ringing building in my ears, and the ground feeling unsteady. I think I hear the faint sound of my name being shouted, but I don't stop.

I have to get out here and far away from this place. These memories. *That girl.*

HOT-GUY-SANDWICH

DELIA

"Are you sure you don't mind?" I ask Navy as she's already starting to head toward the door.

"No! I'll be right back!" she calls over her shoulder, leaving me alone with Callum and Fisher.

Callum reaches for my hand, pulling me into him. Before I can react, Fisher comes up behind me and I'm trapped between the two of them, a flush creeping into my cheeks.

Callum spins me so I'm facing Fisher, and then he presses into me. If Clara could see me now, in the middle of this hot-guy-sandwich, she would be squealing in delight.

Fisher drags a hand through my hair, before settling his grip on the side of my face. He strokes his thumb over my cheek, speaking just above the music, "Really is a shame that there's nothing more than lust between us." He spins me back to Callum who gives me a cheeky grin.

I glance around for Cadence, and when I don't see her, I

realize I also don't see Griffin anywhere which makes me let out a small *hmph*.

"I think they're outside," Callum answers my unspoken question, moving to drape his arms over my shoulders as Fisher puts his hands on my hips. We all sway for a little, until Fisher has to head back behind the bar.

"What's going on with you and her?" I ask, moving my hands to rest around Callum's neck. He shifts his down my sides to my waist and we slow dance to the next karaoke song which is a love ballad.

"Your guess is as good as mine, peaches," Callum says, giving me a smile that doesn't quite meet his eyes.

"Right…Well, there is something there, or am I crazy?" I look over his shoulder at the back door, wondering how long they'll be outside. Not that I care, or at least, I don't think I do.

"I'm not sure anymore. Something changed over the last week and she isn't talking to me like she was."

I hear the sadness in his tone, but don't want to pry too much, so I offer some affirmation instead.

"Maybe it has nothing to do with you. And if it makes you feel any better, she hasn't told me anything. Have you asked her?"

"It's tricky with Cady girl. We do well going back and forth, it's part of our game. It's always been like that, too. Until that night, we saw you in the street? Her and I had a moment. But, we never talked about it. Just went back to playing cat and mouse, and I'm worried if I bring it up, I'll cross a line that I won't be able to come back from. "

I consider his words, dropping my hands from his neck and stepping back, his hands falling from my waist.

"Do you have feelings for her? Or is it more of a hook-up thing?" I tilt my head, hoping I finally get some answers about the two of them.

He scrubs a hand down his face, and reaches for my hand, pulling me closer to him again. "Fuck, I don't know why I'm telling you this, but…" He lets his words trail off, glancing around the room, before looking at me again. "Nothing happened that night, like you're thinking."

"Okay…" I narrow my eyes, waiting for him to elaborate.

"We just stayed up all night talking. That's it. I kissed her once before we left the bar, and she asked if she could come home with me, but nothing happened. We just…talked. Eventually we fell asleep and when we woke up, she drove me back to my truck, and we haven't talked about it again."

"In my professional, unprofessional opinion, I think you should talk to her about it—this past week, the night after the bar. I think it would really mean a lot to her to know someone cares. I think it would maybe mean more to know that someone is you."

He starts to open his mouth, when the announcer calls my name for karaoke, and at the same time, the back door opens again, Griffin and Cadence coming back inside.

Cadence heads directly for us, while Griffin ducks off for the bathrooms.

I walk to the stage, bummed that Navy isn't back yet, but there's always next time.

When I take the mic, Cadence screams and cheers me on, Fisher and Callum adding in their own whoops and hollers.

I take a deep breath, waiting for the song to start, and when it does, I immediately relax. I can't explain why I love this song so much, other than the first time I heard it in high school, it stuck with me. It became a song I could listen to and let my mind drift off, my emotions and feelings entangling with the lyrics to create this beautiful but melancholic dance in my heart.

I start to sing the few first lyrics, closing my eyes, and that's when I realize the crowd has gone deadly silent.

I quickly open them, and find everyone watching me. Cadence and Callum have their phones out, I guess recording, and I can't see Fisher back at the bar. But all my attention is suddenly ripped away from everything, falling onto Griffin pushing his way through the crowd.

He stops long enough to meet my eyes and the look he gives me cuts through my very being.

He turns away, shoving to the door and I don't even think about what I'm doing. I stop singing, setting the mic down, and start to push my way after him.

"Griffin!" I shout, but he doesn't stop, the door swinging shut behind him. I move faster, ignoring the murmuring of the crowd.

I make it outside and frantically search for him, my eyes catching sight of the back of his head. He's moving toward his truck across the street so fast, I have to start jogging.

"Griffin, wait!" I call after him when he's seconds away from his truck. I make it to the edge of the gravel lot a few feet away from him, when he whirls around. I stop dead in my tracks, the look of pure agony written all over his face.

Not just that, but the charge of his anger in the air stuns me.

"Who told you?" he demands, spit flying with his words.

"What…?" I hope the confusion is visible on my face because I'm at a complete loss for what's going on.

"What's the matter with you?" he shouts again, his shoulders rising and falling at an alarming rate.

"Griffin, you're not making any sense," I say, trying to keep my voice calm.

"Was it my sister? Grams?" He clutches at his chest like something is trying to claw its way out.

"No one told me anything. I don't know what you're talking about. Can you please tell me what's going on?"

"The song!" His words come out choked and it makes my heart break.

"Okay…What about it?" I ask, gently, starting to move toward him again. He glares at me like a caged animal, but I keep moving until I'm nearly in front of him.

He starts mumbling to himself and pulling at the ends of his hair. I reach out and tentatively place my palm against his cheek, and that's when I hear it. Among his murmuring, while his eyes dart around unfocused, I hear the voice of a very broken boy.

"Mom. My mom."

Life as I know it ceases to exist.

"Griffin," I whisper. "Look at me."

When he doesn't, I place my other palm on his face and carefully direct his gaze to me.

"What about your mom?" I ask and his eyes finally snap to mine.

"Her funeral," he mutters and I can only assume what he's implying.

I notice his breathing starting to slow down as I rub my thumbs on his cheeks. I don't want to push, but I want to try and see if I can help talk him through what is likely a massive panic attack.

So, I share my assumption while keeping my voice quiet. "They played it at her funeral?"

He slowly nods and the emotions that overwhelm my body threaten to take me out. A potent mixture of his grief collides with my empathy, forming a devastating ache in my chest and I can't help the tears that leak out of my eyes.

"I didn't know," I whisper.

"You didn't know," he repeats as if finally registering that this wasn't some planned attack on him.

"I didn't know," I say again, because at this point, I don't really know what else to say.

"My mom," he chokes out and then stuns me, wrapping his arms around my back and pulling me into his chest, clinging to me like his lifeline.

And I wonder if I just might be...but I should know better by now.

Because another beat passes and he must realize exactly what's happening and he quickly pushes away from me. I watch as his eyes shift back into that familiar distant look.

"You don't breathe a word of this to anyone," he says in a low voice.

"Griffin, don't do that," I plead. "It's okay to–"

"I mean it, Delia. You don't tell anyone about this. You don't tell anyone about the song. They weren't there for–they don't know. You go back inside and enjoy your night and let me leave."

I want to fight. I want to dig my heels in and not let him do this again. Especially because now that I've seen this side of him, my empathy is whining and screaming at me to not let him go.

"Griffin," I say with a little more demand in my tone. "You can't keep running from this."

"I don't know what *this* is," he clips. "But I do know that I can't have this conversation with you right now."

My heart latches onto those two words.

"Right now?" I repeat. "So, later? Please?"

"Why, Delia?" He practically roars, and I steel my shoulders.

"Because I can feel it, Griffin! I can physically feel your pain. It radiates off of you, it emanates from you, and it calls to me. You call to me! You have since the second you found me in the kitchen that night." I exhale with my last few words, closing my eyes and summoning the courage for what I need to say next. I open my eyes again, and speak my truth. "I'm drawn to you, okay? And I've tried to fight it, ignore it, and respect your wishes for me to leave you alone. But I can't keep fighting with my empathy, when it's the most natural and instinctual part of me."

Griffin just stares at me. He presses his lips together, and I watch his shoulders rise and fall with every deep breath he takes. After a few more seconds of silence pass, I shake my head and let the feeling of defeat take over me, once again. But there's also something else in the air. Something I don't quite understand. An electricity that crackles and makes my heart stutter.

"I'll go," I say, my voice barely above a whisper. Griffin still doesn't speak, so I give him a soft smile and turn on my heels to head back into Tombstones.

"Delia," he calls after me in some sort of strained plea.

Chills race down my spine at the way he says my name. I stop midstep and look over my shoulder, not wanting to give him my full attention again.

He runs a hand through his hair, and I notice him tugging on the ends of it, before he says, "I'm sorry I don't know how—"

"Is everything okay?"

I whip around to find Navy standing at the end of the parking lot with my Polaroid camera in hand. Her eyes moves back and forth between Griffin and I, before pinning her gaze on me. And in those couple seconds, I hear the retreating footsteps of Griffin followed by the opening and slamming of his truck door.

"Yeah, it's fine," I lie through my teeth while my stomach pitches knowing I just lost maybe one of, if not the only moment, where Griffin actually tried to open up to me. At least, I think that's what he was about to do.

"You sure?" Navy asks as the truck starts and I continue on toward her, linking my arm through hers.

"Positive."

"WE GOT YOU"

DELIA

We walk back to Tombstones and I try to ignore the sound of the truck driving off. I try to forget the feeling of Griffin's touch still buzzing on my skin from the brief hug. It was different from the one I gave him at the cookout.

When we go back inside, I see Cadence sitting on a barstool with her phone out, raking her hand through her hair. Callum and Fisher are leaning against the bar top and they both look distressed.

Shit. This is all my fault.

We get closer and before I can say anything, Cadence jumps up and wraps her arms around me. She pulls back, grabbing my hand and tugging me outside to the back patio where it's quieter. Everyone follows along until we're at the farthest picnic table and away from all noise.

"Is everything okay? I wanted to follow you outside but the guys wouldn't let me," she says, looking me over as if she thought maybe Griffin and I got into a literal fight.

"Yeah, it's fine," I repeat the same thing I told Navy, unsure how to share what actually happened.

"It's not that we wouldn't let you go outside," Callum starts, reaching for Cadence who swats away his hand. *Uh-oh.* "We were worried it would make things worse if G felt like we were all ganging up on him."

"I'm sorry, *what* happened?" Navy interjects.

"It was Delia's turn for karaoke and she started her song, and Griffin busted out of the bathroom and bolted out the door. Delia stopped singing and went after him," Fisher supplies.

"Because he looked at me like he was shooting daggers with his eyes," I add under my breath but a stifled chuckle from Callum lets me know it was still audible.

"Okay, but in all seriousness, did you guys talk? Did you find out why he left?" Cadence presses and I feel all of their eyes on me, waiting with bated breath for my answer.

But I know I can't tell them, at least not everything. And then I hesitate further because these are *his* friends.

"This is a really weird place for me to be in," I choose to say instead.

"What is?" Fisher asks, crossing his arms.

"I don't feel like I should share what we talked about, but y'all are his friends, and I'm not—"

"You know we have your back, right? All of us," Callum cuts me off and my eyes widen.

"You guys don't really even know me," I retort.

"Maybe not for as long as we've all known each other, but sometimes you just meet people that you click with," Fisher adds.

"You fit in. Here, with us. We got you," Cadence says with a genuine smile.

"We're your friends now, too," Navy finishes off the sentiments from each of them and I can't stop my eyes from welling up.

"Thank you," I say as Callum loops an arm around me and tugs me into his side.

"We don't want you to let Griffin get to you. We're all used to it by now, but we know it can be hard," he says.

"He'll be okay," I tell them. "I think he just needs some time."

"That's all he's been getting," Fisher tosses out in a sarcastic voice and Cadence smacks him in the stomach.

"If you need to talk about it, we're here. But I just wanted to make sure you knew we weren't leaving you to wolves by letting you go after Griffin alone," Cadence says and I peel away from Callum to lean into her.

"I appreciate that. I hope I didn't ruin the night, especially with my less than graceful exit during karaoke," I say with a wince.

"I'd actually like to circle back to that," Cadence says. "You will definitely be singing again because I need the full performance."

"That's the last time I offer to be helpful because I clearly missed everything," Navy huffs.

"I recorded a little," Callum says, pulling out his phone, but before he can press play, I put my hand over it.

"Maybe just text it, yeah? I don't really want to relive that quite yet," I say, the ache from earlier seeming to settle in my chest and making it clear that it's not going anywhere.

"I have to get back behind the bar, but I'm glad you're okay, Delia," Fisher says, brushing past me and kissing the top of my head.

"Yeah, thanks," I call after him, turning to face Callum, Navy, and Cadence again. "I don't want to be a Debbie Downer, but I think I'm going to head back to the house."

"Damn, G really did a number on you, huh?" Callum scoffs. "One of us can talk to him, if you want–"

"No!" I cut him off, a little too quickly. "No, that's okay," I say in a more even tone.

"If you say so," he replies, putting his hands in his pockets.

Navy gives me my Polaroid camera and I curse under my breath, frustrated that I still have yet to use it. I thank her and hug them all, promising to text them when I get to my car and if I need to talk tomorrow.

When I pass through the bar, Fisher gives me a knowing look. I say goodnight to him too, heading out the door and starting toward the car.

I spend the walk to Lasso the Label and the drive back to the house in silence, my mind going a hundred miles a second.

When I make it back, I park the car and turn it off, sitting in the front seat paralyzed by the questions that won't go away. I pick up my phone, planning to call Clara or maybe my mom, but decide against it, not wanting to have to explain what's wrong. Because where would I even start? With the connection I feel to Griffin and how it's rattling me to my core? Or the feeling that maybe coming out here to try and find myself was a lofty idea? Seriously, what *am* I doing?

I get out of the car and start walking toward the front steps, so many emotions pulsing through me.

Why did I think that I needed to come out west to figure out this longing in me? What is a change of scenery really going to do to help me understand my purpose? Why can't I just be normal and take life as it comes and not feel like there's this deeper hidden meaning to it?

Before I can stop it, tears fall down my cheeks and I drag the back of my hand across my cheeks.

"Stupid, stupid, stupid," I mutter to myself as I reach the front steps and nearly jump when I see a figure in the dark sitting there.

"What's stupid?" Griffin's voice is rough; I can't make out much of his face.

"What are you doing out here?" I nearly shriek, not taking another step. He stands and comes out from under the shadow of the roof, stopping a foot from me.

"Cadence texted me that you left," he says. "Along with a few other choice words."

"And you thought you'd just linger here." I motion to the steps. "In the dark?"

He shrugs. "I wanted to talk about tonight and what happened before my friends start sniffing around."

I pinch the bridge of my nose, sighing. "I didn't tell them anything."

"I know you didn't," he replies, shocking me.

I sniffle before I can stop myself, and he asks me again, "What's stupid?"

"Nothing. I'm going to go to bed," I say, starting to walk around him, and stopping when the implication of his words dawn on me.

"Were you waiting for me?" I ask, turning to look at him.

"I was," he says, in that gruff tone that makes my stomach do cartwheels.

"Okay, well, I'm here," I say a little too harshly, but I really need to try and get my thoughts together.

"You are here," he murmurs and I can't help but notice the odd inflection in which he says it.

"So…" I start, rocking back on my heels.

"You said you're drawn to me. What did you mean by that?"

I blink a few times, not expecting his question. The moon casts just enough light for me to see his face at this distance and I don't like the way he's looking at me. Because I can't tell if he's angry again or genuinely curious, but the energy around him tells me it's the latter.

"Do you know what it means to be an empath?" I ask, continuing toward the house and sitting on the steps. I'm shocked yet again when Griffin not only follows me, but sits next to me. The proximity of him has my skin buzzing again–I seriously need to get a grip.

"I'm assuming it has something to do with feelings." He deadpans.

I turn my head and narrow my eyes at him, hoping he can see the irritation on my face with what little light there is. "Okay, no. See, you're not going to do that if you want to have a real conversation. We get it. You hate feelings, they're the devil. So don't ask me to talk about what I said if that's going to be your response."

He stiffens before letting out a breath and dragging his fingers through his hair, tugging on the ends.

"Stop that," I say, reaching for his hand before I can even realize what I'm doing. When I clasp my fingers around his, I swear I hear his breath catch. "Sorry," I whisper, releasing my grip on him and folding my hands into my lap. "I really need to work on that."

"On what?" he asks, resting his hands in his lap and mirroring me.

"Acting without thinking," I reply, and then mutter, "among other things."

Griffin laughs, actually laughs, and I turn my head with wide eyes, finding him already looking at me.

"Why did you pick that song?" He holds my stare and I'm reminded of why we're in this position to begin with.

"It's one of my favorites," I start to say when Griffin scoffs.

"Of course it is."

The disbelief and frustration with his words also reminds me who I'm talking to.

I push up from the stairs and turn around, enjoying the feeling of him having to look up at me, even if he can't fully see me right now.

"I'm being serious. I came across it in high school and it resonated with me, so it was like a no-brainer to let it become my karaoke song." I put my hands on my hips. "Why is that so hard to believe?"

"Because what are the odds?" Griffin rushes out. "What are the odds the song you'd sing is—"

"We don't have to talk about it," I'm quick to say. "Honestly, when I asked you in the parking lot if we could talk about what happened, I was referring to your reaction. I already know you're not going to like what I have to say, but I think it's important. I'm worried about you."

I watch Griffin square his shoulders with my last statement, no doubt already trying to think of what defensive remark to make, but I don't give him the chance.

"I know, crazy, right? Someone is worried about you. Wow. I'm sure that's the last thing you want to hear. But I want to make sure that doesn't happen to you again. I think you had a panic attack, and even though I doubt you'll tell me the truth, I want to know if that's happened before?"

He tilts his head, pursing his lips, and lets out a deep breath.

"It's never been that bad. I mean, I've never had that happen," he admits, and I try to keep my face neutral, even though I'm shocked he's sharing this with me.

"Was there something different about today?" I take a step closer to him, the toe of my boots almost meeting his.

He raises his hand toward his head, but catches himself, pressing his palm into the wooden step instead.

"Good boy," I taunt and immediately regret it, because not even the dark can hide the way Griffin's eyes bore into me. The energy in the air shifts and I find myself stepping back again, putting space between us. "That was a joke," I whisper. "Sorry."

"No you're not," Griffin deadpans, and stands, causing me to shrink away from him.

"Okay, maybe I'm not, but I shouldn't have said that. I don't want to do this back and forth thing right now. I want to talk about what happened tonight."

"And I want to know why you care," he challenges.

"*And* I think I made that pretty clear in the parking lot—"

"I want to hear it again," he cuts me off, taking another step closer, swallowing what was left of the space between us.

"I can feel your pain, physically." My voice comes out unsteady and he narrows his eyes. "What I was trying to say earlier about being an empath? It means that I'm highly sensitive to emotions—mine, and others. I feel things differently, I see life differently."

"I see..." He lets his words trail off.

I don't like the position we're in right now. This stand off we're having in front of the house. And what's worse is that damned desire to touch him is building in me again. Demanding, like an itch that I can't *not* scratch.

I ball my fists at my sides and try to resist the urge. Griffin, of course, notices and gestures at my hands with his head.

"And *that*, why are you doing that?"

"We're getting off track," I grit out.

"Tell me and I'll tell you something," he presses.

I groan, letting my head fall back, and heave out a sigh. I meet his gaze again, unsure what is happening between us right now. Wondering if this conversation will be forgotten tomorrow, and he will go back to avoiding me despite our talk this morning.

"I just…I want–need–I don't know. I'm having a hard time not touching you, and it's probably because I just want to help. I want to take away some of what you're feeling," I admit.

"Like when you hugged me at the cookout," he says, but it seems like he's talking more to himself than me, as if piecing together the events of that night.

"Yes," I answer. "Your turn."

He chuckles, before looking around the property as if he's worried someone might hear him.

"I did something this morning that…opened me up more than usual. I was already not feeling like myself and hearing that song, I just…I couldn't fight it off like I normally can." The strain in his voice twists my stomach into knots. I know this is hard for him.

"When you say 'it', am I to assume you mean feelings?" I soften my voice and hope he doesn't immediately go into defense mode.

"Yes," he says, a tick forming in his jaw, and that's when I take the hint to not push any further, even though I didn't really get to talk to him about the panic attack itself.

"Okay," I state. "Thank you for sharing that with me."

"That's it?" he asks, his tone suspicious.

"That's it," I parrot.

"You don't want to know what the feelings are or why I felt that way?" He raises his eyebrows, and I roll my eyes.

"Of course I *want* to know, but I also know when…or at least I'm trying to be better at knowing when to walk away."

"Interesting," he drawls.

"Very much so," I say, smacking my lips, and wanting nothing more than to dart past him and go to bed. "That being said, I think I'm going to head inside. Did you, uh, get what you needed or—actually, I'm still not sure I know exactly why you were waiting for me to get back. Anyways, I'm sorry you had a rough day, and that I made it worse for you."

I start to walk past him and when I make it onto the porch and flick a light on, he calls after me.

"Thank you. I wanted to say thank you for what you did earlier. I don't know how you got through to me, or I guess maybe I do now, your empath stuff or whatever, but I wanted to say thank you."

I turn back around, the screen separating us and giving me a feeling of safety to speak my next few words. "I really want to hug you again."

We stare at each other, his face visible now with the porch light, and allowing me to take in the way he's looking at me. An unspoken electricity seems to form between us, like that moment before you finally get to hold your crush's hand, or your leg brushes up against theirs under the table. The anticipation of what happens next hanging in the air, suspended in the silence.

Except, I doubt he feels it, and I'm not sure I want to ponder on why *I* feel it, so before he can say anything, I turn back around and bolt inside.

Deels!

How has it been a month?! And your birthday is coming up. I can't believe I'm missing it, but we will definitely be celebrating if I get to visit around the Fourth of July. That sounds like fun and I'm excited to meet these hot guys you're getting to hangout with. Also I'm looking forward to meeting the two girls who are trying to take my spot as best friend. Although, it seems like Cadence is who I really need to worry about. Kidding! I'm kidding! Kinda...

I have SO much to fill you in on with the store. But I won't waste my paper space with that. If I get to visit aka pass my background check, is there anything you want me to bring you? Maybe some lingerie to wear for Griffin? Get him to lighten up? I'm hilarious, I know.

kisses pookie–
C. xx

"HAPPY BIRTHDAY, DELIA"

GRIFFIN

"I really want to hug you again."

Seven words that have been replaying in my mind for the last seven days.

Seven days since I've seen the girl who said that one sentence before bolting inside. Leaving me to figure out what the hell had just happened over those last couple hours.

And while I haven't been able to figure out everything that went down, I did come to the sobering realization that if Delia hadn't followed me out of Tombstones and helped me calm down, I don't know what would have happened.

All week, I've been trying to understand what took over me.

I did a few online searches and it seemed she was spot on about it being a panic attack. What I didn't understand though was *why* it happened.

For the most part, I've been able to avoid things that remind me of my parents' passing.

I don't listen to the radio stations that might play songs I associate with them. I go the long way when driving into town. I've changed routines and broke away from habits that made me think of them. I don't have any social media because I got tired of the random messages or comments I'd get from people telling me they knew my parents and wanted to stay in touch.

The two things I have been able to handle are occasionally visiting their graves and keeping Dad's phone number open.

But over the last few weeks, it's like Delia showed up and all of a sudden it didn't matter what efforts I put forward to keep those memories at bay.

When she walked into the stable wearing my mom's boots, I'd been sucker-punched. It also didn't help that her hair was braided how Mom wore it when she'd ride.

I was just thankful Cathy brought out Maven, because if I'd had to see Delia on my mom's horse too, I wouldn't have been able to give Libby her lesson.

Those few things–*among others*–that physically remind me of Mom, coupled with her emotionally reminding me of my dad…I feel like I'm slowly losing control.

And that was the whole issue with Delia from the jump.

From the first interaction with her, I left the house feeling rattled. Like I didn't have a handle on things the way I thought I did.

So now, I'm trying to figure out if maybe there's some truth to everyone's warnings about shutting off my emotions. But mostly, I've been thinking about how Delia said she didn't want what happened in the parking lot to happen again.

That's really what I've been stuck on. That word: 'again'.

As it's not that I don't want it to happen again, it's that it *can't* happen again. So I should probably find out how to make that a reality.

It's clear to me at this point that it doesn't matter if I try to shove shit down, or act like my problems don't exist. Because, for some unknown reason, it appears as long as Delia is here, she'll be forcing me to face the noise. And the worst part is, it's not even intentional.

But it's something I need to accept, and attempt to be okay with, until she's gone.

My first order of business is to slowly try and get in her good graces.

My thought is, if she thinks that we are "friends", maybe she won't feel as drawn to me. I don't know if that makes a whole lot of sense, but I had the idea that if she's around me more, my presence won't be so alarming for her–with the whole empath stuff or whatever.

Okay, I know what empathy is, thanks to my dad. But the concept of someone *being* an empath was also something I did a little online digging for. And what I learned from those searches was also like a sucker-punch. It became clear that it won't matter how hard I try to mask my emotions, like Delia said, she will still be able to feel them.

Which fucking sucks.

Once upon a time, I was well acquainted with my emotions.

My dad was a great role model for embracing how you felt, and the importance of being vulnerable with the people who care for you, and that you care for.

But I've slowly turned off that part of me and hoped it wouldn't come back. Though, I'm starting to wonder if I even have a choice anymore, and I *really* don't want to linger on what that could mean.

For now, I'm focusing on something a little easier:

Project make Delia think I'm turning over a new leaf, so she will think I'm okay, and stop trying to get close to me.

The first order of business is to break the silence and bring over my peace offering to the house.

When I push through the door with the paper box in my hands, apprehension takes over. But this felt like a good first step, and I need to go with it.

I round the kitchen table and set the gift on the counter.

Cathy, Grams, and Libby are downtown with Delia for her birthday today, but should be getting back in the next couple minutes.

I start to wander around the living room, when my eyes catch on something resting on the coffee table.

Not something, Delia's junk journal.

I don't know why but my feet start to move on their own accord and I pick it up, turning it over in my hands like I've found treasure.

For the girl who seems to always have the upper hand with me, this right here could be her downfall. This could give me some sort of insight on how to turn the tides and not feel so out of my depth with her.

It crosses my mind for the briefest second that this is kind of fucked up.

Okay, it's *really* fucked up.

I'm definitely invading her privacy, and call it pride or ego, but I can't keep losing to her in this emotional warfare.

I decide to start from the back, looking at the most recent ones. Karma immediately kicks in when I land on the one that is clearly recapping the night after Tombstones when I drove her home, the receipt I gave her taped down and a small chunk of writing next to it.

Tonight I went out with some girls I met, Cadence & Navy, and it was fun...
until it wasn't.
When they invited me, I didn't realize Griffin would be there. After the moment in the stables with him, I honestly thought I probably wouldn't see him around much anymore. But, surprise!
It was so obvious he didn't like that I was there. And then, he drove me home, and unfortunately I let some things slip that I really wish I didn't. He already thinks I'm weird and I'm not helping my case. But then I saw him this morning after the events of last night and he was actually a little nice. He gave me this receipt from the bar and I hate how it gave me hope. I should know better that I can't convince everyone to be my friend, and I also should probably stop trying to prove that I'm worth being friends with. One day I'll be sure of myself and who I am, and won't quietly obsess over all the what ifs. But who knows when that day will be? At least rejection doesn't break me the way it used to.

Song for the page: "Keep The Rain" by Scarous (fourth line)

I close the junk journal and set it back where I found it, making sure it isn't obvious that I touched it.

Guilt immediately consumes me from what I've done, from what I've read.

For fuck's sake, am I thirty-one, or fifteen? Going through what is basically someone's diary and hoping to find something to use against them?

This is what I'm talking about, though–when it comes to Delia, I lose my damn mind.

I take my phone out, however, needing to look up that song. Needing to know what the fourth line is. I'm sure it has to do with guys being assholes or something relating to how the night went, but my stomach pitches when I pull it up and read the lyrics.

I can't do this, I think to myself, quickly moving back to the kitchen and grabbing the box off the counter.

I start to head toward the door, ready to go back to my house and re-think everything.

Why would Delia not like herself?

My mind starts to sort through what little information I have of her and I curse myself at the same time for not making somewhat of an effort to find out more about her. Maybe *that* would have leveled the playing field, and not me just stringing together my own assumptions and perceptions of her. *Or going through her personal things,* a nagging thought comes from the back of my mind.

The only thing I can land on is her comments about her exes, the reference about me thinking she's weird, and I guess the fact that she did admit to wanting to go back to Georgia. But still, even among those things, the concept of her not liking herself doesn't align with what I've experienced with her. She seems so sure of herself, always able to put words to her feelings, and speak what's on her mind.

I'm seconds from opening the door to the porch when I hear the car pulling up. I consider going out the back door, but remember I drove up here 'cause I didn't want to carry that damn box, worried I might drop it or something.

"Shit," I mumble under my breath as I set the box on the kitchen table. I have to pull it together. I don't need Delia sniffing out any of these emotions and somehow figuring out what I've done.

I hear the creak of the porch door, and I realize I'm standing in the middle of the room like an idiot. I quickly dart toward the kitchen, leaning against the kitchen island, and pulling my phone out to occupy myself with.

The door to the house swings open, Libby bursting through and already yelling for me.

"I know you're here, Griffy! I saw your car!" she says, immediately running and throwing herself at me.

I quickly scoop her up and squeeze her, before setting her back down and all my attention zeroes in on Delia.

She's laughing at something Cathy said, the sound bouncing off the walls of the house and reverberating into my bones.

She's wearing a strapless white dress with small light blue and pink polka dots scattered on it, and it molds to her body as if it was custom made for her.

Her hair is curled, a few pieces pinned back, a few pieces still hanging around her face, framing it in a way that forces you to look at her features. Sitting on top of her head like a crown is a headband that's the same shade as the sweater she always wears. I'm starting to wonder if that's her favorite color. A part of me wants to ask, but I ignore that, while also trying to ignore how good her legs look with heels on. Not to mention how short it makes the dress look, hitting her mid-thigh.

Damn. She may be difficult to deal with, but I think I like looking at her.

"Griffin! What are you doing here?" Cathy asks, pulling me from my stupor.

Oh, yeah. *What am I doing here?*

"I was heading out and saw this on the porch. I guess it got delivered while y'all were downtown? I figured it was for Delia, so I brought it inside. I was about to head out when you guys made it back," I lie.

Grams narrows her eyes on me, but says nothing.

"Why would it be for me?" Delia says, tilting her head and finally placing her hazel eyes on me and making my brain short circuit.

"It's a cake. Uh... Grams said she was getting a cake for your birthday. Something about a tradition," I rush out, looking at my grandma with wide eyes and my jaw set.

Grams' eyebrows raise before she quickly schools her expression, Delia's head whipping to the table before she rushes over to the box, opening up the top and smiling down at the contents.

"Wait, Marge, you found someone to make me a Coca Cola cake? You didn't have to do that," Delia says, her voice breaking a little and Grams' eyes dart back to me, Cathy looking between the two of us.

I widen my eyes even more, and I'll be damned if this is the one time my grandmother's intuition doesn't work.

"Yes, yes, I did. Surprise!" Grams announces with a lilt in her voice.

"I didn't know you did that," Cathy remarks and I swear under my breath.

Libby has found her way into the chair in front of the cake, peering at it with Delia.

"I must have forgotten to tell you." Grams waves her hand in the air, dismissing the words.

"Where did you order from?" my sister asks and Grams gives me another pointed look.

"Oh, you know," Grams starts, and I quickly jump in.

"Cadence. She had Cadence make it."

Delia's head perks up at that. "Isn't she out of town?"

For fuck's sake.

"Navy probably dropped it off," I say, realizing I'm going to have to send some texts after this.

"That makes sense," Delia responds. "How thoughtful of them."

After a few more glances around the room, Cathy orders us all to sit while she gets plates and starts cutting everyone a slice. But Grams abruptly stands, pinching my arm as she walks by, motioning with her head toward the far side of the kitchen. She also picks up Delia's plate and I get up to follow her over there.

"You have some serious explaining to do," she mutters under her breath.

"I'm sorry," I whisper.

"You can make up for it by starting with this," she says, and produces some birthday candles from the drawer, sticking them into Delia's slice of cake.

"What are you doing?" I clip out.

"Making you own up to at least one thing tonight," she declares, handing me the plate while she lights the candles, and swatting me in the direction of the table.

I turn around, my eyes connecting with Delia, and my stomach knots. As I start to walk toward her, Cathy begins to sing "Happy Birthday", Libby and Grams joining in.

The candles flicker as I move closer to Delia and when I'm almost to her, she stands, the plate in front of her chest.

The shadows dance on her face, the flames sparking the gold of her eyes, her hair, and her nose ring. I'm holding onto the plate like I'm holding onto much of everything else in my life–tentatively but faking confidence.

With her gaze transfixed on the cake, she reaches up, placing her hands over mine as if I need help holding the plate. The second her skin connects with mine, a strange sensation washes over me, and something in my chest tightens.

I try not to think about what I did earlier, what I read, the song, but I can't help it. I'm caught between guilt and this new emotion, and for a second, my hands go slack. The plate would have dropped, but Delia's hands are there to support mine and keep the plate from falling and shattering. And if that isn't the biggest metaphor for mine and Delia's whatever-this-is, I don't know what is.

The singing stops and Delia peers up at me, those big hazel eyes saying more than I can fathom.

"Happy birthday, Delia," I whisper, not sure where my voice has gone.

"Make a wish!" Cathy yells, and Delia closes her eyes just briefly before opening them again to look at me.

And with her eyes locked on mine, she leans forward and blows out the candles. The flames disappear, and with it, some part of my resistance to her seems to flicker out as well.

"Thank you, Griffin," she whispers back.

She takes her hands off of mine, grabbing hold of the plate, and I feel the loss of her touch immediately. I don't waste any time trying to understand that feeling, though, and sit next to Grams who gives me another knowing look.

I spend the rest of the night chancing looks at Delia, wondering what she wished for, thinking about the journal, and realizing that once again, everything I thought about her was wrong.

But a strange warmth fills me from how much joy is radiating from her as she recounts her past birthdays, and once again expresses how grateful she is for the cake.

I like seeing her like this, and knowing I'm responsible for Delia's happiness floods me with goodness and purpose, like I haven't felt before, seemingly rattling the parts of me that long lay dormant.

It's as if some innate piece of me takes over, my old project of faking some sort of friendship falling away and a new, much more simpler one slipping into place.

I want Delia to feel like this all the time.

But more importantly, I want to be the reason she's happy, even if she doesn't know I'm the one who's causing it.

twenty-seven
COCA COLA CAKE

DELIA

Why do I always cry on my birthday?

I thought I'd broken the curse, making it all day without shedding a tear, but now that the day is ending and I'm tucked away in the guest room, I can't stop my eyes from welling up.

Fat tears spill down my cheeks as I unpin my hair and take my headband off before pulling it up into a messy bun.

Pausing in front of the bathroom counter, I grip the edge as a sob racks through me. Like a fissure has opened up inside my chest, in the most beautifully painful way. I let my head fall and watch the droplets land on the tile.

I thought my twenty-fifth birthday was going to be insignificant, unremarkable, and unmemorable. Swept under the rug and moved past since I wasn't home and around the people that love me and that I love.

But today was significant. It was remarkable and memorable. After the events of the day, I'm left wondering why I feel like I *am* home and around people that love me and that I love.

ELLE F. SUN

I don't know why, but that notion both excites and frightens me.

More tears fall as I realize my well thought out plans for *the big twenty-five* might be falling apart. They might be changing, because I'm changing.

When I finally pick my head up and stare down the bleary eyed girl in the mirror, I think back on the last few years of my life. I think about the loss of self I experienced, letting others' words define me. When in my heart, I knew I wasn't the things they said I was.

I've spent so much of my life trying to prove to others that I'm worth their time. That I have something valuable to offer them. But more often than not, I'm still left questioning if I'm enough.

But tonight at dinner, Catherine and Marge spoke life into me. They expressed their wishes for me, as they told me how incredible I am, what a joy I am to be around, and how *they* were honored to spend my birthday with me.

They encouraged me that in this next year, I should unapologetically be myself.

I didn't and still don't know how two women I just met a month ago could see so much potential in me, but the conviction with which they spoke told me there's no denying they mean what they said.

And as I sat there at the table, listening to them—Libby coloring and oblivious to the heartfelt conversation taking place—the call I had with my mom earlier to wish me a happy birthday replayed in my mind.

She reminded me of her words before I left. "It doesn't matter where you are, Delia. Life will still be life, unless you make peace in your heart with who you are." Then she said, "And I hope in this next year, you will be able to do that."

And at that moment, it was like a switch flipped.

I realized that maybe it's not that I was chasing after something. Maybe I was trying to run from something instead.

I thought that the distance I could put between myself and a life stained with hurt and self-inflicted regret would give me clarity on what it is I'm meant for.

But is it possible, like my mom said, that it doesn't matter what job I pursue or if I move to a bunch of different states, none of it will matter until I face my fears and doubts. Until I confront the hurt that still lingers inside me, that I tell myself is gone, but clearly isn't.

It seems I've put a small bandage over a massive wound and convinced myself it was healed. Only to act surprised when it was picked at and still bled.

I splash some water on my face before walking over to the dresser, taking out a sweatshirt and some boxer shorts, and changing out of my dress so I can sit comfortably on the floor while working on my junk journal. But when I open the nightstand and find it empty, I remember that I left it in the living room this morning.

I tip-toe back downstairs, making a small detour through the kitchen to sneak one more bite of that amazing Coca Cola cake Grams got me.

I grab a fork and plate, cut off a small slice, and am mid-bite when I hear a door down the hall creak open, and shut again. Setting the cake down, I come out from the corner, expecting Catherine or Libby, but find Griffin looking as startled as I feel.

"You're still here," I whisper.

"Libby wanted me to read to her until she fell asleep," he says with a shrug.

I hum my acknowledgement, turning around and walking back toward my plate. I pick it up, and lean back against the counter, shoving another bite of the delicious goodness into my mouth.

Griffin follows me, resting against the kitchen island, and folds his arms across his chest.

I'm not sure how to act around him anymore—how I feel around him.

We still haven't spoken since last week after I darted inside. And, there was the moment earlier when he brought me my slice of cake with candles. Something about the moment felt so important, that I tried to commit every detail to memory. Even now, thinking about the way he looked at me while I blew out my candles makes my stomach do a pirouette.

"Are you happy with the cake?" he asks, pulling me from my jumbled thoughts.

I smile around the fork and nod.

"Did you have a good birthday?" He tilts his head, sweeping his gaze over me, his eyebrows furrowing. Before I can answer, he speaks again. "Have you been crying?"

I swallow, the cake suddenly feeling like sludge, and turn to set the plate and fork on the counter. When I face him again, I find myself unsure of how to answer. I'm not afraid to admit to Griffin that I was crying–he's seen me cry. I think I'm just confused as to why he's asking. Because he certainly doesn't...he can't...care?

"I'm okay," I say instead. "And yeah, I did have a good birthday. I still can't believe this cake." A smile slips onto my lips and Griffin takes a step toward me. On instinct, I go to take a step away from him, but the edge of the counter bites into my back, reminding me I have nowhere to go.

"You didn't answer my question," he insists. "Were you crying?"

I cross my arms in front of my chest protectively, forcing myself to lift my chin up and meet his gaze.

"Why do you want to know?" I counter.

"Just answer the damn question, Delia," he says, taking another step closer to me, and my breath catches at just how close he's getting to me.

"Tell me why you're asking, Griffin."

A low growl comes from him, before he runs a hand down his face.

"I don't want to do this with you anymore," he states.

My arms fall to my sides, his words stunning me.

"I've been thinking about last week," he starts, pausing to contemplate his next words. "And after tonight, I don't want there to be any more hostility between us."

"There isn't," I'm quick to say. "I'm sorry, I'm not trying to be difficult. I guess I'm just not sure why you'd want to know if I was crying, unless it was to make a remark about me being emotional or something."

"I'm going to try and be better with that," he says. "I'm asking because after seeing you so happy tonight, I don't understand why you'd be crying."

A mix of a laugh and a scoff falls from my lips.

"Well, that's the thing about emotions. They're unpredictable and sometimes all over the place. You can also feel more than one of them at a time, which is kind of what I've been dealing with." I sigh before continuing. "You're right, I was really happy–still am–but I also had a moment of sadness, or maybe sorrow, for the time lost to being so consumed with trying to please everyone around me. I'd also talked up this birthday in my head. Told myself, 'Twenty-five, that's a milestone. Need to start figuring shit out.' And tonight, I realized that everything I thought I wanted, or I guess believed would come to fruition with this birthday, is changing." I cover my face with my hands, groaning. "That's a lot, I know."

"How do you understand it all?" Griffin asks, genuine curiosity laced in his tone.

I slide my hands down my face, wrapping my arms around myself.

"The emotions?"

"Mhm," he hums.

"I mean, I don't always. Yeah, maybe I have more emotional intelligence than most people, but I'm still learning and figuring it out. I went to therapy for a few years after my parents split up, but I don't understand it all. I think the biggest issue is that I…" I let my words trail off, not sure I really want to give Griffin more of myself.

"You what?" He takes another step and now he's impossibly close–too close. And my hands are starting to itch again with the desire to reach out and make contact with his skin. I hug myself tighter, and absentmindedly bite my bottom lip in thought.

I swear Griffin's gaze flickers down to my mouth, but it's so fast, I might have imagined it.

"Why do you want to know?" I ask again, my voice now quiet.

"I'm trying to understand you," he states and I let out a sarcastic laugh.

"Funny, that's what I said about you to Fisher and Navy at Tombstones the night you drove me home."

He raises his eyebrows, before laughing himself. "Don't know why I'm surprised, but don't try to distract me. What's your biggest issue?"

"I don't know what to make of you like this," I say, playfully pushing him in the chest. But I instantly regret it, as lightning zings through my body and I know my cheeks are flushed.

Griffin looks down at the point of contact, before pretending to be knocked away by me and stumbling back.

"Like what?" He tilts his head as he moves to close the distance between us again.

"I don't know...nice?" I laugh.

"Yeah, I've been a real–what did you call me?"

"Jerk," I deadpan.

"Riiight," he says. "But again, you're trying to distract me."

"Fine," I grumble. "My biggest issue is that I have this desperate need to convince people that I'm worth something. That I'm not just an overly emotional person. That I'm not too much. I meant what I said that night you brought me back here– I think I'm special. The issue is I want everyone else to think that too, even though that's not plausible. Yet here I am, still struggling to let my opinion of myself be enough."

"And how does the birthday girl see herself?" he says, a playful but thoughtful tone to his words.

"Griffin, you're freaking me out. Seriously. Did you get body-snatched?"

"No, Delia. I'm just trying to treat you the way," he pauses and clears his throat, "the way I should have from the start. The way my mom and dad raised me."

Something shifts in the air at the mention of his parents. I didn't anticipate my journey downstairs turning into this late night confessional, least of all with Griffin.

"I appreciate that," I whisper.

He searches my face for a second, maybe trying to see if there's more I want to say, probably expecting that there's more I want to say, but I don't have any more words. I'm too perplexed and thrown off by this entire encounter.

"I'm going to go back upstairs," I start, glancing beyond him to the living room. He follows my gaze before turning back to me.

"I came down here for my junk journal and got distracted by the cake."

At the mention of my journal, he stiffens.

"Right, yeah. I should probably head back to my house. I've got a project I picked up for tomorrow," he says.

I want to ask him more about what he does, what the project is, and honestly, just keep talking. But the words that fall from lips instead are, "Yeah, sure."

We stand there for a second, looking at each other, like we're meeting again for the first time. And maybe that's what this is.

He breaks the moment, turning and heading for the front door, and I squeeze my eyes tight, scrunching up my whole face and wincing at how badly this could go.

"Hey, Griffin," I call after him.

He stops and turns around, and I move toward him before my mind can comprehend what I'm doing and stop me.

"My birthday could be better," I say a little unsteadily as I come to stand in front of him.

"How?" he asks, his voice low.

"A hug. You could–can I–what I said on the porch." I trip over my words, losing my confidence.

"Yeah, okay," he murmurs, taking a step toward me, reaching his arms out. But I move faster, bouncing on the tips of my toes to push myself up and wrap my arms around his neck, forcing his hands to fall around my waist.

For a second, his arms just hang there, but then he wraps them around me and pulls me into him. I squeeze my arms tighter, too, and our cheeks brush.

I'm being so selfish right now, taking this hug for myself, wanting to fulfill the urge I've had for weeks now to truly embrace him. But I didn't anticipate how it would make me feel. How much I would like it.

I thought I wanted to hug him for *his* benefit, giving him some of my good energy and hoping it lifted his spirits. But holy hell, this feels like so much more, and I need to reel it in.

I slowly pull back, my nose accidentally grazing along his jaw, and his hands flex for the briefest second around my waist before he lets go.

I step away from him, my body feeling like it's both on fire and connected to a live wire.

His eyes fixate on me, the blue peeking through, and an intensity in them that makes me shiver.

"Thank you," I whisper, a little breathlessly, and do what I seem to do best–I bolt toward the stairs, swiping my journal off the side table as I pass it.

When I get inside the guest room, I pad over to the window, tucking myself behind the curtain, and watch Griffin get in his truck. My heart still beats erratically and his touch feels seared into my skin.

I can't stop thinking about how badly I did *not* want to break that hug. I also can't stop thinking about what was going on in his head during it.

The only thing I know for certain is something changed between us.

As the red glow from his tail lights grows fainter, I finally step away, grabbing my journal and getting back to my original task at hand.

A few minutes later, I have all my art supplies strewn out on the sleek wooden floors. I crack open my junk journal and flip to the next blank page. My head nods along with the music playing from my phone, the messy bun on my head bobbing in time. I get to work, taping down all my treasures from the last few days, a little smirk overtaking my lips when everything is placed where I want it. *Perfect.*

I pull out my pen, ready to write the thoughts, musings, and feelings that accompany the items, but I lose my grip on the journal and the paper flitters to a previous page. The smirk slips off my face as the memories stare back at me. I reach out to touch the corners of a fading concert ticket, but hesitate at the last second as if it might bite. With my fingertip hovering over the crinkled paper, I think better of it and quickly flip back to my spot. But the uneasiness lingers.

I try to ignore it. I try to tell myself what I am starting to know as truth, especially after today. I wanted–want–this change. I need it. I can't stay where I'm comfortable and expect to grow. But seeing that ticket, remembering that day with Clara, my stomach twists.

When I get back to Atlanta, will things be different? Will the change last? Or will I slip back into familiar patterns and routines?

How will I know when I've found that peace my mom keeps talking about?

And even if I were to move here–or anywhere else–would I be able to handle being away from my parents? Clara?

I try to shake off all the what if's that start ping-ponging in my brain and focus on something more exciting–Clara is going to visit for the Fourth of July like Fisher suggested.

Catherine thought it was a great idea, and once Clara's background check came back clean, she requested the time off. She let me know this morning when she texted me for my birthday that she booked her flights.

I return my attention to my journal, biting off the cap of the pen and balancing it between my lips, and scrawling out a few sentences. I sit back and re-cap the pen, scanning the collage and scribbles about this past week, when Navy and Cadence came over for the day. They hung out with Libby and I, and we went swimming in the lake. It's up there as one of my favorite memories from this trip so far.

A yawn escapes me and I glance at my phone to realize it's nearly midnight. At least tomorrow is Sunday and I have off. Although, I'm sure I'll end up doing something. I don't want to waste a lot of my free time because before I know it, the summer will be over and I'll be going home. But why do I suddenly feel sad about that?

Making quick work of cleaning up and getting in bed, my mind wanders back to the ticket as I settle under the covers. More so the day it's from. The memories that come with it. My chest aches with a twinge of homesickness. And that sadness from just moments ago about leaving isn't helping.

"It's just been an emotional day and I need to go to sleep," I mutter to myself.

But I toss and turn for the next few hours, feeling caught between this chapter of my life and the ones that have passed. All while wondering where I'll end up, but also feeling drawn back to the former.

I give up on trying to get some rest, staring at the ceiling and stewing on my emotions. So much has happened in such a short amount of time.

At some point, my eyelids begin to feel heavy again, and I eventually slip into a dreamless sleep. When I wake up the next morning, the last thought I had before drifting off floats to the front of my mind.

Maybe it's nostalgia that is the thief of joy, not comparison. Because every time I think I'm happy right where I'm at, flashes of my past seem to detonate in my mind and steal my bliss.

I worry I won't ever be able to find that peace my mom keeps talking about.

"THE BIRTHDAY THING"

GRIFFIN

"Turn around. Turn around. TURN AROUND," my mind screams at me the further away from the house I drive.

What the hell just happened?

I went from reading Libby a bed time story–*five* bed time stories, actually–to having maybe the most meaningful conversation with someone in years.

Not someone.

Delia.

I bring my truck to a stop outside my house, my feet carrying me to my front door, while my mind still fixates on the last few minutes. I unlock my front door and walk over to my couch, collapsing onto it.

Running a hand through my hair, flashes of Delia start going off in my mind.

Her innocently biting her lip, making my gaze fall on her mouth. The moment she pressed her hand into my chest to push me away and how something came to life under her touch.

Her soft laughs still echo in my mind.

But the moment that replays most vividly is the hug she gave me. Except it felt like she stole it from me, along with some piece of me that I was sure I'd locked away.

I thought it would be a hug similar to the one at the cookout, but it seemed she had other plans. When she pushed up and wrapped her arms around my neck, pressing herself into me, my brain stopped working. She was so close to me. It was like instinct took over and I quickly pulled her tighter against me.

The waves of emotion that came over me the longer she touched me soothed aches deep in my chest, while also stoking embers I thought would never ignite again.

All that from a *hug*.

And now, my mind won't stop spinning.

I want to go back.

But why? To say what?

"Delia, I need you to hug me again so I can see if that was a fluke."

What am I even talking about.

No. Absolutely not.

I will not, I *cannot*, let Delia have this effect on me. Especially when I have more important things to do.

Shaking my head to clear my thoughts, I take my phone out and call Cadence. It connects after only the first ring and she screams into the speaker.

"Griffin! I've been waiting to hear from you! How'd it go? Did she like her cake?"

"Hey, Cady. Yeah, it was great, Listen, I need you to do me a favor," I say, getting straight to the point.

"Um, okay? Boo, you. You're so boring, but what's up?"

"If Delia asks, because I'm sure she will, my Grams ordered the cake from you and Navy delivered it."

"What? Why?"

"I don't want her to know it was my idea."

"And why is that?"

"I just don't, okay? I don't need the credit."

"Right, okay. So basically, after like the last decade of your life, you finally do something nice for someone, and you don't want them to know. Right, yeah. Makes total sense."

I scoff. "I've done nice things for other people."

"Your sister, grandma, and niece do not count."

"Whatever. Will you keep this between us?"

"Fine, but I want something in return."

I roll my eyes. "What?"

"I don't know, but when I think of it, you best believe I'll come calling."

"Whatever. How is the trip going? Did you find out anything in your meeting today?"

Silence falls between us and I pull my phone away from my ear to make sure the call didn't drop.

"Cadence?"

"No," she says, her voice catching. "It's not looking good."

"I'm sorry. I'll keep looking into it."

"Thanks, Griffin."

"Anytime. Alright, I need to text Navy and tell her about this whole thing."

"Give us a heads up next time you plan to make us your accomplices, yeah?"

"Bye, Cady."

"Bye, Griff."

I hang up, opening up my messages.

I need a favor.

NAVY

Wrong person?

Funny.

You and Cadence should take up comedy.

NAVY

Omfg

A favor and jokes? What is going on?

I don't have time for this.

If Delia asks, you dropped off her birthday cake at our house today, got it?

NAVY

Uhhhhhh

Sure, but am I allowed to ask for more info?

No.

NAVY

Then no favor

Navy.

NAVY

Griffin <3

Fine. I'll tell you the next time I see you.

NAVY

I'll hold you to that

I get off the couch and walk into my room, stripping down to my boxers and getting ready for bed.

Once I'm settled, I grab my phone again and call my dad, the beep coming instantly.

"Hey, Dad. Not sure if you noticed, but I've had to call you a lot more recently. Well, there's a reason for that. Her name is Delia. Cath hired her to come live here for the summer, help out with Libby and Grams, and work at Lasso. I was really upset at first, because Cathy and Grams got one over me. They let me think she was an older woman, when she's in her twenties. She turned twenty-five today, actually. Honestly, you would have probably thought it was funny, too."

I pause, and swear I can faintly hear his laugh. But silence surrounds me, and I sigh.

"I'm wasting time. Delia gets under my skin, Dad. It's like she knows every button of mine to push. Always challenging me, calling me out, all while also bringing me this profound sense of peace that I don't understand. This is one of the few times I wish you could actually talk back, because I need your advice. I'm trying to be her friend now that I've set my pride aside, but I don't know if I actually want to get any closer to her than I am now. Cadence told me that she thought Delia might be the person who could help me come back from my…"

I close my eyes, choking out my next few words.

"…grief. And I'd never admit it to anyone else, but I think she might be right. And between you and I, that scares the hell out of me. Delia scares the hell out of me. You'd probably like her, think she's good for me, and that also scares me. She reminds me of you in some ways, Mom too. Think you could send me a sign or something and help me figure out what to do? That would be great. Love you."

I hang up, setting my phone on my nightstand before rolling onto my side.

The next couple of days will be busy, and I can use that to my advantage while I sort out how to approach Delia.

For now, I'll try not to think about everything I just said to my dad, more so, how speaking everything out loud confirmed something that I've been trying so hard to fight.

I'm drawn to Delia, too.

* * *

"Appreciate you helping me out today," I say to Callum while we load our tools into my truck bed.

"You know me, I've never met a porch I didn't want to screen in," he replies with a goofy grin.

I raise my eyebrows and scratch the side of my neck. "Sure, Cal. Whatever that means."

He laughs, hopping into my passenger seat and we drive back to the ranch. He doesn't linger, getting his truck and heading straight to the Kofford's since Cadence got back a few hours ago.

I head inside, rinsing off, before walking up the main house. I'm not sure what the girls and Delia did today, but there's someone I need to have a conversation with.

I walk up the steps to the porch, pleased to find Grams already sitting out here, as if she knew I was coming.

"About time," she drawls, and I take a seat next to her in Pop's chair.

"Where's everyone else?" I ask, looking beyond her to the window to see if anyone is inside.

"Your sister and Libby went to go get ice cream, and Delia is out exploring," she says with a wave of her hand.

"Exploring?" I echo, a hint of concern in my voice. "Not like the mountains or hiking, right?"

Grams reaches over and grasps my hand. "It's nice to see you care, but no. She wanted to drive around and find some things to do when her friend, Clara, visits."

I skip past her comment about me caring, although a little

relief does wash over me knowing Delia isn't alone doing something that could be dangerous. I also want to ask about her friend visiting—that's the first I'm hearing of it—but I need to focus on why I actually came here.

"So, the birthday thing," I start.

"Yes, the birthday thing. Let's hear it," she says, putting her hand back in her lap.

"I'm sure you've noticed that there's been some hiccups between Delia and I. Part of it is because of what you and Cathy have been saying, she is definitely different for me. And the other part is, I don't like how–"

"She seems to see through all those walls you have?" Grams fills in for me.

"Something like that," I mumble.

"I had a feeling from the very first couple of conversations I had with her, that she would be quite the challenge for you. But I'll be honest, that made me even more excited to have her here," she admits.

"Hm," I hum in response, thinking on her words. "She is a challenge, that's for sure. Want to hear something crazy?"

"I would love to," she sings.

"When we were at karaoke the other night, of all the songs Delia could sing, she chose the one we played for Mom at the funeral," I say, my throat tightening at my words.

Grams turns to look at me, her eyes widening. "Well, my goodness. I bet that was both shocking and calamitous."

"I've just been trying to figure out what the odds are. Of all the songs? She happened to choose that one? I don't know. There's just been these moments where it's like, I don't know, she's programmed or...that's not the right word."

Grams smirks. "You've met your match."

"Whoa, okay. That's not what I'm saying." I point at her. "Don't do that."

She laughs. "I have to say, I'm shocked we are even having this conversation. I don't know the last time you shared this much with me."

I frown, guilt swirling inside me.

"I'm sorry, Grams. I really am. It's been wrong of me to treat you and Cath the way I have. I'm not suddenly changed or anything, but I am working on it," I say.

"That's all we can really ask for," she remarks. "I just want you to be happy, Griffin. I know we have all been through so much, and I know it affected you differently because of the business, but we never wanted you to feel like you had to do it all on your own."

"I know that. It's just...hard."

"Well, we don't have to talk about it much more. I want to hear about Delia and the birthday cake," she says, a mischievous glint in her eyes.

So, I tell her the truth. How the cake was originally supposed to be a ploy, but I couldn't go through with it. I leave out the junk journal part, but explain everything else on a somewhat surface level. The conversations Delia and I had, the things she'd said to me, what really happened at the cookout, and I find the more I talk with my grandma, the more I realize how much I missed this.

"I'm proud of you, Griffin," she whispers at the end of our conversation. "They would be too."

I nod, unable to think on those words for too long. I may be trying to make progress in some areas, but I'm not ready to just tear down all my walls entirely.

"I told you that night you carried her into the house, and I'll say it again since your mom can't. Life loves to surprise us when we least expect it, but need it most," she recalls, chuckling. "Did you ever hear what your father said back to your mom when she would say that?"

I stiffen. "No?"

"Oh, goodness." She pauses again, pressing her hand to her forehead and shaking it back and forth. "She'd make that comment and he'd say, 'And what if that surprise scares you? Do you still need it?' and she'd say, 'Those are typically the best type of surprises.'"

Her eyes flicker with emotion.

"Thank you for telling me that, Grams. It means a lot," I say, but not for the reason she thinks.

Because of what I'd said to my dad last night. Except she had no idea. And somehow, I got the sign I asked for. It might not have brought me the clarity I hoped for, but it was something. Now I just need to figure out what it means.

I close my eyes and rest my head back on Pop's chair. I know I need to try and talk to Delia again, but if I open myself up to the idea of actually becoming friends, I'm worried that I won't be able to stop opening up to her.

And *that* scares me, most of all.

twenty-nine

TWO NEW BOXES

DELIA

The next couple days fly by and before I know it, it's Friday–only four days until Clara gets here. I'm so excited I could scream.

Navy and Cadence have been giving me suggestions on what we should do, but I also have been making plans with them, too.

Navy is going to cover my shifts at the boutique, and Cathy said she'd bring Libby with her to the store, but I told her that Clara and I would be happy to spend at least a couple mornings with Libby.

I think it's going to be so much fun and I already know that Clara is going to fit in so well.

Although, I'm curious to see if Griffin will hang out with us at all.

I haven't been able to talk to him much since my birthday, but the few passing moments we've had have been good. I'm planning to try and talk to him before Clara gets here, but I just don't know when that moment will be.

It's weird to think that in the span of about six weeks, I've made such sincere relationships with the people here. Just last night, Marge and I ended up talking on the porch until about ten at night–which is way past her bedtime.

Catherine came out and joined us after she got Libby settled, and we had another one of those, if not the most, meaningful conversations. I shared with them the epiphany I had on my birthday and they gave me some of their own insights on how to seek out that peace my mom mentioned.

Marge said that even in her old age, she still doesn't have it all figured out. Yet for her, what matters most is she knows who she is, the characteristics and attributes she holds, and that's what brings her contentment.

Cathy opened up about her struggles of not having her mom during some of the toughest years of her life. How hard it was to not have her there when Libby was born, but how grateful she was and is to have her brother and grandmother. And of course, I cried for her. She continued to say that she found peace when she stopped trying to figure out the "why" behind everything. I relished in the knowledge that like myself, Cathy struggled with all the "what if's".

I will carry that conversation with me forever.

Every day that I wake up here, I feel a little lighter, the part of me that was feeling lost slowly fading. I still have moments of uncertainty, but I'm feeling more confident about going back to Atlanta and having a new perspective on things.

Except, when I think about going home, that strange sadness starts to creep back in.

My phone starts buzzing in my pocket and I take it out, seeing it's Cathy.

"Hi! I'm closing up now."

"No worries! I was calling to ask if you'd bring my laptop back with you, I left it in the back room."

I walk out from behind the cash wrap, heading in that direction, and grabbing it while I'm on the phone so I don't forget. "Got it!"

"Thank you. I need to go through some of the newest applications I received, so I can try to get some interviews done while I have the help. You'll be gone before we know it!"

My stomach drops at her words.

"Oh, right. Of course. If there's anything I can do to help, let me know."

"I appreciate that! Are you coming straight to the house?"

"Yes, unless you need anything else?"

"No, we're good. I'll see you in a little."

"Sounds good."

I end the call, putting my phone into my back pocket and sliding Cathy's laptop into my bag.

As I lock up the shop and head out to the car, I can't shake the feeling that came over me at the mention of her looking for my replacement. That's always been the plan, so I don't know why hearing it came as a surprise.

When I get back to the house, I walk in and find Cathy at the kitchen table finishing her dinner, Libby and Marge settled into the sofa watching something on the TV.

"Here you go," I say, taking the laptop out of my bag and setting it on the table next to her plate.

"Thank you again!" she remarks as she tilts her head, looking me over. "Is everything okay?"

"Yeah, of course. I'm just tired." I take my crimson boots off, placing them by the front door with the other pairs, and hanging my purse on one of the hooks.

I pad into the kitchen, not sure what I want, and upset that I ate my last Pop-Tart the other day. But when I open the cabinet to see what else I can snack on, I find two new boxes of the breakfast pastry. I let out a little squeal, grateful that Cathy must have gone grocery shopping and picked them up.

"I could have gotten groceries if you needed me to," I call to her, worried that maybe I missed one of her Post-it notes or a text.

"I'm planning to go on Sunday," she answers and I frown. *Weird.*

Walking back to the table, I sit and open up the Pop-Tart, biting off the corner and a sigh of contentment leaves my lips.

"You don't toast them," Cathy states.

"Eh, sometimes. Depends on my mood," I say with a shrug. "Did you, uh, want my help with hiring at all? I do it back home, so if it would be helpful for you, I don't mind." I take another bite.

"I might take you up on that," she remarks, giving me her full attention. "Can I ask you something? And I don't want you to feel on the spot or anything, it's just something that's been on my mind."

I roughly swallow the last bite. "Of course."

"Have you thought at all about staying?"

I blink a few, times, my mind seeming to buffer at her question.

"H-here? As in the house? Wyoming?" I stammer.

"All of it," she replies. "Here, the boutique, Jackson. I didn't want to ask and put any pressure on you, but I'm curious. I have my own thoughts, but, of course, it's not up to me."

"What are your thoughts?" I ask, my stomach doing somersaults.

"Honestly? I think you would do well here. That you fit in. That I would love to have you around for the store, but also for us. I truly didn't know what to expect when I hired you, but this last month has far exceeded any expectations I might have had." She pauses, tilting her head. "I thought whoever I found for the summer would come, do their duties, and leave. But, Delia, you've become a part of our family."

My eyes well up, a lump forming in my throat.

"Cather-Cathy," I say, my voice breaking. "I don't know what to say."

"I'm sorry, I didn't want to make you feel uncomf–"

"No, it's not that," I cut her off. "I'm not uncomfortable. It means more than you know to hear that. It's just… It was never in my plans to stay."

"I know," she says, clearing her throat. "I know. But I just wanted to let you know that if you change your mind, if you want to stay, you could–you can."

"Thank you," I choke out.

"I know you're going to be busy with Clara when she's here, and after she leaves, you'll only have four weeks left. It'll fly by, so I wanted to make sure I told you as soon as possible, so you could think about if it was something you might be interested in."

I nod. Not knowing what else to do or say, I get up and walk over to her, bending down and hugging her.

"Thank you," I say again, because I'm at a loss for all other words.

"Of course," she replies, hugging me back.

I continue on toward the stairs, stopping before going up them. I turn around, taking in the house that has become so familiar to me. The three people who have become paramount to my life.

Cathy's words–her offer–already start to weigh on me.

So instead of going up to my room, I walk over to the couch and find a spot next to Libby, squishing her between me and Marge.

"Can I watch TV with you?" I ask Libby, who's already moving to situate herself and lie her head on my lap.

"Of course, Deely," she says as she snuggles into me.

I glance over at Marge who has a serene look on her face, and my heart clenches. It's exactly like Cathy said, it feels as if we're family. For the briefest of moments, I let myself slip into the feeling of what it would be like to stay. I imagine what my life would look like.

Getting up early to go feed the chickens or water Cathy's flowers. Coming back inside to greet Marge and chat over coffee and tea before waking up Libby. I don't know what it would look like when she starts school, but I assume I'd be dropping her off and heading to the boutique after.

I'd definitely be a regular at Boulder Brewing Co., like I'd daydreamed about. Maybe I could pick up part-time work there if Cathy still wanted to work at Lasso in the mornings. Or would she step back from that all together and let me run the show? My heart gallops at that thought. And I find the longer I sit in these feelings, these wistful "what if's", the more I consider it.

Could I actually move here?

But a face flashes in my mind—stormy blue eyes and hardened features. As much as I maybe want to stay here, I don't know if I would ever be fully welcome.

I'd never make a decision for myself because of someone else, but I have to consider Griffin and everything he's been through. And the truth is, it's pretty obvious that he's chomping at the bit for the summer to end and me to leave. No matter the talks we've had or what moments I think we might have shared, there is no world where Griffin Aberdeen is okay with me moving onto his family's ranch. And, with all the loss he's suffered, I refuse to add to that by possibly coming between him and the three most important people in his life.

Tonight, though, while I'm settled on the couch with Libby

and Marge, Cathy in the kitchen working on her laptop, I'll let myself pretend that this is what my life will be like from now on.

"I'm glad you're here," Libby murmurs as if somehow sensing what's on my mind.

"Very glad," Marge adds.

"I wish you could stay forever," Libby says, and I wonder if maybe she heard some of Cathy and I's conversation.

"Me too, Libby," I whisper. *Me too.*

Mom,

I don't know when you'll get this and I'm sure by then we will probably have talked on the phone about this already. But I'm going to write it all down anyways, so I can capture my thoughts and feelings in the moment.

Cathy asked me if I would want to stay. And mom...I think I want to. But I can't, right? It doesn't make sense. It would be crazy and there's so many people expecting me to come back. Like Clara, who will be here soon and I'm sure this feeling of wanting to stay will fade. I don't think I could leave her for good. I would miss you and dad too much. And Diane would probably be upset if I ended up quitting. This was supposed to be temporary. I also can't stay because of a certain someone I told you about, who would probably lose his mind if that happened. I told Cathy I would think about it.

What would you do?

love you mommy.
pp Delia

"FRIENDS?"

GRIFFIN

Of course the one time I actually need to be somewhere, I hit every single red light.

There's only a small window of time in the afternoon when Delia is free while Libby naps, before Cath gets home, and she has to head downtown. And with every red light I hit, that window gets smaller and smaller.

It's killing me that I still haven't been able to talk with her.

I've been busier than usual with my projects and we keep missing each other with our schedules. Which is why I can't lose this last chance to talk before her friend gets in tomorrow, and what happened between us fades into background noise.

It's not like me to take a break from work in the middle of the day, but something tells me that things are about to change. Maybe they already have. And I need to make sure that the air is clear with Delia before *whatever* else happens.

No more open ended conversations. No more letting her bolt

off like she has in the past. But most importantly, no more getting defensive.

Grams and I have had a couple more conversations since last Sunday on the porch, and each one has given me a different perspective on the events of the past.

I still have a hard time talking about my parents, but it's getting easier.

I've also been talking to Cadence more as we work on figuring out her situation. She won't let the birthday cake thing go, but is also happy to see that *something* is different in my demeanor.

It's not lost on me that most of these changes have been spurred on by Delia and her arrival, and it's time I own up to that.

Today, I'm going to ask Delia if she will be my friend.

Which is comical, given that when she first posed that idea to me, I really thought that would never happen.

I park behind the house, coming through the back door and looking around for her. In hindsight, having gotten her number at some point would probably have made this easier, instead of trying to track her down.

I see Grams on the porch through the window, so I start walking toward the door when a faint but familiar sound reaches my ears.

I stop in my tracks, certain that I'm imagining it. But, there it is again, the faint chiming of bells and tinkling of glass.

As if being lured outside by the sound, my feet start moving again and when I open the front door, it feels like I've been transported back in time.

I close my eyes as the breeze picks up again, the soft melody floating throughout the porch.

But how is this possible?

"Beautiful, isn't it?" Grams says, and I open my eyes to look at her as she points over to the corner where my mom's wind-chime is back in its place.

"How?" I whisper, stepping toward it.

"How do you think?" she asks.

Delia.

"She found it the other day and asked me about it. Her and Libby have been working on putting it back together all week," Grams says, reading my mind.

I stand and marvel at the wind-chime, still not convinced it's actually there. It's been glued and strung back together, a few pieces replaced, but for the most part it's exactly how I remember it.

Another breeze passes through, making the chimes and glass dance, an ache ricocheting in my chest. I didn't think I'd ever hear that sound again, forced to accept that the wind-chime was just another piece of my mom that I'd lost.

Of course it would be Delia who found a way to give that back to me.

"Where is she?"

"The dock," Grams responds, closing her eyes and letting a smile settle on her face. "You have about fifteen minutes."

I quickly open the screen door, rushing down the steps and taking off toward the lake.

As I get closer, I steady my pace, not wanting to run up on her and scare her. When I reach the end of the dock, I also take a second to just observe her. Her hair is braided and it no longer annoys me seeing it that way.

A smile slips on my face, instead. She's wearing jean shorts and a white tank top, mirroring my jeans and white T-shirt.

Heading toward her, she turns when she hears the creaking wood under my feet.

"Oh, it's you," she says, returning her gaze back toward the water.

"Yeah, just me," I echo, sitting next to her on the edge.

"It's so calm out here," she whispers. I follow her line of sight over the lake and to the mountains in the distance. The clouds are hanging lower today and the whole landscape resembles a painting.

"Can we talk?" I ask, hoping she doesn't say no for some reason.

"What about?" She responds, still not meeting my gaze and that's when I notice her posture and the dimmed energy coming from her.

"Are you alright?"

"I'm just having an off day." She sighs.

"What does that mean? Sorry, I'm not the best with this–as you know," I say with a small laugh.

Still not giving me her attention–as if talking to the water and not me–she answers, quietly, "I woke up and everything just felt wrong."

"Everything?" I repeat.

"Yeah. I'm sure that doesn't make sense to you, but sometimes this happens. I'll wake up and it's as if I'm on the outside of my body, disconnected from my emotions and feelings. I *hate* it."

She finally looks at me and for the first time, I don't find that glimmer of gold in her eyes. You want to talk about hating something? Well, I hate that.

"What did you want to talk about?"

"I'm not sure exactly, but I think I want to start by telling you a few things," I say, hoping I can get through this without my defenses flying up.

"Alright, well, I'm all ears," she declares, turning her body toward me.

"Right, okay," I start. "I guess I'll just come out with it."

She nods and gives me a soft smile.

"My parents died in a car accident. I had just graduated and there were all these plans for me to work with my dad and Pop. But all that fell to shit."

"I'm so sorry," she interrupts, her voice cracking. "Really."

"It was storming, the same way it was a few weekends ago. They hydroplaned and went off the road..." I trail off, remembering how it felt to get that phone call. "I've never told anyone this, but I blamed myself for a while," I admit. "They were driving to meet me for lunch."

"Griffin," she breathes out. "That doesn't make it your fault."

I notice how her hand flinches, no doubt wanting to reach out for me because she balls them into fists after.

"But they were on the road because of *me*. And I've replayed that day over and over. It wouldn't have happened if they–"

"It wasn't your fault," she cuts me off, her voice firm.

"I tried to move past it. I threw myself into working with Pop, moving onto the ranch with him and Grams because Cathy wasn't living here at the time. I slowly started to deal with what had happened, but Pop passed and I couldn't handle it. Even with Cathy moving back, then Libby being born, there was something in me that was never the same. I started shutting off any part of me that could feel something. I locked away memories, and I shoved down my emotions. Everyone around me started to accept it. They started to give up on trying to help me because I pushed away anyone who tried. Besides Grams, Cathy, and Libs, I didn't go out of my way to see or talk to anyone I didn't have to. I lived behind my walls." I let out a breath, one that feels like it's been trapped inside me for the last ten years.

Delia holds my gaze, smirking. "And then I showed up with a sledgehammer."

313

I chuckle, grateful for the light-hearted remark, instead of asking more questions and causing me to relive more than I have to.

"Basically. But the way I reacted to you, it was because that was all I knew how to feel. I've been so angry for so long, Delia. It's like I see red sometimes."

She looks away from me again, casting her vision over the water and mumbles something under her breath that I don't catch.

"What?" I ask.

"I sat with my anger long enough until it told me its name was grief."

My eyes widen and I blink a few times as I process her words.

"My therapist told me that a few years ago after one of my friends died. I think it's a quote or something. She told me that as session after session, I kept saying I wasn't sad, I was angry. But she was right, underneath the anger was grief so vast it consumed me."

"That's how it felt," I murmur. "Like I *was* my anger."

"Yeah, it's hard to separate yourself from your emotions sometimes. Especially when they're connected to something so monumental to your life."

"You do," I'm quick to say.

"Hm?"

"You know how to handle all your emotions. I think you're the most emotionally intelligent person I know," I answer truthfully.

"It hasn't always been like this," she states.

"What do you mean?"

She sighs. "You told me something nobody else knows, so I guess it's only fair I do the same."

I tilt my head, not sure what she's getting at, when she stands and starts to unbutton her shorts.

"Ummm," I stammer.

She rolls her eyes, moving her hand to the side of her hip, hooking her thumb into the edge, and folding the fabric down. She moves the edge of her underwear with it and that's when I notice a series of thin white lines–no, scars–along her hip bone. She pulls everything back up into place, buttoning her shorts and sitting back down next to me.

I just sit there, my eyes wide and mind blank. I am, however, able to say one word. "Why?"

She rubs her hands up and down her thighs, letting out a breath.

"In my early twenties, I really started to struggle with being an empath. I didn't know how to manage my emotions, how to figure out which ones were mine and which were other people's. It got so overwhelming that I decided to do what you did and shut it all off. Numbed myself until I basically felt nothing." She pauses, and lets out a sigh.

"It didn't last long, and *this* happened," she says, pressing her hand over her hip bone where I now know–and will never forget–are her scars. "Before you ask, I haven't done it again. I went back to therapy after and found healthier ways to manage my emotions."

"But why that?" I question, not liking the idea of her harming herself, but relieved to know she hasn't done it since.

"It just became too much. I needed to get it out." She hesitates, before continuing. "It's similar to why you had that panic attack."

"What do you mean?"

"It's not sustainable to shove down your feelings. It'll always backfire," she states, and turns to look at me. "Because that's the thing about emotions, they demand to be felt. We can try all we want to ignore them, turn them off, shove them down, but one way or another, they will make themselves known, and we will have to feel them."

"Damn," I say under my breath.

"Damn," she echoes.

"I didn't expect the conversation to turn into this," I say.

"I'm sorry, I hope I didn't mess it up," she rushes out.

"No, it's not a bad thing. I actually have been enjoying our talks lately, up until the point of you bolting off." I grin.

Delia blushes and it makes me grin wider.

"This is nice," I say. "I finally feel like you don't completely have the upper hand here."

"Hey," she quips, reaching over and smacking me in the chest. I catch her hand with mine, holding it against me, and she inhales sharply. Her fingers curl under my grasp, fisting my T-shirt, and a look passes between us before she lets go and slides her hand out from under mine. She folds her hands in her lap, facing the mountains once more.

We sit there for a few seconds in silence, a million thoughts racing through my head, and my skin buzzing.

"I have to tell you something," she says, an unsteadiness in her voice that makes me uneasy.

"Alright…"

"Your sister asked me to stay," she whispers.

I rear my head back, blinking rapidly as that statement washes over me.

"When?" I demand.

"Friday night," she says with a wince.

I wait for the flare of fear and anger I felt a few weeks ago to appear. This is exactly what I worried about. But those feelings never show; instead, a weird sort of erratic sensation starts to build in my stomach.

Before I can say something, she speaks again. "I'm not going to."

"What? Why?" I blurt out.

She turns to face me, scrunching her face up. "Because I'm pretty sure you've probably been counting down the days until I leave since you met me."

I choke-cough at the accuracy of that statement, quickly recovering. "Okay, maybe the first couple of weeks I felt like that, but now, I don't know. It's clear how much you mean to my family, and you've been really helpful."

I can't believe I'm saying this. And clearly neither can Delia, because her eyes just about pop out of her head, but she schools her expression.

"Even if things had changed between you and I, it was never in my plans to stay," she says. "I was always going to go back to Atlanta."

I contemplate her words, and I don't know why but there's a part of me that wants to argue with her on it. Maybe it's because once again, after our conversation, I'm left feeling like there's still more to unfold between us.

"Plans change," I challenge.

She narrows her eyes. "I don't know what you're playing at."

"Nothing," I scoff. "I wanted to talk to you today and try to actually have a conversation with no bolting, no fighting, and try to get on some sort of level playing field."

"And was it successful?" she asks, her voice getting quiet.

"I don't know, what do you think? Friends?"

She bites her lip in thought, and like the other night, my eyes fall to her mouth. This time, though, I'm not as fast flicking my eyes back up and the look Delia gives me tells me she noticed.

Her cheeks flush and she leans back, resting her hand on the dock near mine. Her pinky brushes my fingers, and she glances down at the small point of contact, and back up at me.

"Friends?" she repeats, her voice taking on a breathy tone.

"Friends," I echo, trying not to focus on how it feels like my skin is buzzing again where we're touching. What is happening?

"I'd like that," she says, giving me one of her soft smiles.

We sit there like that for a couple more seconds, her finger lightly resting on mine. A breeze picks up and it reminds me of something else I wanted to say.

"Thank you for fixing the wind-chime. That means more to me than you know."

"Grams told me your mom made it," she says thoughtfully. "I hope it was okay that I had to replace a few things."

"It's perfect, and Cathy will think so, too."

She nods, finally moving her hand and starts to stand up. "I need to get ready, but I'm glad we talked."

"Me too," I say, getting up with her. But before she can walk away, I stop her.

This is my moment to figure out if the other night was a fluke.

"I'm going to give you a free pass, if you want. One hug, since I know how badly you–"

I don't get to finish my sentence before Delia lets out a small squeal and throws herself at me, wrapping her arms around my neck like the other night. I catch her, pulling her into me and holding her tightly.

"Thank you," she whispers against my neck, and chills break out on my skin.

And it's at that moment I know I fucked up.

The other night wasn't a fluke.

There is an undeniable electricity between the two of us, and I don't know what it means, or what to do about it.

I set her down on the dock and she slides her hands down

from my neck, leaving them on my chest, while mine rest on her waist.

"See, that wasn't so bad," she says with a smirk.

"Whatever you say," I mumble as she pulls away and starts to run toward the house.

"See you later, *friend*!" she yells, leaving me on the dock, my thoughts running wild.

I run a hand through my hair, tugging on the ends. I was right, things are about to change, just not in the way I expected them to.

Cathy asked her to stay, and she said no, because of *me*. And now for some reason, I'm trying to figure out if there's a way to change her mind–for Cathy, Grams, and Libs, of course.

But a faint voice from somewhere deep in my mind whispers that I'm lying to myself, and despite the conversation I just had with Delia, I shut that off and shove it down.

I take my phone out, sending a text.

> Cathy asked Delia to stay.

CADENCE

Shut up

That's the best news of my life

> She said she's not going to.

CADENCE

Uh why?

Let me guess...

You had something to do with that?

> Yeah, so you have to help me change that.

CADENCE

Holy shit

You totally want her to stay don't you

For my family, not me.

CADENCE

Yeah, okay, Griff

Whatever you need to tell yourself

Look, are you going to help or not?

CADENCE

Might be hard with her best friend coming into town

But I'll do what I can

Thank you.

I put my phone back in my pocket and head toward the house, a smile on my face as I think about the progress I made with Delia today, and feeling like maybe I'm turning a corner.

When I get to the porch, Cathy is pulling up, and when she gets out of her car, she freezes. I watch her experience the same moment I had earlier, the wind-chime still singing from its place.

We talk for a few minutes before she walks inside, leaving me on the porch with Grams. But she soon gets up and heads back in the house, claiming it's tea time.

I head down the steps, about to walk around back and get in my truck when the screen porch door flies open and Delia comes down the steps in a blur a color.

She's wearing the outfit from the night I saw her in the street for the first time, and an unknown feeling slams into me so hard, I actually stumble a little.

"You good?" Delia asks, stopping next to me and reaching for my hand to steady me. The scent of her that's had some sort of a hold on me since the night we met catches on the breeze and floods me with warmth.

"Yeah, lost my footing," I mutter, righting myself and for some reason, I turn my hand over and hold hers for a second. She glances down, interlacing her fingers with mine for a brief second, her thumb skimming across my knuckles, before squeezing and letting go. Then of course, she bolts toward the old 4Runner.

I watch her drive off, that tugging sensation in my chest mixing with that unknown feeling. The loss of her hand in mine startling me, as a thought comes to the forefront of my mind, my stomach dropping.

That's how you feel about friends, right?

thank you

Thank you so much for reading *Chasing After More*!
This book was a passion project that turned into a love letter and
I'm so grateful you've given it a chance. I can't wait to take you
back to Aberdeen Ranch next year!

acknowledgments

To my beautiful grandmothers, who were both named Margaret and are no longer earth-side, thank you for leaving a legacy that moved me to write a character that represents who you both are to me.

To my mom and dad, who continue to champion me in all seasons of life, thank you for loving me unconditionally. I know you both have always loved my writing and I can feel how proud you both are that I have taken my talent and done something special with it. I love you both so much.

Shay, I don't even have words. There will never be a project I think up and won't immediately bring to you, your support and encouragement unending. With your help, magic is always made and you leave my stories better than you found them. But more than that, you are such a good friend to me. Thank you for not letting me give up this summer when I almost lost all hope. Love you big.

Ellie, you have such a gift. I'm so grateful to have had you alongside me with this book. You didn't just edit it, you helped breathe life into it. Love you dearly, to oz and beyond.

Maeghen, where do I start? From your canning updates to cookie pics, I'm so grateful that we connected through SIYL and now I always have you in my corner with each project. You always help me get through the dark times that arise during the months of writing and editing, and I cannot say thank you enough. Love you so much.

Jess, thank you for your care and help with this project. Your words and feedback encouraged me to finish this story and I'll always be so grateful for your talents.

Alice, my comma queen, thank you for being the most incredible beta reader. You contributed such incredible feedback that made me feel confident in my manuscript! Your edits also brought life to this story that made it even more real than I could have imagined.

Maddy, I'm sorry I read you so many parts of this book that it probably got annoying, but thank you for always listening and believing in me. *thumb and finger crossing heart emoji*

Katy, thank you for being my friend and always answering my many questions while I work on my books. I'm so thankful for you and that you're in this space with me. There's no else I'd rather share it with. I can't wait to see you and Max be such an amazing parents.

Sal and Ollie, do you two know that no project would be what it is without you both? Always being eager for sneak peeks, supporting me when I change what I'm writing, and being the best cheerleaders I could ask for. You both are so special, talented in your own ways, and have so much potential. I'm so proud of you both and that amidst all the adversity you've both faced, like Delia, you continue to keep your heart soft. I will always be here to root for you both and I can't wait to see where life takes you.

Kay, thank you for taking the time to talk through so many things with me during this process and always being so kind. You pushed me to take leaps with this and do things that felt scary, all while being encouraging and gracious. Thank you xx

To my ARC team, thank you for your excitement for this book. You've already received so much of my gratitude, but it always means the world to me that there are people who would take the time to read my story early because they're so excited for it.

Bap, thank you for letting me ramble and rant about this story. Read chapters to you (only to change them and then re-read them). But most importantly—thank you for being my best friend.

Am I allowed to thank my dogs? Because I am. To Dazzle and Millie, the most loyal writing and editing companions—especially into the wee hours of the night. No doubt you both were sick of staying up until 3 a.m. but you got the treats you deserved and then some.

Last but not least, to myself. Girlfriend. You almost gave up on life itself during the production of this story, but I'm so glad you didn't. If you ever find yourself in a dark place like that again, come back here, and read through this to remind yourself there are so many people who love you, are proud of you, and need you.

about the author

Elle is an indie author based in Charleston, S.C. She loves writing about intense emotions, heavy feelings, and things that make her heart feel alive. When she reads, she enjoys supporting other indie authors, powerful stories, and relatable characters.

Elle hopes to use her passion for mental health, trauma recovery, and emotional healing, in her writing to connect with other readers' souls. Her dream is to restore hearts she didn't break and make the lost feel seen.

When she isn't writing, shopping for more books, or working through her endless TBR, she is snuggling her two rescue pitbulls or finding a cozy coffee shop.

For author updates, upcoming projects, and sneak peeks, follow Elle on Instagram: @ellefsun.author

also by elle f. sun

The Nature of Emotions: a poetic novella

Stay in Your Lane: an emotional, swimming romance